DEATHBLOW

DANA MARTON

DEATHBLOW

By Dana Marton

My sincere gratitude to Sarah Jordan, Diane Flindt, and all my wonderful readers.

First Edition: 2013

Updated Edition: 2022

ISBN-13: 9781940627038

CHAPTER ONE

THE WORST TIME FOR A POLICE CRUISER TO FLY OFF A BRIDGE IS when you're handcuffed in the back.

For a moment the railing held the back tire. Then the Hummer behind the cruiser crashed into it for the final time, and the Crown Victoria plummeted into the night.

Joe Kessler put his head between his knees, like the flight attendants recommend in case of an emergency on airplanes. "Brace!"

The two Philly cops up front yelled all the way down, "Hang on! Hang on!"

Joe and Gomez Hernandez, a teenage crime-lord-wanna-be, cursed up a storm, until the car hit the Schuylkill River with a bone-rattling crash, stealing the air from their lungs. Joe smashed into the metal screen that separated him from the officers who were scrambling for their seatbelts. Gomez fell on top of him, the kid's pointy elbow stabbing Joe's face.

God, he hated undercover work.

Then the rear end of the car slammed down, and everyone dropped back into their seats, the driver shouting into his radio unit. "Officers in the water! Men in the water!" He jabbed at his window button. "We went off the bridge! We're sinking!"

The dark river churned around them, swollen from the spring rains.

Joe kicked hard at the door on his side. "Open it! Let us out!"

The cop in the passenger seat pounded the window button on his own side, grunting. "Water's gonna short out the electrics!"

"Open the back!" Joe delivered another kick, in vain.

Gomez was fighting to get out too, cussing at the cops, his eyes bugged out with panic.

"Undercover officer," Joe said through gritted teeth. *A month of undercover work down the drain.* His gaze met the driver's in the rearview mirror, and he shouted louder. "I'm an undercover officer!"

Gomez's yelling and the rush of the raging river drowned out the words.

The ice-cold water was up to their knees in a second, then up to their chests, a shock to the system. *Ho-ly hell.*

Joe twisted to kick the wire mesh divider—that ought to get attention—but the officers were focused on ditching their ride, ignoring the panic in the backseat.

The car filled up in seconds, only a two-inch air pocket hanging on stubbornly under the roof where Gomez was sucking air, quiet at last. Joe too fought for every last gulp. They were still going down. How far was the bottom? Underwater, the headlights' eerie glow provided only a foot or two of visibility; nothing but murky river beyond that.

The driver wiggled free then kicked away, disappearing in the dark water in seconds. The other officer was squeezing through the passenger-side window inch by inch. He was rounder in the middle, but he heaved himself through at last. He glanced back.

Joe looped his arms around, over his ass and legs—hands to the front—then banged his cuffs against the mesh divider, holding the man's gaze. *Don't you fucking leave us here!*

Desperation twisted the officer's face. He reached back in, pressed the button and waited the three seconds for the back window to retreat most of the way.

Then he was gone, fading into the roiling water as he swam for air.

Joe grabbed Gomez and shoved the kid free. He followed close behind, forcing himself through the stingy gap. Any skin he scraped off would be a small price to pay for escaping a watery grave.

He was barely through when the water rolled the car. And then it rolled him. *Which way up?* Zero visibility. He went with his best guess, kicked as hard as he could, his cuffed hands extended above his head, palms pressed together.

The current was a killer, strong enough to drown him. He fought against the overwhelming force, his lungs threatening to burst.

Hell no. Not today. Not like this.

He toed off his water-logged shoes, then propelled his body forward harder, his legs scissoring without a break.

Kick. Kick. Kick.

He breached the surface, his ears ringing, the Schuylkill River filling his mouth with dirty water on his first gulp for air. He choked. Seconds passed before he managed to draw a full breath.

"Help! Hey!"

Unforgiving cold and darkness surrounded him. Nobody rushed to his aid.

His hands cuffed, he couldn't swim for shit. He angled his body toward the river bank. *Stay on the surface, ride the current.* He could see no sign of the cops, or anyone else either.

"Hey! I'm here! Help!" he called out again. "Gomez!"

No response.

The current had separated him from everyone else. Not a single boat on the river nearby, nothing ahead and nothing behind him. He was alone in the night.

The lights of the Schuylkill Expressway glowed high above, the bridge now several hundred feet away, the distance growing by the second. The water was rapidly carrying him downriver.

He paddled as hard as he could, numb from the cold.

"Help!" he yelled again, then silently cursed. Every time he opened his mouth, he gulped as much water as air. He coughed, fighting to stay afloat. "Gomez!"

He couldn't hear anything but the rushing river. Something caught around his legs.

He reached down and pulled hard.

Gomez broke the surface, limp as a dead fish.

"I've got you." Joe shook him. "Breathe!"

The fifteen-year-old coughed up water as he revived, clamping on to Joe and trying to climb him.

"Stop!"

The kid yanked him under instead.

Joe fought his way back up. "Hang on, dammit." He kicked hard to keep them afloat. "You're okay. I'll hold you up. Stay still."

Not a chance. Gomez couldn't rein in his panic. He wasn't the tough guy he wanted to seem, no matter how big a gun he usually carried. He wanted to be just like his older brother, wanted desperately to belong. He'd been faking it till he made it, but there was no faking it tonight, not in the river. Here he was just a scared kid.

Joe struggled to keep him above water. "Move your feet."

Gomez gurgled and flailed. "Don't—"

Joe held on to him. "I won't let you go. Calm down. All right? Kick and breathe. Don't panic."

The river's frigid cold seeped into his bones. He was freezing. And then, when Gomez kneed him in the gut, he was hurting too.

"Umph."

Might be easier to keep the kid afloat if he was knocked out. But before Joe could act on his desperate idea, a dark mass appeared upriver, a hundred feet away and rapidly closing the distance.

One of the officers?

No. Longer and lumpier.

"Hey. That's a log. Try to grab on."

Their emergency rescue vehicle caught up to them in about thirty seconds.

Joe grabbed after a ragged stump of a branch, but the river rolled the log and the stump smashed into his face. He tasted blood.

"We gonna die!" Gomez screamed.

Like hell. They'd made it out of the submerged police cruiser. They were on the surface. They had a flotation device. "Grab on!"

He shoved the kid toward the log, then looped his own handcuffs around a gnarled root and held on for dear life as they hitched a ride, choking and coughing.

He kicked to give the log direction, angling toward shore, toward the lights of the city. Then he prayed. The river ran rough. If the log rolled again, they might go under, get tangled. They might never come up.

Even if the log didn't roll... The gnarled root ball they were holding on to kept dipping under. Gomez almost slid off.

Joe eased his weight off the back. That helped the log regain buoyancy, and the stark truth became rapidly clear: only one person could catch a ride, the log couldn't handle the both of them.

"Keep this thing steady," Joe yelled to the kid as he let go. "Keep it in balance. Kick toward shore. You'll be all right."

"Don't leave me, man!" Gomez shouted.

In seconds, he and his raft were nothing but a dark blob on the water, rapidly disappearing downriver as the current sped them away.

Joe looked back toward the bridge, but no other logs came his way, not a chunk of driftwood, not so much as a twig, nothing to hang on to, nothing to save him. He turned onto his back and worked to stay afloat, kicking with his feet.

He made more progress without Gomez hanging on to him. He swallowed a lot less water, too. Still, an eternity passed before he reached the muddy bank. The Schuylkill River had carried him past Philadelphia by then.

He crawled out on his hands and knees, coughing, then he flopped into the mud. Nothing but barren land around him, no sign of life anywhere, not down the riverbank or farther in, just scraggly bushes and broken reeds. He hoped Gomez landed where people would find him and save him.

A fat raindrop hit Joe's face. Then another. Then a dozen. *Really?* All he needed was freaking lightning to strike him.

He shivered, unsure if he was blinking rain or blood out of his eyes. The log had hit him hard. He struggled to sit, then to stand. He had to get going.

He was wanted by the Philly police because they thought he was a member of the infamous Brant Street Gang. Worse, the rival gang had just tried to kill him—he'd caught a glimpse of a Twentyniners bandana hanging from the Hummer's rearview mirror. But that wasn't even the *worst*.

If he didn't find someplace dry and warm, hypothermia would get him first.

CHAPTER TWO

I SHOULD HAVE BOUGHT THAT GUN, WENDY BELLE THOUGHT. SHE'D researched small firearms online but hadn't made a purchase. *My mother killed my father* wasn't the kind of legacy she wanted to leave for her baby.

Keith pushed her roughly against the kitchen wall, his whiskey breath fanning her face. His pale reptile eyes watched her with a predatory gleam as rain drummed on the windows of her two-bedroom Wilmington apartment—miserable weather for a miserable day.

"Keith." She said his name as she squirmed. Saying *no* would only make him more determined. "Listen, want to watch the game on TV? I recorded it yesterday."

Once when he'd been like this, she'd successfully distracted him with football. She kept recording games, even if the trick hadn't worked since, just as a person keeps insurance that might or might not pay when trouble hits. A slim chance was better than nothing.

He grabbed her hard between her legs. She winced, and he laughed. "You know what I want, babe."

The overhead light glinted off his short blond hair styled into the standard "successful businessman" cut with a touch of gel. His expensive suit was custom-tailored to fit the shoulders that boxed her in. *Most Eligible Insurance Broker. With a Temper.*

She pushed back.

"Come on, don't be like that," he said in the low-toned voice Wendy used to think was seductive.

Now that tone sent a cold shiver down her spine.

At least he isn't shouting. Her two-year-old slept in the next room, the door open—she hadn't had a chance to shut it before Keith barged in. And she couldn't tell Keith to keep it down so he wouldn't wake Justin. She didn't want to bring her son to Keith's attention at all if she could help it.

He ground his body against hers. "You like it rough? I'm going to give it to you rough." He wrapped her hair around his wrist then yanked until tears sprung into her eyes.

She didn't like it rough, and she didn't like *it* any way at all from him, but he'd been gunning for her from the moment he'd shown up at her door uninvited.

Fighting back was futile. Every time she'd tried that in the past, she'd failed. Keith had the physical advantage. He spent countless hours at his country club's gym to meet potential clients.

Say something.

"Wait! Are you hungry? I have a charcuterie tray in the fridge. Sophie's coming over."

"Why is she here all the time?"

"Just girl's night. There's an America's Next Top Model marathon on TV."

"Nobody loves you like I do. I'm the only one you can trust. You know that, right?" Keith held Wendy in place and slid one hand to her waist. Stopped. "Are you off your diet? You don't want to get fat and lose your gigs, do you? I'm trying to help here." He pinched her skin, hard. "You have to pay attention to your weight!"

She held her breath, praying that Justin wouldn't wake. If he woke, he might cry, and that might set Keith off even worse.

"Come on, babe." He dropped his voice again. "Weekend's over. I have to go to work tomorrow, stupid meetings back-to-back all day.

You're my girl. Make me feel better. After all I've done for you, you owe me this much."

She *wasn't* his girl. At the beginning of their relationship, when she'd still had stars in her eyes, she used to daydream about the day when he would propose to her. Now she was grateful he never had. All she wanted was for him to be out of her life forever.

Careful. Show neither fear nor revulsion. She kept her expression friendly. "Why don't you sign the papers before we forget about them?"

He reached up to her breast. He squeezed until it hurt. "I could make you feel sooo good."

He could not. "It's not the right time for me. I'm having my.... Sorry."

Fury flared in his eyes. "Why the hell are you teasing me then? You know that shit grosses me out." He shoved her to her knees, onto the hard tile floor.

She swallowed a cry of pain.

He was usually more careful not to leave bruises. He knew how to hurt her so no one could see the signs later.

"Keith—"

"Shut up and get to it." He rolled his hips toward her face.

"Could we sign the papers, please?" She wasn't beyond begging. She would have done anything to get him out of her and her son's lives forever.

He shot her a meaningful look. "Maybe."

He'd promised before. This wasn't the first time they'd played this game. She'd let him touch her, for Justin's sake, hoping and praying that Keith would sign over full custody.

When she'd given in, he used her then promptly forgot about his promises. When she'd stood up to him, he'd beaten her down. Nothing seemed to work. But she couldn't give up.

She shifted to rise. "I really need you to sign the papers today. I mean it, Keith."

He smacked her so hard she fell sideways, knocking a kitchen chair over, which knocked a second chair to the tile floor, one loud crash after the other.

Justin wailed in his bedroom, long sharp cries of displeasure at having been so rudely awakened.

"Shut that stupid kid up!"

She scrambled across the living room and pulled the door closed as quickly as she could. She didn't go in to soothe her baby. Keith would come after her. She didn't want him anywhere near a bed.

Don't cry, baby. Don't cry. If Justin didn't quiet down, Keith would get angry and go in there anyway. She could deal with being pushed around, but if Keith hurt her son...

Justin quieted after a final wail, thank God, but Wendy didn't have time to relax. Keith stalked her, eyes glinting with anticipation.

She evaded, stepping around the ottoman, skirting the couch, then putting the kitchen island between them.

"Here they are." She opened the top drawer and pulled out a battered manila envelope. She laid the custody papers out on the island, then searched for a pen.

"Are you trying to piss me off?" Keith caught up with her and grabbed her wrist, his tone as cold and hard as his gaze. "I bet you put out for the photographers. Are you whoring for your agent? You don't think I'm good enough now?"

She was a small-time model these days, posing for the weekly department store circulars, barely making enough to pay for the apartment and basic necessities for herself and Justin. She'd never had an inappropriate relationship with her agent—who was gay—or the photographers. At least a dozen people milled around at a shoot, everything timed to the minute. There wouldn't have been an opportunity if she'd been looking for one.

And she wasn't. God knew she'd learned her lesson, again, the last time she'd let her guard down with a man. She definitely couldn't tell Keith about *that*. If he found out that she was pregnant again, the news would send him into a rage. "I don't have time to date."

"You're a liar." He let her wrist go, but before she could step away, he grabbed her elbow in an iron grip.

"Please stop."

"Or what? You'll blabber to the cops again? You think it'll work better this time? Do you know how much money my company donates to the police department? You think the cops would mess that up?"

"Please let me go. I'm sorry."

She had zero trust left in the police. The officer who'd responded to her last call told her any accusation of battery would be her word against Keith's. And then he advised that she should stop provoking her guy. *"Go along to get along. Know what I mean?"*

Keith had trapped her, in more ways than one. She couldn't fight back physically and win. He was stronger; she'd just get hurt. If he put her in the hospital, who would take care of Justin? And if she bought a gun, she'd have to use it. He wouldn't stand for being threatened. Once she pulled a gun on him, there would be no turning back.

Then the police might or might not believe her claim of self-defense. If she went to prison, where would her son go?

And if she went for a restraining order against Keith, he'd fight back by demanding time with Justin, an official, enforceable shared custody agreement. The prospect of sending Justin to him on the weekends, on unsupervised visits, scared Wendy more than death itself.

If hers was the only life at risk, she would have fought back, would have run a long time ago. But they had a child together, which meant custody laws came into play. She couldn't find a way around that. All she could choose was who got hurt, her or her son, and how badly.

When Keith shook her, this time, she didn't resist. She steeled herself for the rest.

A loud rap sounded at the door, granting her unexpected reprieve.

"Is everything okay? Wendy? I just heard a crash as I was coming up." Sophie's voice coming through the door was nothing less than a lifeline.

Oh, thank God.

Wendy stepped forward to let her in, but Keith pushed her back. "I don't want to find out that you've been complaining about me behind my back." His tone dipped low, heavy with threat. "Our relationship is nobody else's business."

"Wendy?" Sophie Curtis, pretty much the only friend Wendy had left, knocked again.

Keith silently shook his head.

Another rap on the door. "I'm coming in."

She *could*, thank God. She had a spare key for emergencies.

Keith stepped away as the door opened, the smell of fresh paint rushing in with Sophie. Building management was having the hallways painted.

Keith plastered on a charming smile, the hostility melting off him in an instant. He changed roles faster than a professional actor.

"Hey, no need for alarm. We got a little carried away." He winked at Wendy as if sharing a private joke, as if they'd been caught in a careless moment of passion.

Sophie stayed in the doorway. "Bing is coming up in a minute. He's parking the car. He just got off shift at the police station."

Keith turned to Wendy, and as soon as he had his back to Sophie, pure hate flashed on his face. He grabbed the custody papers from the kitchen island and crushed them in his fist. "A boy needs his father," he whispered with a warning look. Then, in a normal tone, back to friendly, "Need to drop my car off for detailing. You girls have fun."

He even gifted them with a cheerful wave as he passed Sophie.

Sophie shot an equally fake smile his way.

She was a head shorter than Wendy, wrapped in a stylish black wool coat, her cheeks pink from the cold. It was good to see healthy color on her, after her health issues for the past few years.

Her wild red curls bounced around her face as she walked into the kitchen and dropped her purse on the counter. "Are you okay?"

"Failed to get Keith to sign over custody once again." Wendy swallowed her despair. "I'll get him to sign next time. I'm glad you're here." *Keep talking. Maybe Sophie didn't notice anything.* "How was traffic?"

She'd never told anyone Keith had turned abusive—not her friends, and not her parents who lived in Florida and already worried endlessly about her.

Keith Kline was *somebody* in Wilmington. He held memberships in all the right business clubs. His company gave a ton of money to charity, including the Police Association. The people who loved Wendy would just get hurt if she dragged them into her screwed-up relationship. Sophie couldn't find out. Nobody could. Wendy was the one who'd picked Keith. He was in her life because of her bad judgment. She had a child with him. She had to figure out how to deal with that. Handling Keith was her responsibility and nobody else's.

She walked over to the smaller bedroom, pushed the door open a few inches, and peeked in. Justin had fallen back asleep, an innocently snoozing little angel in the middle of his bed. She closed the door and turned back to Sophie. "I have some snacks. Hungry?"

"Later. Could I have some water, please? I didn't realize Keith was coming over today. How are things with you two? Other than the custody issue."

Wendy pulled two bottles of water from the fridge. "Okay." Keith would kill her if he found out that she talked about him behind his back. "Is Bing really coming?"

"No." Sophie shrugged out of her coat and folded it over the back of the sofa. She wore dove-gray slacks with a white top, her style always flawless. She had a good eye for color and design, could have worked in the fashion industry. Not that she'd ever been interested in that kind of thing. Computers were her passion. She was smart and strong, everything Wendy wanted to be. Sophie had her own web design business.

She walked over to the table with a tentative expression. "I thought—"

"How was your checkup on Friday? I forgot to ask."

Sophie flashed a brilliant smile. "Passed with flying colors. The ticker keeps on ticking."

Wendy set the bottles on the table, then she picked up the fallen chairs.

Sophie helped, caressing a translucent acrylic dining chair that had the sleek lines of a sports car. "These look fantastic. I have serious furniture envy."

"Scored them from Mia." An interior designer who often worked on the same sets as Wendy. "A millionaire client's castoffs."

They were modern design; pieces of art that Wendy could never have afforded otherwise. Her table didn't match, a minor detail. She'd get there eventually.

Sophie meandered back into the living room. "Hey, the pictures are new too."

Wendy's photographs caught Justin in the early morning light, sitting in front of the window, dust particles floating in the air, sparkling like diamond powder in the sunlight. The images had a surreal feel to them, the magic of childhood made visible.

Sophie kept looking. "If you ever quit modeling, you could be a professional photographer."

"That's the dream." A successful business, so she didn't have to worry about the future. *Strong and independent.* Goals that felt light years away.

Sophie watched her. "You can tell me *anything.* You know that, right? I'd support you. That's what friends are for."

Wendy forced a smile. Sophie would support her, but Sophie didn't deserve Keith's nastiness dumped on her. As a heart-transplant recipient, stress was the last thing Sophie needed. "Everything's fine."

"Then why is your knee bleeding?"

"I didn't realize..." Wendy glanced at the bright red drops just below the hem of her wool skirt that was new, a perk of her job. Unlike high-fashion shoots, department-store flyer jobs let models keep the clothes, which her small budget appreciated.

She grabbed a napkin and dabbed her knee clean. *No big deal.* She could cover that with makeup for work.

"I tripped. You'd think, as a model, I'd be less clumsy." She rolled her eyes, slipping on her public-Wendy persona, the mask that showed her in control of her life and happy. She'd been modeling since sixteen; she could act. She'd become good at hiding her scared, weak core even from those close to her.

Sophie waited, radiating patience, love, and support. She wouldn't push. She never did.

The mood shifted between them.

The mask slipped.

Wendy dashed away the tears that were suddenly blurring her vision. She wasn't going to cry. She wasn't a crier. Tears just made Keith angrier, and anyway, crying never solved anything.

"Hey." Sophie hurried over and put her arms around her.

The comfort felt incredibly lovely, especially after the confrontation with Keith. Wendy drew a deep, shuddering breath, and whispered, "I didn't really trip."

"I know," Sophie whispered back, holding her tightly. "We're going to figure out what to do about this."

CHAPTER THREE

JOE WOKE WITH A SCREAMING HEADACHE. THE BANGING AT HIS front door didn't help. He grabbed his jeans from the floor and dragged them on, then shrugged into a wrinkled T-shirt.

Socks? He grabbed a pair from his dresser.

The doorbell rang.

The Brant Street Gang didn't know he lived in Broslin, but he shoved his gun into the back of his jeans before he dragged his tired ass down the stairs.

He'd meant to sleep until noon, then spend the rest of his day at the nice, warm station, catching up on paperwork. The chill of the river had stubbornly lodged itself into his bones. As he passed by the thermostat, he punched up the heat.

"Calm down! I'm coming." He yanked the door open, ready to send away his insistent visitor, then swallowed the words when he came face-to-face with his boss. "Captain."

Ethan Bing was only an inch shorter than Joe, solidly built. Not a man to mess with. He might have been fifteen years Joe's senior, but he could still whip serious ass. He expected his men to keep in shape, and he didn't ask anything of them that he wasn't willing to do himself. He put in his time at the station's small gym.

He took in the four-inch cut on Joe's left cheek, courtesy of the log that had slapped him in the river. "With all those stitches sticking out, it looks like you have a giant red caterpillar on your face."

"That'll disappoint the ladies."

The captain shook his head. "Doubt it. On you, they'll probably like it, think it's all manly." He peered behind Joe. "Anyone naked in there?"

"I'm having an off morning." Joe stepped aside to let him in.

Captain Bing was the only person he couldn't send away, especially since the man was holding a tall cup of coffee. He had a Main Street Diner paper bag in his other hand, which likely held a slice of pie. For coffee and some of Eileen's famous strawberry pie, Joe would have let the devil in.

The captain walked straight to the kitchen table and set down his gifts. "How's the concussion?"

"Feels like a thousand tiny lumberjacks with a thousand tiny axes are competing in my head over who'll get to my last nerve first."

"You didn't answer your phone. Haven't talked to you since you called from the emergency room. Thought I'd stop by to see if you needed anything."

"I was trying to sleep in. Any news on Gomez?"

"Chief Gleason has a man watching the kid's house. He'll let us know when Gomez shows." Bing sat and looked at the muddy clothes tossed on the floor in the corner. "You're not supposed to sleep with a concussion. You should take a couple of days off."

Joe reached for the coffee and enjoyed a long swallow of liquid heaven. "I was planning on going in for my shift."

The captain pushed the paper bag toward him, across the table. "I don't think so."

"Nothing's wrong with me. If you think I'll scare people, I can slap on a bandage."

Bing shook his head. "I'm sorry I got you into this mess."

"I volunteered," Joe reminded him. He wanted to make detective. He'd spent most of his youth playing competitive sports. Pushing to get to the next level was an ingrained habit. "Anybody call the hospitals to look for the kid?"

"Nobody was brought in matching Gomez's description, according to Gleason."

Neither of them said what they were both thinking...that Gomez might be dead.

Joe's fingers tightened on the Styrofoam cup, until some of the golden-brown liquid came up through the hole in the lid. *Should have tried harder, dammit.*

"Don't be too hard on yourself." The captain handed him a napkin from his coat pocket. "We feel responsible for the people we protect. It's hard to lose someone. You never forget any of them, especially your first. Mine was a car accident. She died after I arrived at the scene. I started CPR, couldn't bring her back. Twenty-seven, mother of two. Her name was Jillian Lin."

Joe set his cup down. "I shouldn't have left the kid alone in the water."

"You couldn't have saved him. You were both cuffed. It's a miracle you made it back. And I'm the one who got you involved. I'm sorry."

The Philadelphia Chief of Police had wanted someone to infiltrate Ramos Hernandez's crew. Ramos was Gomez's older brother. Chief Gleason had reason to believe that Ramos had an inside man at the Philadelphia PD. The chief wanted an undercover guy from the outside. He'd attended Police Academy with Captain Bing, so he called up his old friend for help.

Joe had jumped at the opportunity. He liked action, and most action at Broslin PD went to the detectives: Harper, Chase, and Jack. This was Joe's chance to prove himself.

"Chief Gleason wants a full briefing," Bing said. "I gave him the basics, but he wants you to call in."

"Now is good." Joe looked around for his cell then bit back a curse. "My phone's in the river."

Bing pulled out his own and dialed, set his cell phone on speaker, and slid it to the middle of the oak farm table between them.

"Morning. I'm with Officer Kessler," he said when the other end picked up. "He's been resting."

"Kessler. I heard you had a rough night." Gleason's voice boomed through the phone. He was a big guy, built like a linebacker. "How are you, Officer?"

"I'm fine, sir. I lost Gomez in the river. I'm sorry."

"Let me worry about that. I have the officers' report on my desk about the accident, but I'd rather hear it from you. Why don't you start at the beginning?"

Joe gulped his coffee. "The kid wanted to pick up a car. I went with him. It's not easy to pry him away from his brother. Figured I could get some information out of him about the dirty cop on Ramos's payroll."

"Did you?"

"Not enough time." Joe leaned toward the phone so Gleason could hear him better. "The kid found a nice BMW. Barely popped the lock when Philadelphia PD showed up. We were in a dead-end alley, no chance of running." He cleared his throat. "Officer Tropper was driving after they picked us up. Officer Washington rode shotgun. They start questioning us, name, address, the usual. And when Gomez said his name, Officer Tropper looked at him in the rearview mirror, asked him if he was Ramos Hernandez's little brother. The kid says yes."

That had been when things had gotten interesting.

"Tropper asked the kid how old he was. Kid told him, fifteen. Then Tropper said he was going to let us off with a warning. Officer Washington protested, but Tropper overrode him. Before Tropper could pull over, a Hummer showed up behind us. Twentyniners bandana in the window. Tropper couldn't let us out in front of the rival gang, without guns, without a ride. He kept going, waiting for the Hummer to turn off on a side street. It didn't. Once we were on the bridge, the Hummer rammed us."

Joe rubbed his hands over his arms. He couldn't shake the memories of the freezing river.

"Sounds like Tropper might be our guy." Disappointment echoed in the chief's voice. "Did you see who drove the Hummer?"

"One of Racker's enforcers, according to the kid. He didn't mention the guy's name." J.T. Racker was the Twentyniners' leader.

"Why would the Twentyniners hit a police cruiser?"

"The BMW we tried to steal was in their territory. J.T.'s guy could have seen us, wanted to teach us a lesson, police car or not. Could have been high, not thinking straight. Felt like a big boy in that Hummer."

Silence on the other end.

"Or," Chief Gleason said after a few seconds, "he knew Officer Tropper was on the Brant Street Gang's payroll. The guy saw a chance to take him out along with Ramos's little brother, a double blow to Ramos. What did you think of Officer Washington?"

Joe closed his eyes and ran through the events from the arrest to the crash into the river. "Like I said, he looked surprised when Officer Tropper said he was going to let us off. Then when the car went under, Officer Tropper panicked and left us in the back. Officer Washington opened the window for us. We would have drowned without his help."

Gomez might have drowned anyway. Somebody would have seen him by now if he'd made it out of the water.

Joe rolled his neck to ease the roaring headache at his temple. He compartmentalized the pain and answered every one of the chief's follow-up questions.

When they finished, Captain Bing put his phone away. "I appreciate your help. I wish the op ended differently."

"Me too. Believe me." Joe reached for the paper bag with the pie at last.

His stitches itched, but he wasn't about to complain about them. He'd have a scar, while Gomez likely got a watery grave. The kid had trusted him. He'd held on to the log because Joe had told him he would be all right.

The strawberry pie tasted like river mud in Joe's mouth. As he set it down, the captain's shoulder unit went off.

"One eighty-seven at the medical center." The dispatcher's voice crackled through. "Suite 1025. Repeat, that's a one eighty-seven."

Homicide.

The captain was on his feet. "On my way."

"Wait. Did she say suite 1025?" Joe jumped up too, stepped into his sneakers and grabbed his coat. He followed Bing to his car. "That's Phil's office. Philip Brogevich."

They were on Baltimore Pike by the time Joe explained his connection to Phil, that they'd gone to school together.

Bing flipped on the siren. "Isn't he the shrink?"

"Yeah. Hasn't been at the medical center that long. His wife had a baby. He wanted to be closer to home so he moved his practice back to Broslin from West Chester."

Bing's family had been in Broslin for as long as Joe's. They knew most people in town, a double-edged sword. They knew who the troublemakers were, but then again, the troublemakers knew them and played the *Dude, we were on the same baseball team. You gonna arrest me for a little drunk driving?* card. Or the *Our mothers go to the same church* card. Or, *You dated my sister in high school, man.* Which came up a lot more often for Joe than for Bing, to be fair.

"Does your friend keep drugs on the premises?" The captain had to shout to be heard over the siren. "Benzodiazepines?"

"Don't know." Joe glanced at the dashboard clock. *Eight thirty.* "Do you think someone broke in overnight for pills and OD'd? Phil found him when he got in?" The victim didn't have to be Phil. A knot formed in Joe's stomach regardless. "We grabbed a couple of beers the other night at Finnegan's to celebrate his daughter's birth." A three-week-old baby girl, Isabella, a miracle after multiple grueling IVF tries. Phil had a hundred baby pictures on his smartphone. "His wife's a shrink too. On maternity leave."

Cars pulled out of their way, giving them a clean shot at the road.

They reached the Broslin Care Medical Center in ten minutes, an old strip mall that had been converted into doctors' offices when the owner had decided to repurpose it, giving the property a face-lift. The new setup drew a better clientele than the tattoo parlor and the pawnshop had. The previously empty spaces were filling up too, only three left empty.

Bing parked in front of suite 1025. No other cruisers yet. Before business hours only half a dozen cars were scattered around in front of the various doctors' offices, belonging to people who worked there.

Joe jumped from the cruiser.

The captain right behind him. "No rush. You never get a second chance to get a first impression of your crime scene."

Joe slowed down. Bing was right. They wouldn't want to miss any details.

Philip Brogevich, MD the brass plate announced discreetly next to the entry, then below that, *Psychiatrist.* The handicap ramps were new. The sign on the railing warned of fresh paint. The door stood half-open.

"Looks like the pawnshop's security cameras were removed during renovations." Bing cranked his neck. "Your friend hasn't gotten around to putting up new ones yet."

"Maybe he doesn't think he needs security. I doubt he has significant cash on the premises." Joe followed the captain into the reception area where the receptionist sobbed by her desk, wringing her hands.

Doris Paffrah was in her late fifties, a grandmother of six, widow of a local fireman. She made a limp, helpless gesture toward the half-open door that led to Phil's office. "He's—he's—"

She began sobbing again, and the knot inside Joe's stomach grew harder.

He took her by the arm. "Why don't you sit down, Mrs. Paffrah? We're here now. We'll take care of it."

He brought her a cup of water from the cooler before he hurried after Bing, stopping on the threshold as if he'd hit an invisible wall. "Aw, man..."

Phil lay sprawled on his back on the floor, his head bloodied. He'd gained a good twenty pounds since they'd played on the high school football team together, had a receding hairline now. He had circles under his eyes, wasn't getting much sleep with the new baby.

Joe could barely get a single word past his gritted teeth. "How?"

Bing, crouching next to the body, glanced back over his shoulder. "A single deathblow. Delivered with a blunt object, judging by the damage."

No matter how long Joe had been a cop, he didn't think he'd ever get used to senseless violence—it was an affront to him, always personal. Broslin was *his* town. He'd sworn to protect and serve the people who lived here. And Phil had been a friend, dammit. "He was a decent man who deserved better." A bloodstained, antique black desk phone lay in the corner of the office. "Looks like we have the murder weapon."

"The killer used what was at hand. Not premediated." The captain kept his attention on Phil. He must have seen the phone already. "Fresh clothes."

Bing liked to talk cases out. He believed it made investigators think more clearly.

Joe went along with the method. "Phil didn't spend the night at the office. He was attacked after he came in this morning. Suit and tie neat, shoelaces in tidy loops. Doesn't look like he rushed or was upset when he dressed. He didn't know he was walking into trouble." He glanced toward the door patients used to leave after their sessions so they wouldn't run into the next patient waiting at reception. The system helped avoid any awkwardness. Broslin was small enough that everyone knew most everyone else. "Back door open or locked?"

"I want to dust for fingerprints before we try the knob." The captain straightened. "The coroner will determine time of death, but I'd say your friend was killed within the last hour."

Joe agreed. The blood hadn't coagulated yet. "Office hours are from nine to four." He stepped back to call out to Doris. "Do you know if Phil had an emergency call to meet a patient before the office opened?"

Doris sat collapsed in her chair. "Not that I know of. But those don't go through me." She blew her nose. "High-risk patients have Phil's cell phone number. People who have a history of suicidal thoughts. Things like that."

"You have a list?"

"Sorry. No. But it'd be marked in their individual files."

"How many active patients did Phil have?"

"Around a hundred and fifty?" Her voice shook. "I'm not sure. I can check. They aren't all regulars. Some people only see him *as needed*. If and when old problems come back."

Bing walked over to the door to join the conversation. "I'm going to put in for a warrant for the patient files. I'd appreciate it if you could get them ready for hand over."

Tears flooded Doris's eyes. "You think it was a patient?"

"Can't rule out any possibilities, at this stage. But it could have been someone else he knew. Or an act of random violence. You keep any drugs here?"

"No. The pharmaceutical company reps drop off samples now and then, but we give those to the free clinic."

Bing nodded then turned back into the office.

Joe strode to the front door. He needed to look at something other than Phil's lifeless body.

No sign of forced entry.

"Was this door unlocked when you came in?" he asked Doris.

Doris stared, lost. She needed a few seconds before she recovered. "I had to unlock it."

"How about the door to Phil's office?"

"Closed. I opened it to see if he had anything in his *Out* bin. I had to leave early on Friday to drop my car off for an inspection."

"I don't suppose you tried the back door?"

"It should be locked. He always locked it before he went home."

Bing popped out again. "I'm going to need you to cancel today's appointments," he told the receptionist. "As soon as possible. I don't want patients showing up and contaminating the crime scene."

"Of course." Doris reached for the computer mouse.

"Joe." The captain tossed his keys to him. "Grab a roll of crime-scene tape from the trunk and string it up. And start the crime-scene log. Then you can begin canvassing the other offices, in case anyone saw or heard anything."

"On it." Joe cordoned off a twenty-foot-by-twenty-foot area in front of the entrance, tying the tape to the railings on the new handicap ramp. Then he checked the ground. Slowly and carefully. No cigarette butts that they could send to the lab, no garbage. No footprints either, since the entire lot was paved.

He grieved, but he went on being a cop, doing the cop thing. He was going to figure out who killed Phil.

He wrote up the crime scene log. *Time of call. Time law enforcement arrived on scene, with names. People already on scene. Etcetera.* Then he strode over to the pediatrician's office next door. Still closed. Most he could do was peer through the window. Nobody behind the reception desk. He moved on to the endocrinologist, then to the ob-gyn.

He questioned the staff already at work—two receptionists and a nurse—but nobody had seen or heard anything. The offices were soundproofed for privacy.

The news of the murder, Phil's death, shocked everyone. They had questions and wanted answers. Joe put them off as politely as possible. Even if he had information, which he didn't, he couldn't discuss the case at this stage.

By the time he strode back to suite 1025, Detective Harper Finnegan was driving up.

Joe added him to the crime-scene log.

Harper was a couple of years older, whiskey-brown hair, square jaw, nose broken in a bar fight a few years back. There'd been a time when he'd been the Finnegan family's black sheep. It was a miracle he'd ended up working for the police, and everybody said so. He pulled his cruiser up next to the captain's, shaking his head as he inspected Joe's face. "Ran into a jealous boyfriend last night?"

"Ran into an argumentative phone pole on the four-wheeler."

Since Joe had gone undercover to catch a dirty cop, the assignment was strictly confidential. Only one person at each station knew about the undercover op—Captain Bing in Broslin and Chief Gleason in Philadelphia.

Harper looked skeptical, but he didn't push. He ducked under the yellow police tape flitting in the wind. "Dispatch said homicide."

"Philip Brogevich." Joe updated him on what little they knew so far.

Inside, Doris was still on the phone, calling patients to cancel appointments, crying quietly.

The captain looked up when they walked into the office. "How is your caseload, Harper? Can you take lead here?"

"Yessir."

Joe stepped forward. "I'd also like to be assigned to the case."

"The victim was your friend."

"It's a small town. Everybody is everybody's friend."

"I'll think about it. How did the canvassing go?"

"Barely anyone's here. None of the three people I interviewed has seen or heard anything unusual."

Bing stood up. "I need something from the car. Come with me."

They stepped outside in time to see Officer Mike McMorris pull up. Joe added him to the crime-scene log too.

Mike stared at Joe's patched-up face as he hopped out of his cruiser, the morning sun turning his red hair pure copper.

"Rough date? Hey, I got a joke for you." When Mike grinned, his Irish freckles danced. "Guy comes home and finds his wife in bed with another man. He shoots the guy, turns to the wife, and asks, 'What do you have to say about that?' The wife says..." Mike paused a beat for effect. "'Keep it up and you won't have any friends left.'"

Joe groaned, while the captain shook his head with resignation on his way to his car.

Mike mock-punched Joe's arm. "Seriously, who smacked you? Losing your touch with the ladies?"

"Never gonna happen." Joe shrugged. "Four-wheeler accident."

The captain popped the trunk of his cruiser and looked back. "Mike, you can go ahead and secure the premises."

"Yes, sir." Mike stationed himself at the door.

Joe went to help the captain who was hauling out his crime-scene kit, a large black plastic container that had an orange handle and a million compartments inside to stash all the swabs and bottles of chemicals.

Bing cast a sideways glance at him. "Grab an extra box of gloves." Then he added, "It's not just about you and the victim being friends. I don't want you to jump straight into a homicide after last night."

"I'm fine."

"There's another thing." The captain paused. "I didn't come to your house this morning just to check on you. I have a personal favor to ask. I need you for an unofficial protection detail. Woman and child. She moved away from a nasty ex. He probably won't find her, but I'd rather err on the safe side."

Joe thought of Gomez, the panicked look in the kid's eyes as the current had carried him away. "I don't think I'm a good bet in the protection-detail department."

"She's a friend of Sophie's. Sophie said you might remember her. Wendy Belle."

The name hit Joe like a sledgehammer. His fingertips tingled. It was the weirdest thing. "We've met."

"Where?"

"Ran into her at Sophie's place when I was providing protection detail to Sophie." Back before Sophie and Bing had gotten together.

Wendy Belle was a professional model. She had the looks to twist a man into a lust pretzel, lips that begged to be kissed, and those mysterious gray eyes that Joe hadn't been able to forget since he'd first looked into them.

As a small-town football hero, now a policeman, he had his share of dates. Uniforms were a chick magnet. And he'd been raised to be a gentleman, took good care of his dates in and out of bed. He kept in shape, put in more time at the police station's gym than anybody else. He appreciated women, and they appreciated him right back.

More often than not, women walked up to him with their phone numbers. *Not Wendy.* Joe had been dazed by the instant attraction at their first meeting, but she hadn't taken him seriously, not for a second. She'd taken one look at him, and she'd *dismissed* him.

"I went to a fashion-show fundraiser she was in." He hadn't been able to forget her.

He'd put big money in the plate—at least, big for his police salary. His gesture hadn't impressed her, as he'd stupidly hoped, but impressed some of the other models, and they'd invited him to the after-party.

He'd caught Wendy sneaking out early, into pouring rain and not a cab to be had. He'd offered her a lift home. She offered to brew him a cup of coffee, so he wouldn't fall asleep driving back to Broslin. He'd gone up to her apartment, which had turned into—

"Good." Bing gave a brisk nod. "If you two know each other, she'll be more comfortable with you."

Wouldn't bet on it.

The captain kept talking. "Her ex, Keith Kline, has a tendency for violence, from what Sophie says. Wendy's apartment in Wilmington is out of our jurisdiction, unfortunately, but she and her boy will be staying here in Broslin for a few days, at Sophie's old place. Sophie's out at the log cabin with me, anyway." He lost himself to a startlingly uncaptain-like smile for a second. Then he caught himself and his lips flattened. "Wilmington PD isn't doing anything because the guy hasn't committed any crime that can be proven. From what Sophie tells me about him, my gut says he will. Sooner or later, he'll hurt her bad, past the bruises she's been hiding."

Joe tried to line up that batch of new information in his head, fit it into the picture he'd formed of Wendy Belle already. Their first meeting had lasted five minutes, the second an hour and a half. Obviously, there were a lot of gaps.

Yet all that darkness the captain was talking about didn't seem possible. Wendy had been nothing but light both times Joe had met her.

The thought of some asshole laying hands on Wendy didn't sit well. The ex sounded like he could use a stern talking to. Wendy Belle wasn't going to get hurt again. Not on Joe's watch.

And not on Bing's either, it seemed, because the captain's next words were, "If the jerk shows up and tries anything, I'm going to come down on him like a ton of bricks."

"Shouldn't she have an official protection detail?"

"For one, she won't ask for it. Kline has her too scared. She wouldn't even talk to me about him. But even if she reached out, I couldn't justify assigning resources to a domestic violence complaint about past events that were never substantiated and didn't take place in my jurisdiction."

"Right." *Sometimes, the rules could be stupid that way.*

"I figured, since you'll be taking a sick day or two, you could drive by a couple of times. But since you say you're friends, maybe you could hang around at the house with her. That'd be better."

"No problem." Even if Joe didn't need time off. He was sore from the crash, but he'd taken beatings ten times worse on the football field.

"I appreciate it. If you can do that today and tomorrow, it'll give me a chance to figure out what I can do to keep her safe long-term."

"Consider it done. You think I could be the one to notify Marie? Phil's wife." He couldn't bring himself to call his friend *the victim.* "She might take it better from someone she knows." Since Joe had a free hand, he opened the door for the captain. "I could drop by to talk to Marie, on my way to Sophie's place."

"All right."

"Thanks." Joe set the box of gloves on the little table that held magazines for waiting patients, then turned to leave. Stopped. "I don't have a car with me."

"Take mine. You have the keys. I'll ride back to the station with Harper when we're done here. You can drop my cruiser off when you get a chance and switch over to yours."

"About working the case—"

"I'm assigning it to Harper, but I'll make sure he keeps you up-to-date. Right now, focus on recovering from last night and watching over Wendy and her son." Bing flashed Joe a pointed look. "She's a nice young woman. Vulnerable right now. I don't want her feelings hurt."

Not so subtle code for *Don't hit on her*.

Joe flinched. "No worries."

He nodded at the captain before he walked away.

His last encounter with Wendy.... Hell, she'd been the one to hurt *his* feelings.

The best sex of his life, and she'd kicked him out as soon as it was over, told him not to bother with calling because it was strictly a one-time thing. Told him, actually, *while* he'd still been inside her. The woman had shaken Joe's unshakable self-confidence.

He tugged off his rubber gloves and tucked them into his pocket, then got into Bing's cruiser. *Phil. Marie. Wendy Belle.* His day was shaping up to be an ass-kicker, which was saying something, considering that the day before included his arrest, a concussion, and a near drowning.

CHAPTER FOUR

KEITH STOOD IN THE MIDDLE OF WENDY'S APARTMENT, A VEIN throbbing at his temple.

She had moved out on him again.

Her mismatched furniture and most of her clothes remained, but it didn't fool Keith. All the baby stuff was gone, and the fridge stood empty. She didn't plan on coming back for a while. She wasn't just off somewhere shopping.

He kicked a toy car out of his way hard enough so it bounced off the wall. "I'm going to teach you respect, bitch."

He never should have let her leave his place, to start with. Shouldn't have agreed to her renting her own apartment. He had, after the baby was born, because the brat cried all night, and she was no good for sex anyway. He was a man. He had needs. If he had other women, it was her fault, nobody else's.

Her absence had been fine for those first few months. He'd expected her to beg him to let her back. She hadn't. She always had some excuse for why she couldn't return—the lease she'd signed, whatever.

Keith hated her damn place. He wanted to see it burn. Maybe he would.

Not today.

Today, he wanted to find her. She needed to learn that she could *never* outsmart him.

He opened her garbage can. Empty. Nothing to tell him where she'd gone. He walked into her bedroom. No clues in there either. The top drawer of her dresser stood an inch ajar. He opened it. Underwear. He ran his fingers through the jumbled mess of silk.

She'd left behind his favorites.

"Where have you gone, Wendy?" He whispered to her empty room that refused to give up her secrets.

No matter. He was smart, he was determined, and he would find her.

Who did she have other than him? Not that many people. Her parents in Florida and her bitch friend, Sophie, in Broslin.

—————

"I don't need a babysitter." Wendy kept her voice down.

Justin was sitting on the couch in Sophie's living room, watching his favorite TV cartoon about three tap-dancing sheep. He looked fully absorbed in the show, but if Wendy had learned anything about motherhood so far, it was that little ears always heard everything.

"I don't want Joe Kessler to come and take over," she whispered to her best friend who was standing by the door, ready to leave. "We barely know each other."

Sophie was picking up old work files she'd left behind when she'd moved in with Bing. She was setting up her office out at the farm, and she wanted to keep all her paperwork in one place.

She shrugged into her coat. "And if Keith shows up?"

Anxiety burned in Wendy's stomach. "I keep thinking he might not have stopped by the apartment yet. He's going to be furious when he finds me gone." Temporary safety was all well and good, but there'd be hell to pay when he eventually caught up with her. "Maybe I could go back before he realizes that I left."

"He has a key to your apartment. You're not safe there."

Sophie was smart and usually right about things, but maybe she was wrong about this. Wendy pushed back against her rising panic, but it wouldn't go away. Letting Sophie talk her into moving out to Broslin the day before had been a mistake. "It's not like I can stay away from him forever. We have a son together. I don't have sole custody."

A fact that filled her with dark desperation.

She rubbed the heels of her hands on the side of her pants. She was a model; she could smile on demand, so she did. She didn't want Sophie to worry. "I was shaken up yesterday. I was too tired. I made more of things than what they really were. We'll be fine at home."

Sophie was the only close friend she had left. All the others had dropped off one by one over the years. They didn't like Keith. And Keith hated them. According to him, they weren't really her true friends anyway. They just pitied her because she was such a screwup.

If Sophie found out how weak Wendy was, what a mess she'd made of her life, maybe Sophie wouldn't be her friend either.

Nobody cares about you like I do, Keith must have told Wendy a hundred times. *I'm the only one you can trust.*

She brushed invisible lint off her pants. "I just needed a good night's sleep. I got that last night. Thank you. I'm fine now."

Sophie's expression was the picture of patience and support. "Stay for a day or two. Give yourself a chance to think. At least you get out of the paint fumes. Those hallways at the apartment building are toxic. I swear I was high by the time I made it up to your floor. You can always go back in a few days, after the painters are finished. In the meanwhile, you'd be helping me out. It's nice not to have the house stand empty. I still have furniture and computer equipment here. Treat this like a mini vacation."

No such thing as a vacation from Keith, but Wendy couldn't tell Sophie that. Part of her desperately wanted to stay, but she was afraid she was making everything worse. And the idea of a private bodyguard made her even more nervous.

If Keith tracked her here and found her with a man, he'd probably kill them both.

"I don't want to put anyone out." She fixed her model mask on, the one that showed no emotion, certainly not fear.

"I'm scared for you and Justin."

"Keith had a bad day. He knocked me over by accident. You'd think if I could walk down the runway in six-inch heels, I could stand steady barefoot in my own kitchen. I was a little lightheaded. I skipped breakfast."

"Are you dieting?"

"No." Just watching calories. Keith had said she was losing her shape. She wasn't as strong or as smart as Sophie. Her figure was all she had. She earned her living with her body. She couldn't afford to gain weight right now. She'd be showing soon anyway. She could only work for a few more weeks, and she needed those paychecks.

Sophie watched her silently for a few seconds, then decided not to press the issue. Instead, she went with "Joe is pretty good at the body-guard thing. He kept an eye on me when I needed help." A quick smile flashed across her face. "He's so hot, he has his own Broslin fan club. *And* he likes you."

He does? Did he say that?

"I'm not in the market for a romantic fling." Out-of-this-world-hot one-night-stand with Joe notwithstanding. "No offense, but Joe Kessler is a total jock, small-town football hero with an inflated ego."

If Wendy ever let another man into her life, he was going to be the exact opposite of Joe, someone who would be a great stepfather for Justin.

Whatever had gotten into her the night of the fundraiser, the first night Justin had been away from her staying at the log cabin with Sophie and Bing.... Something like that could never happen again.

Sophie wrapped her pristine white silk scarf around her neck, her eyes reflecting worry. "Not every guy is like Keith. It'd be a shame if you couldn't trust anyone because of him."

"He wasn't always like this." He'd been attentive when they'd met. He'd spoiled her. "Since his promotion, he's responsible for more than his fair share of accounts at the office. The stress level is incredible."

He told her that every time he apologized for flying off the handle. *"I'm sorry, babe. I'm exhausted. I love you so much, you drive me crazy."*

"Does he still do drugs?" Sophie asked in a carefully neutral tone.

"It's not like that. He only took stuff for a little while, to be able to keep up with work." That was when she'd gotten her own place, shortly after Justin was born. "It was just a phase. This is a phase. He can be romantic too." He used to be. There'd been gifts and flowers and lavish dates.

Sophie buttoned her coat. "I wonder how much of that romance was true. Maybe he needed a model girlfriend to round out his hotshot moneyman image. I'm sorry, but how does someone suddenly turn abusive? It had to be there all along under the surface."

"I don't think so." If Sophie was right, that would mean Wendy had been too stupid to notice. And she wasn't stupid. "It's the stress. He changed little by little."

The first time he'd grabbed her and screamed at her after a grueling day at work, he apologized profusely. She'd believed when he said it was never going to happen again. But as time went on, he lost it more and more often, becoming more controlling. She knew she had to leave. She'd planned it—but then she found out she was pregnant with Justin.

She'd been on the pill, and she always insisted on Keith using protection. He wouldn't always comply. He'd start playing with her, then push inside, claiming afterward that he'd gotten carried away. And the pill was only 99% effective....

Not that Wendy could ever regret Justin. She glanced at her son. He was clapping madly at the tap-dancing sheep, a bundle of innocent joy. He was the very best of her.

Yet Keith had never been happy with their son. He'd hit her for the first time shortly after Justin was born.

"You were smart to move out of his place." Sophie took Wendy's hand and squeezed it. "And you're smart for moving out of his reach again. Smart and brave."

"The first time, I was naïve."

Wendy had thought she would be safe from him across town. She couldn't have been more wrong about that. Keith kept showing up at her place, and the violence kept escalating.

She forced a smile. "All right. Enough with the pity party, or I'm going to have to look for some cheese to serve with all this whine. How is life at the farm with Bing?"

Sophie frowned at the sudden change of subject, but the frown quickly disappeared, as if she couldn't help but smile every time he was mentioned. "Pretty great. You could come and stay with us there. Peaches would be happy to guard you."

Peaches was the stray Rottweiler mix Sophie had adopted.

"That dog and Justin have their own mutual admiration society, but you and Bing need your privacy. You just moved in together."

"Wendy." Sophie tucked her wild, Orphan Annie hair behind her ears. "We're friends. I love you. I care about you and Justin. I want you to be safe. So I'm going to say this at the risk of overstepping my boundaries. Either you agree to protection here, or I'm taking you two back to the farm with me. I'm not leaving you in danger."

"Hey. Just because you moved in with the police captain, it doesn't mean you get to do the tough-cop talk with me." Wendy tried for light-hearted. She didn't want to fight with Sophie. "Honestly, I don't see this working with Joe. Is he going to fit us in between dates?"

Joe had the sexiest smile in three counties and trouble glinting in his dark eyes when he looked at her. Sadly, she had a feeling he looked at every woman the same way.

The sexual attraction between them had been instantaneous, had knocked her back a step. She'd given in to Joe's sexual allure once, so she knew what being with him felt like. He was a wild ride. He left her breathless, with her hormones humming. But the two of them together would never last beyond a week. A few years ago, maybe that would have been fine with her, but now with Justin, and a baby on the way, everything had changed. She wasn't interested in a casual relationship.

"He's going to hit on me." Wendy rolled her eyes. "He can't help himself. And then things will get all awkward. He's a womanizer. You know he is."

"I said women like him. It's not necessarily the same thing. Let him help. If for no other reason than because worrying about you stresses me out, and stress is bad for me."

"Really? Playing the heart-transplant card? You'd sink to that?"

"You bet your ass, if that's the only card you leave me."

"Fine." Wendy bit back a smile. "Joe can drive by when he's out and about. But I don't want him here all the time. I don't want to confuse

Justin. I don't want to be the kind of mother who has a revolving door for all the *uncles*."

"You won't even notice that he's here." Sophie hugged her, with undisguised satisfaction.

Wendy groaned. "Because at six feet and built like a football player, with a chiseled jaw and devilish dark eyes, Joe is so easily overlooked. If this turns into a total fiasco, I'm blaming you."

"Give the guy a chance. That's all I'm asking. He'll drive by a couple of times a day, maybe park across the street and hang out. He won't be any trouble." Sophie flashed a brilliant smile as she picked up her box of files.

Wendy opened the door for her, looked out, got distracted by the bright, happy yellow of the forsythia bush in the front yard. "Mind if I take some photos of your place? The garden looks great. And in here too." She looked back. "I like the way the sunshine from the back hits everything."

"Knock yourself out."

"Thanks. I'm trying to upload some work onto online stock photo sites." Small businesses that couldn't afford their own photo shoots used the images for their ads and websites. "If someone buys my pics, I receive royalty payments. If I could bring in an extra couple of hundred dollars a month, it'd be great." She nodded toward the fireplace. "That could make a great romantic backdrop for the cover of an indie romance novel." Stock photos were a way to test the waters, to see if someday she might be able to earn her living with photography.

Sophie paused in the doorway. "I hope your pictures sell like hotcakes."

"Thank you for always being supportive." Wendy followed her outside and opened the car door for her but didn't linger. She didn't like leaving Justin alone. Little boys got into way too much trouble at Justin's age. She backed toward the front door. "I'll call you later."

As Sophie pulled away from the curb, she waved.

A middle-aged woman in an oversized brown coat was walking her Dalmatian. She stopped in front of the house and looked after Sophie's car as it turned at the end of the street.

"I was hoping to catch her." The woman sighed. "I guess she rented out the house, then?"

"Hi, I'm Wendy. Are you one of the neighbors?"

"Terry. We live at the end of the street. I talked to Sophie about renting the house for my parents. They lost their home to a scam artist. All of us living together is not ideal. They're older and need peace and quiet, not four ADHD grandkids. There's only one guest bedroom, so they have to share. They hadn't shared in years. My father snores like a machine. My mother hasn't slept through the night for weeks."

"I'm sorry."

The woman eyed Sophie's house with raw longing. "When my mother is on the edge, everybody is on the edge. Especially my husband." She looked back at Wendy. "It's such a lovely place. You're lucky."

"I'm only here temporarily. You should give her a call." Was Sophie losing rental income? "Sorry. I have to go. I have an unsupervised kid inside." Wendy hurried up the walkway.

She was going to straighten things out with Keith. They couldn't hide from him forever. The end of April was four days away. If she could figure out her life by then and move back into her own apartment, Terry's parents could start renting Sophie's house from the first of May.

Justin was singing the Sheep Shimmy song with the TV, oblivious to trouble, as he should be. Wendy picked him up and covered his chubby little cheeks with kisses. "Ready for lunch?"

"PBJ!" he squealed. He wasn't the type who had to be talked into eating. "I do it!"

She loved his sweet voice. He'd come to talking late, but once he'd started, he picked up vocabulary fast. He was a smart little peanut.

Wendy switched him to her hip and carried him to the kitchen. "Let's wash our hands first."

Sophie's kitchen was larger than the one at Wendy's apartment, comfortable and homey with the kind of country chic décor that matched the rest of the house. Sliding glass doors led to a deck. Justin loved watching squirrels race along the top of the fence in the back.

They washed their hands in the sink, then Wendy collected the jars of grape jelly and peanut butter, and a plastic knife so Justin could try spreading. "Can you hold this? You are such a big boy." She got out the bread. "Thank you for helping."

"I can do it. I can do it!"

She let Justin put two slices of bread into the toaster, then push down the lever. Toast wouldn't fall apart so easily when he went at it with the plastic knife. Sophie had the kind of toaster that printed smiley faces on the side of the bread, which amused Justin to no end.

Wendy was settling her son onto his chair when the doorbell rang.

"Sounds like Aunt Sophie forgot something. Don't make a mess." She smacked a loud kiss on the top of his head before she walked to the door.

She would have been happy to see Sophie. She was not happy to see Joe Kessler.

"Oh. It's you." She immediately regretted the tone. She wasn't normally rude. "Hi."

When she'd first met him, he'd been all boyish charm mixed with pure masculine charisma, as close to physical perfection as any of the male models she'd worked with. In his crisp uniform, he'd looked more like a stripper cop heading to a bachelorette party than a real police officer. Then that second time at that charity ball, in a sharp tux....

Now his dark hair fell in disheveled locks across his forehead, several inches past regulation length. He wore faded blue jeans and a white T-shirt, both wrinkled, as if they'd spent time sitting in his dryer. An angry, red wound stretched across his left cheek, the stitches still in it. He had a different energy, a different aura. He had a hard edge to him that made him look older, as if he'd aged several years in the few months since she'd last seen him.

Only his eyes were the same—the color of strong, black English tea. The cocky glint in those eyes was what had gotten her in trouble in the first place, those eyes and the way he'd smiled at her when he'd offered her a ride home from the fundraiser at the Ritz.

He wasn't smiling now. "Wendy. May I come in?"

She was so stunned by the change in him that she stepped back without arguing the need for his presence. "What happened? How did you get hurt?"

"Captain said you need help." He strode past her, a dark blue gym bag in his hand.

She had a bad feeling about that. "I'm okay. Sophie is being overprotective. Are you okay?"

"The captain filled me in on what's going on. I thought about it." He glanced at Justin making an unholy mess in the kitchen, and dropped his bag by the coatrack. "I'm moving in."

CHAPTER FIVE

WENDY BELLE DID NOT LOOK AS IF THE NEWS THRILLED HER.

"When did you talk to Bing?" she asked Joe, her mysterious gray eyes narrowing.

"This morning." Not that he saw what difference that made.

"Sophie just left here." Wendy wore jeans and a white knit top with azure threads shimmering through it. Her outfit was as relaxed as her no-fuss ponytail. She was a knockout without half trying.

So sue him for noticing.

She was whip smart, too. And a great mother. She was the first woman Joe had ever met who made him feel like she was out of his league. If he had a vain side—very small, miniscule—he might have found that disconcerting. But he wasn't vain. And he wasn't going to let her get to him. Not her, and not the fact that they were the same height, that in heels she was taller than him.

"We've been set up." Aggravation snapped in her tone.

Joe wasn't an idiot. He was going to be a detective. He could put two and two together. He nodded.

"We don't have to fall for it," Wendy rushed to say. "I don't need protection. My ex and I had a fight. It was my fault. I was upset, and Sophie misunderstood."

Defense of the abuser was common from victims of long-term abuse. Joe looked at her more closely, noted the wariness in her eyes that he'd missed before because he'd been too busy staring at her kissable mouth. "What did you fight about?"

She pressed her lips together and took a step back. "I would like full custody of Justin, and I pushed too hard. Keith had a rough day at work. We'll work it out. Honestly, you don't need to be here. *I* don't even need to be here. I should go back to my apartment."

Every time he stepped forward, she stepped back, keeping a safe distance between them. He didn't think she even noticed she did it, just acted on reflex. The small, ingrained defensive habit pissed him off. *Should have caught that sooner.*

"I'll just hang around for a while. In case you need me."

"I don't *need* you," she said with a syrupy sweetness. "You're confusing me with your other women. Won't they go into mourning if you disappear suddenly? I wouldn't want to be responsible for all the wringing of hands and gnashing of teeth in Broslin."

She offered a patronizing smirk of a smile that he would have dearly loved to kiss off her lips, if he weren't there specifically to protect her. She was stonewalling him. He'd been a cop long enough to recognize victim behavior. It made him incredibly sad for Wendy, and beyond pissed at the man who would do this to her.

Sugarcoating wasn't going to help. "Do you think Keith Kline is capable of hurting you? Has he hurt you before?"

"He didn't mean it—"

"I'm moving in." He held up a hand to cut off further, futile protest. "Listen, after the night and morning I've had, I don't have the energy to go through the whole song and dance. Give me your cell phone."

She folded her arms and did her best to stare him down.

He spotted the phone on the sofa table, stepped past Wendy, and grabbed it, held it up to her face to have facial recognition unlock it. He'd picked up a new cell phone on his way over, since his old one was in the river. He entered his new number, then put her phone back down. "I'm going to stick as close to you as possible for the next couple of days, but if your ex shows up when I'm not with you, I want you to call me."

"I'm not sleeping with you again," she said through clenched teeth.

That she thought that was why he'd come, that he was the kind of guy who would take advantage of her problems, ticked Joe off another notch.

He raised an eyebrow. "Rocked your world, huh?" He shook his head. "I'm not here for a repeat. Sorry. I'll be sleeping on the couch. Alone. Don't get any wild ideas."

Then he strolled into the kitchen, leaving her sputtering.

Sophie's kitchen was smaller than his but homier, had a woman's touch—houseplants and flea-market art, little sayings like YES, YOU CAN painted on signs she had hanging all over the place. Sophie was big on positive thinking.

At the table, Wendy's little boy was making what might be lunch, absorbed completely in the task.

"Hey, buddy."

"Hi," Justin said without looking up. He was spreading jelly everywhere but the slice of bread in front of him, sticking his tongue out in concentration.

"I'm Joe. Do you remember me? I'm a friend of Sophie's and your mom's."

Justin spared a glance, shook his head, went back to smearing everything in reach. A glob of purple jelly glistened on his ear, dripping on the green T-Rex on the front of his shirt.

"I'm going to hang out here for a while."

"Why? Do you live here with Aunt Sophie?"

"No. I have my own house, but a dinosaur sat on it."

Justin's attention snapped to him, eyes wide with interest. He pointed at Joe's face. "You have a boo-boo."

"The dinosaur smacked me with his tail by accident."

The kid frowned. "Does it hurt?"

"Nah," Joe said. "Piece of cake. I'm a tough guy."

"Me too, I'm a tough guy. Did the dinosaur make a mess?"

Joe gave an exaggerated eye roll. "You wouldn't believe it. The dishes are in the bathtub. The chairs are hanging from the ceiling."

Justin giggled.

"My socks are in the toilet."

The little boy's squeals bounced off the walls.

"My pillows blew away when he sneezed."

The kid laughed even harder.

Joe stepped closer. "What are you making?"

"PBJ," the little boy said with pride.

The mess was insane. It didn't seem possible that anything was left in the jars. Half the table was frosted with a sticky brownish-purple substance.

Joe glanced at Wendy. "He's thorough. Definitely goes above and beyond. Not to mention sideways."

The tension slipped off her face, replaced by an indulgent smile as she walked up to them and ruffled Justin's hair. "How about I help?"

She fixed the PBJ, cut it into wedges, then cleaned up. She wasn't afraid of a little dirt, even if she *was* a city girl. She only got one smudge of grape jelly on her, on her neck. Joe would have liked to lick it off. If he weren't here to protect her.

"You missed a spot." He indicated the problem with his hand.

She took care of it. "Thanks."

He liked her, but he didn't want to like her too much. She had to have a dark side, or a few bad qualities, at least. Everybody did. She was probably afraid of the woods. And cows too, Joe decided. He was a country boy. No sense in mooning over a fancy city girl and being a total sap for her. She would never fit into his life, so there was no sense it daydreaming about it.

He moved past her. "I'll check out the house."

While Wendy joked and chatted with her son in the kitchen, Joe inspected all the doors and windows. The security was in top shape, the front door brand-new with a new lock and dead bolt. Not that he'd expected any different. When Sophie had had a break-in a couple of months ago, Bing had fortified the place.

Joe circled back into the kitchen. "Everything looks good."

Wendy was washing dishes, so he picked up a kitchen towel to help with drying.

"You don't have to do that." But she shifted to the side to make room for him.

Too much room, he noted the extra distance she put between them. *Skittish.* "Your parents live around here?"

"Florida."

"Siblings?"

"No. And you shouldn't go around accusing people of incest."

The unexpected flash of humor made him laugh. He was a sucker for a sense of humor. "I meant, do you have any siblings?"

"Only child."

Isolated. Exactly how abusers liked their victims.

She handed him a dripping plate, and as he took it, he couldn't help noticing the way the sun shining through the window gilded her in a golden light. His gaze caught on the graceful line of her jaw.

Eyes on your work.

He was there to protect her, not to speculate on how many kisses a determined man could line up between her collarbone and the small hollow behind her ear.

She handed him the next plate. "So how is this going to work?"

"You can go on with your day as you would normally. If you have to go out, I'll follow you in my car. I want to keep you in my line of sight. You need to keep that in mind. Think of me as a bodyguard."

"I'm sure that won't be an intrusion into our lives whatsoever." She pressed her lips together and shook her head. "This is such an overkill. You know that, right?"

"I'm a professional. I can do my job so you won't even notice."

"Yeah? That's what the beauty technician who did my first Brazilian said. I'm not falling for *that* line again."

CHAPTER SIX

"I'm warning you." Wendy put her hands on her hips, dishwater be damned. "I've just about had it."

Keith rarely gave her a choice in anything. And Sophie had pretty much blackmailed her into coming out to Broslin, then staying. Now Joe Kessler was laying down the law about playing bodyguard. Everyone was moving her around as if she were a doll. Nobody asked anymore what she wanted. *She* wanted to be in control of her life. She wanted people to respect her wishes.

"You might not have noticed, but I actually have a job. I work." Her frustration tumbled out. "And I take care of a two-year-old, all by myself. I don't just sit around all day and think about pretty clothes, then prance around on a runway when I feel like it. I have appointments for hair and nails and facials, and I have to go to the gym. I have murderously early photo shoots. Then I go out and take my own photos. I have over a hundred images I haven't even had time yet to upload to the stock photo sites. I spent the morning settling us in here, I updated my digital portfolio, and I paid the bills online. I don't want to have to coordinate every minute of my life with you. Believe it or not, I actually have a schedule."

"I didn't mean—"

"What have you done with your morning?" She flashed a pointed look toward his rumpled civilian clothes. "Spent it in bed with a cheerleader?"

Oh God. Shut up! She hugged herself, waiting for the blow back. If she'd said half this much to Keith, he would have thrown her across the kitchen. Was she stupid? When was she going to learn not to provoke men?

Joe put the kitchen towel down.

Wendy rose to the balls of her feet, poised to run.

His eyes softened with sadness. "I was out at the murder scene of a friend," he said quietly. "Then I had to go notify his widow." He looked out the window. Blinked. "She took it badly. I stayed with her until her parents could come over, or I would have been here sooner."

Oh.

Her heels met the floor. Okay, she was a total bitch. She'd been scared and confused and frustrated, and she'd ripped into someone who didn't deserve it. She barely knew who she was anymore, but she wasn't this. "I'm sorry."

"It's all right. You're in the middle of a crisis. You're entitled to feel off-kilter. When I said we'd hang out, I didn't mean I want to lock you in the house. You can do what you normally do. I can protect you while staying out of your way."

He was so damn kind and reasonable, he disarmed her. "All right. I was about to run out for groceries. If we go now, Justin will be half-asleep by the time we get home, so I can put him down for his nap without him protesting too much. Riding in the car makes him sleepy."

Joe's heavy-lidded eyes said he could use a nap himself, but as tired as he had to be, he smiled at her. "Let's do it."

"Who was murdered?" she asked him. "I thought Broslin was small-town paradise on earth. Sophie didn't say anything."

"The body was only found a few hours ago. She might not have heard from Bing yet."

"You said the victim was a friend of yours? I'm sorry."

"We went to high school together. He became a psychologist. Had an office at the medical center."

"You think one of his patients killed him?"

"Too early to tell. Anyway, I can't discuss an active case."

"Of course. Sorry." She wiped her hands on the dishcloth and stepped away from the sink. "So how is this protection detail going to work?"

"You go to the store as usual, and I'll be right behind you. Please park in a spot where I'll have room to park next to you. Don't get out until I get out, until I give you the nod."

And that was exactly what Wendy did, once they got going.

Joe went into the store with them, and picked up a few things for himself: eggs, bread, mayo, tuna, and cold cuts.

"I can take care of the meals," she offered.

"I'm here to protect you, not to give you extra work. You do enough already. My sister, Amber, is a single mom. I know it's not easy."

His acknowledgement further soothed her ruffled feathers. And then he dropped a green plastic dinosaur into his cart, giving Justin a wink. "That's for you, buddy." And Wendy came perilously close to seriously liking him.

She nudged her son. "What do we say?"

"Thank you!" Justin beamed.

Wendy thanked Joe, too, but he just shrugged. "No big deal. If you can make a little kid happy, I don't see any reason not to do it."

His easy smile and warm tone made it clear that he meant the words.

Wendy could have hugged him.

For Justin's entire life, his own father had never given him a gift, not a single toy. Seeing Joe do it so naturally, without giving it a second thought, made Wendy realize how much Justin was missing. Not gifts, that was the least of it, but fatherly care and love. She'd been so focused on navigating their encounters with Keith to keep everyone safe, that she hadn't thought about the fact that children needed more. Her son *deserved* more.

On their way home, Joe stayed behind them once again. Wendy kept looking around too, but if Keith was out there following her, she didn't catch a glimpse of him.

Joe pulled up next to her at a red light, and Justin waved the plastic dinosaur at him with a grin. Joe put on a startled face, as if he'd gone wide-eyed with fear. Justin dissolved into peals of laughter.

When Keith was around, Justin usually stayed quiet.

Wendy glanced at her son in the rearview mirror. "Do you like Joe?"

"Joe!" Justin banged the dinosaur against the window and laughed again.

Maybe having Joe around for a bit wasn't going to be too bad. For the past couple of hours, he'd managed to keep Wendy's mind off being scared, and that was something.

Broslin, too, had a calming effect on her. The town was warm and welcoming, peaceful. Couples strolled down the sidewalk arm in arm; kids rode three-wheelers. The shops were ridiculously pretty, everything clean and cared for, no garbage blowing on the side of the road, no graffiti on the buildings. The quintessential all-American town surrounded by farmland, cows, and horses. The mushroom capital of the country, complete with signs for fresh-picked mushrooms everywhere.

She checked out a selection of mushroom hats in a boutique window as she drove by. *Brown and floppy.*

She pictured herself wearing one. "Not enough money in the world," she told Justin. "We might not have much, but we have style."

"Pie!"

They were going by the diner. Wendy didn't slow. "Not right now, honey. It's nap time." The window advertised mushroom soup as the special. "This town is seriously mushroom crazy. Who gets this excited about fungi?"

They even had a mushroom festival. Sophie had invited Wendy and Justin the year before. They hadn't been able to attend. Keith had dropped by her apartment and refused to let them leave.

That's not going to happen again. "We are free and fabulous, that's what we are."

She smiled at Justin in the rearview mirror. His eyes were closing. As usual, the car ride was working its magic on him.

The drive back to Sophie's place took no more than ten minutes. She carried Justin to his bed. Joe hauled in the groceries. Then he checked all the doors and windows before pulling out his laptop. "What are you doing next?"

"I'm going to edit and upload a hundred new photos. I want to build up as large an inventory of everyday images as I can. Each photo earns only about a quarter per download. The stock photo game is a numbers game."

"Sounds rough."

"There's no such thing as easy money." Wendy focused on the job.

Joe made a dozen calls and kept working on his laptop, tracking down leads for a case. Wendy couldn't tell if it was his friend's murder or not. She stayed out of his way. When Justin woke up, she played catch with him outside for a while. Fresh air was important for kids, and movement too. She didn't want her son to grow up in front of the TV.

She made chicken and rice for dinner, and invited Joe to join her and Justin.

"Are you sure?" He looked up from his phone. "I can fix myself a sandwich. I meant what I said about not making extra work for you."

"It's no hardship to put another plate on the table."

She'd worked hard at improving her cooking skills, since she'd gotten her own place. The kitchen at Keith's penthouse had been for show. He ate out every night, liked to network, liked to show off his model girlfriend. Starting to cook was another way for Wendy to assert her independence and make her own choices.

"I can cook tomorrow," Joe offered. "Give you a break."

"Sure." She wasn't going to hold her breath. He was a nice guy, but according to Sophie, he was always surrounded by women. Wendy doubted he'd done much work in the kitchen.

He did help her clean up after dinner, however, then played ball with Justin until Wendy took her son upstairs to give him a bath. She read him a picture book, then Justin "read it" back to her, more or less. He knew the words by heart. He was so proud of himself.

Then, of course, as his reward, she had to sing the sheep song, complete with the bleating. She sincerely hoped Joe couldn't hear her.

Once Justin was asleep, Wendy padded back downstairs and settled down in front of her computer again.

Joe was watching the local news but glanced over. "Checking out colleges for Justin already?"

Since he'd caught the college logo on her screen, she might as well come clean.

"I'm taking an online class." He didn't sneer, so she went on. "Digital photography. Manipulating digital images."

"Want to know what it'd be like on the other end of the camera?" His tone held sincere interest.

She rubbed her palm over her knee. "Modeling is not a steady, long-term occupation, but photography isn't much better, is it? There's a reason for the expression *starving artist*."

He turned off the TV. "You could check the Broslin Tourist Board's website. They have a photo contest every year with some pretty good prize money. A win might generate commissions for flyers from local businesses. Weather's supposed to be nice this week. I'll show you and Justin around. You could snap a few pictures. And we have art shows twice a year at the high school. You could make art posters from your photos and sell them there."

Multiple possibilities. Something concrete and achievable. She could actually get started. Yet instead of excitement, she felt unease. "You don't think it's stupid?" She didn't trust his unquestioning support. "Why do you want to help me?"

"Why wouldn't I? Not everybody has an agenda, Wendy." He kept his tone mild, didn't bristle at her for challenging him, didn't fly off the handle. "How did you get into modeling?"

Again, why did he care? Why did he want to know more about her? She didn't trust it.

"I was discovered in a shopping mall in Upstate New York when I was sixteen," she responded, to be polite. "It felt like winning the lottery. The agency had me move to New York City."

"Your parents must have been worried."

"My mother cried her eyes out, but I was living in a dream and talked her into letting me go. What sixteen-year-old doesn't think that she's ready for anything?" Wendy caught herself smiling at the memory. "My parents didn't have the energy to fight me. My mother was forty-five when I was born, my father fifty-five. By the time I was a teen, they were planning retirement."

"They must love having a grandson."

"They want us to move down to Florida. How about your parents? Lobbying for grandbabies yet?"

"They passed away last year. Dad had colon cancer. Mom died of a broken heart three months later. Her heart just stopped." Joe's brows furrowed, his tone heavy. "She wasn't even sick."

"I'm sorry for your loss."

He nodded.

She wanted to hug him. *Probably a bad idea.*

After a few seconds, he asked, "How did you like New York at sixteen? Was modeling as glamorous as you thought it would be?"

"As glamorous as expected, but more cruel. I was never tall enough, not skinny enough. If a picture doesn't come out right, it's always the model's fault. You're assumed to be empty-headed and superficial, and definitely *easy*. A lot of the ad executives routinely came around to ask for *dates*. Models who declined were struck from the roster with one excuse or the other."

"Didn't your agency protect you?" His tone dipped low, tight and pissed. "You were a teenager."

"Some people I worked with protected me. Some tried to pimp me out. As long as the money is rolling in, many agencies are willing to turn a blind eye. Anyway, other than that, what I remember most of the early years is the hunger. I was expected to lose weight. Endlessly. If a model has to drink, do drugs, smoke, or throw up on a regular basis, she's expected to do it and keep her mouth shut about it. In the world of high fashion, appearance is everything."

He held her gaze. "That had to be difficult."

"Early on, I was so dazzled by the city, the speed of it, all the wealth, the opportunity, I barely noticed anything else. Later...." Wendy fiddled with the napkin on her lap. "Having no voice, no choice in even the most personal things became difficult. Others controlled the color and length of my hair, the makeup I put on, and the clothes I wore."

Her life ceased to be under her control from the moment she'd signed on the dotted line at age sixteen, next to her mother's signature as guardian.

"My career belonged to the agency. My time belonged to the customer. My body was no longer my own. Once, I was asked to pose naked for a shoot, wrapped in a giant snake. I was petrified, but I had to suck it up and do it. That's what's expected. Big boo-hoo, right? A million girls would kill for a chance at becoming a model and living on the top of the world. It's not like I was working second shift in a factory. I was lucky."

"You were a kid. You had to be scared and overwhelmed."

"Sometimes I was. Other times, the city and the job distracted me from everything else. The work could be grueling, but it could also be exhilarating. I met Keith in New York."

"How old were you then?"

"Eighteen. He was older, educated, sophisticated. He knew about wine and could quote black-and-white art movies." She'd thought Keith was her knight in shining armor. "Once he walked in on a client manhandling me in the hallway. Keith put the jerk in his place and threatened to rip off his head if he came near me again."

"When you say older... How old was he?"

"Thirty-four."

"He seduced you," Joe said in a flat tone.

"It wasn't like that. We were friends first." He'd been kind back then, exciting. "Apartment prices being what they are in New York, I rented with three other models who were more into the party scene than I was. Drinking, drugs, bringing home strange men. Keith offered the spare bedroom in his penthouse. You should have seen the place. All glass, the city right outside. I felt like Cinderella."

He took her to Broadway shows, to nice restaurants. They held hands. Kissed. He'd been patient. And she'd been so incredibly happy for a while. The happiest she'd ever been. But then he told off more of her clients. And then he told off her agent. He went behind her back and canceled photo shoots that he didn't think were appropriate.

"Eventually, my agency dropped me." She'd been heartbroken, lost, hadn't known what to do, where to go. "At around the same time, Keith's company was opening a new office in Wilmington, and he was transferred to a more senior position here. He asked me to come with him."

He'd told her the New York fashion world was for airheaded whores. The two of them could spend more time together in Wilmington. He tossed the word *family* around until she was dreaming about a white wedding. Except, that wasn't what she got after they moved from New York to Delaware. Keith became more and more controlling, and she didn't have her New York friends for support. She had nobody she could turn to for help.

A fierce glint came into Joe's eyes. "When you met Keith, you were so used to others controlling every aspect of your life, it seemed natural to give him control over everything."

"I didn't—" Wendy's first instinct was to deny, but she couldn't. Honestly, she was just trying her best not to cry, because, by some miracle, Joe knew that she had let herself be abused, but he didn't judge her for it. "I've been stupid and weak, and—"

"No."

His suddenly harsh tone made her jerk back.

"Sorry." He pushed to his feet. "I'm going to check on things outside."

He was mad at her. She'd been boring him to death with her silly story. He had better things to do, with people a lot more interesting than her. He was only with her because Bing had asked him. Couldn't say no to his boss, obviously.

Aw, dammit.

She had to blink back tears of embarrassment as she looked after him.

He probably hated babysitting her and Justin.

CHAPTER SEVEN

Joe closed the door behind him and stood on the front stoop for a minute, unclenching his hands. No cars rushed by. Even the dog walkers were done for the day. The clear night sky stretched over Broslin, an onyx bowl dotted with golden stars. He loved his town, loved every damn thing about it.

He didn't want to get kicked out of Broslin PD. And that meant he couldn't track down Keith Kline and beat him, no sense in fantasizing about it. No sense in fantasizing about Wendy either.

Wendy took him for a small-town jock. So maybe he thought about football and his glory days more than he should. Not a crime. And he liked beautiful women, which wasn't a punishable offense either. He didn't care what anyone thought of him. Except Wendy. He wanted her to have a good opinion of him.

He checked his gun, then walked into the cold of the night. He'd spent too much time at work lately, especially with the undercover gig. He needed to go out more. He hadn't been out with a woman in a while. Since that night with Wendy.

That can't be right. Joe turned his face up to the sky. Had it been that long?

Huh.

It had been.

The week before last, the new waitress at the diner had asked him out for coffee, but he'd been busy. Then there'd been that old high school flame who'd been looking to rekindle things. He'd put her off too, had wanted to do more research on the Brant Street Gang.

He needed to rearrange his priorities. A person had to make room for fun in his life, or it wouldn't be worth living.

He walked around the house, checked up and down the street, saw nothing suspicious.

His thoughts circled back to Wendy.

She'd been *eighteen* when she'd met Keith—living alone in a big city, without her parents, nobody but her agent to watch over her. And her agent had only been concerned about how much money she was making him.

She'd been a magnet for a predator.

Keith freaking Kline.

Joe rolled his shoulders. His body still ached from the crash and from the beating he'd taken in the river. He had some stiff tension he needed to work out of his system. What were the chances that Sophie kept a set of weights in her basement? Probably slim to none since she was a heart transplant recipient and wasn't supposed to overtax her new heart.

Joe pulled his phone from his pocket and called into the station.

"Has Gomez turned up yet?" he asked the captain.

"Nobody has seen or heard from the kid. I just talked to the chief a minute ago. Listen, you can't let it get to you. You did what you could."

"Can only hope it was enough."

After Joe hung up with the captain, he stretched his muscles, then he dropped down and did a hundred sit-ups and a hundred squats, followed by a hundred push-ups.

His body felt better afterwards, but the exercise failed to push Gomez from his mind. He kept seeing the desperate look on the kid's face as he'd floated downriver in the night. Joe walked around the house one last time, then he went inside.

Wendy was still in front of her computer, studying, all rapt attention and poised grace.

"Guest bathroom is upstairs at the end of the hallway. If you want to get ready for bed," she said without looking at him.

The word *bed* coming from her lips unleashed a whole batch of X-rated images in Joe's brain, memories of her coming apart in his arms. He saw her naked before him, back arched, dusky nipples drawn into tight buds as he grazed his lips over them... He cleared his throat.

"I'll go take a shower." *Cold.*

Her gaze remained riveted on the screen.

He knew exactly what his fascination was with her. She posed a challenge. He needed to remember that he liked easy. Easy was fine. Better than fine, *great*. Easy was what he wanted.

Upstairs, he let the cold water pummel him and thought about work. He was almost back in a professional state of mind by the time he tugged on his Broslin PD T-shirt and sweatpants.

At home, he slept naked. And alone. If he spent the night with a woman, he usually stayed over at her place. He didn't have a rule about not taking a date home; it just never worked out that way.

He checked in on Justin on his way downstairs, the kid all snuggled up with his new plastic dinosaur as he slept. Joe's nephew, Max, was about the same age. Joe enjoyed hanging out with him, being the fun uncle, how Max's face lit up whenever Joe walked in. He helped his sister when he could. Since they had no parents, Joe took his big brother responsibilities seriously.

"Did he wake up?" Wendy was padding up the stairs, her steps barely audible on the carpet.

"No. He's a good sleeper. I was just checking on him."

She stopped next to Joe. The soft, exotic scent of her perfume mixed with the scent of baby powder. She was a single mother. Joe had done his best to avoid that kind of complication in the past, as much as possible. The fathers tended to pop in and out of the picture and turn themselves into a major pain.

Joe liked his affairs hot and intense, and his women all to himself. He had no interest in playing house. This wasn't who he was. Yet there was something in the thickening air between him and Wendy that reached him on a deeper level.

"You're good with kids." She stood close enough so that he could have easily turned and pulled her into his arms.

"They're fun at this age." He flashed a carefree grin over his shoulder to mask how much he wanted to touch her. "As long as they're someone else's responsibility."

An unreadable expression crossed her face. "Never settling down, huh?"

He shrugged as he turned. "When you have a good thing going, no sense messing it up, right?"

She walked back down the stairs without responding.

He followed her to the living room, dropped onto the couch, and checked his phone. She shut down her computer then pulled the rubber band from her ponytail. Silky strands of her hair spilled over her shoulders in a cascade of gold. When she reached up to massage her scalp, the soft material of her shirt molded to her chest, outlining her breasts.

He wasn't a total dog, he didn't stare. He only watched from the corner of his eye.

Shapely, but definitely not a rack.

There, she wasn't perfect. He was a boob guy, so sue him. But Wendy Belle couldn't be called stacked by any stretch of the imagination. No reason for him to feel all that heat. And yet... Had he just taken a *cold* shower five minutes ago? He might need another one before he went to bed.

"So, what's going on with your ex?" he asked. "Bing was kind of sketchy."

She shoved the rubber band into her pocket and rested her shapely ass against the lucky edge of her desk. "Everybody is completely over-reacting. I don't want to talk about it. Let's talk about you. What happened to your face?"

"Rough night on the river."

"What river? Broslin Creek?"

"Never mind. Nothing wildly exciting." He couldn't share details of his undercover mission. "Back to the boyfriend." He hadn't jumped right into questioning her earlier, didn't want to in front of Justin, but he did need as much information as she would give him. "Keith Kline." The fact that the bare mention of the asshole's name could make her flinch said something right there. "Bing only told me that Keith turned threatening. What does that mean?"

She tucked her hair behind her ear. "He's going to be mad if he finds out that I'm talking to the police. I don't want to make him mad. I need to keep him happy. I'm hoping he'll sign over full custody."

"Is he using Justin to stay in your life?"

She looked at her toes, wiggled them inside her fuzzy purple socks. "He's been difficult. I should have realized earlier... I feel so stupid."

Joe kept a lid on the anger that bubbled up inside him. "Plenty of smart women fall for *difficult* men. Some of those guys are good enough actors to get their own stars on Hollywood Boulevard."

"He used to be different. He changed after I got pregnant with Justin."

"How?"

She shrugged.

Unfortunately, Joe couldn't drop the subject. "The more I know about him, the more I'll be able to anticipate his next move if he means to do you harm. Knowing more about him, about his personality, would be helpful."

He also planned on running a background check on the guy, although, he was pretty sure the captain had run one already. Something to check in the morning.

Wendy rubbed the heels of her hands over her hips. "He's good-looking, charismatic. Driven. Definitely type A. He has a lot of powerful friends. He's a top insurance broker at his company. We met at an art gala where I was modeling wearable art. His company was one of the sponsors of the event. He can put on the charm. When he wants something, he pulls out all the stops, both in business and his personal life. I was blinded by all the flowers and gifts, the lavish dates."

"And then he changed."

Her shoulders tensed. She gave a reluctant nod. "Little by little. Harsh, then sweet again. Each time he lost his temper, I'd just think he was having a bad day, a hard day at the office. *This is not him. He just needs a break from stress.*"

Joe was familiar with the abuser profile. They were all charming at the beginning. Then they took more and more control until they had their victims trapped. "He didn't like your friends, so your friends started staying away. He used to praise your beauty, then suddenly began telling you that you're fat, or ugly, or stupid."

Wendy wrapped her arms around herself, betrayal and resentment flashing in her eyes. "Did Sophie tell you all that? Forget it." She turned away. "I'm not going to strip emotionally naked for your entertainment."

First of all, for love's sake, don't say naked. "Sophie told me nothing. Broslin sees maybe a dozen violent crimes in the average year, and around a hundred and fifty property crimes. The detectives are assigned to the major homicides and burglaries, with the captain stepping in for high-profile cases. Other property crimes and domestic disturbances fall to me and Mike. I've seen my share of abused women and kids."

She looked back at him.

"How long has the physical abuse been going on?" He wished he'd found out about Wendy's troubles when he'd first met her. He could have helped. He could have spared her months of abuse.

She said nothing.

"How badly does he hit you?"

Her arms tightening around her middle. "He doesn't."

A lot of victims lied. They blamed themselves. Joe didn't express his anger through hitting, but right then he would have liked nothing better than to plant his fist in Keith Kline's face.

Wendy pushed away from her desk. "I should go up to bed. I have a shoot first thing in the morning in Philly."

If she didn't feel comfortable enough yet to confide in Joe, that was okay. But he wanted her to know that he was committed to protecting her. "He's not going to get through me. I'm here now. Whatever he's done in the past, I'm not going to let him do it again."

She gave a quick, jerky nod, an acknowledgement purely for his benefit. He could tell she didn't believe him.

"Where will Justin go while you're on the shoot?" he asked.

"I'll leave him with Ginny. She lives in my apartment building. She's a single mom too. She watches kids for extra money."

"Does Keith know that Ginny babysits for you?"

The way the blood ran out of Wendy's face gave him the answer.

Her eyes filled with a deep misery. "I'd like to think he wouldn't take Justin, but.... If he thought it'd make me come to him?" She rubbed her hands against the fabric of her pants, a nervous tick he didn't think she was aware of. "I can't skip the shoot. I need the money to pay bills. And if I cancel at the last minute, they'll never call me again."

"I could watch Justin," Joe offered for no discernible reason, regretting it immediately. He was a police officer on an unofficial protection detail, which did *not* include babysitting. Yet the words kept coming out of his mouth. "I don't mind."

She hesitated. "Justin doesn't know you that well yet. No offense, but I don't know you that well yet either. Leaving my baby with someone is a big deal."

"Of course. I know that. I meant, I was planning on sticking around you guys anyway. If you're going to a shoot, I'm going with you. We could take Justin, and I could watch him right there, behind the scenes, keep an eye on both of you at the same time. Would the shoot director agree to that?"

"She brings her kids and the nanny sometimes." Hope lit up Wendy's face. "You'd do that?"

"He's good kid. I doubt he'll be too much trouble. He'll keep me from getting bored by all those models running around in bikinis."

For a second, Wendy smiled, but the smile quickly disappeared. "You can't hit on the models. I mean it. We'll both get kicked out."

Annoyance bristled through him. "Give me some credit."

She did instantly look chagrined. "I'm sorry. That wasn't fair."

Oh hell. "Technically, it was."

If this had happened three months ago, he would have gone and collected phone numbers. He'd been off his game lately.

She smiled at his admission, then walked to the stairs before turning back for one last look. "Good night, Joe. Happy dreams."

Unlikely. He'd settle for dreams that didn't include Gomez as he floated downriver on that cursed log.

Of course, Wendy caught his sudden change of mood. "What is it?"

"I'm pretty sure someone died because of me last night," he said without meaning to. And then he had to explain it. "I was supposed to protect him, and I didn't. Fifteen years old, dammit."

"I'm sorry. Is that when you got hurt?"

He nodded.

"Do you want to talk about it?"

"No. And I couldn't if I did. It's another ongoing investigation." He had no idea why he'd brought it up. Maybe because he wanted someone to lay the blame on him, since Captain Bing wouldn't.

Wendy wouldn't either. Instead, she said, "Even the best cop in the world can't save everyone."

A damn depressing thought. What if he couldn't keep Wendy and Justin safe?

She held his gaze. "We are safer with you here."

Yeah. But what if "safer" wasn't enough?

He actually *wanted* Keith to show up. Because if Keith came, and he threatened Wendy, Joe could toss his bastard ass in jail and throw the book at him. Problem solved. Except, long-time abusers tended to be cannier than that.

She started up the stairs again.

"Good night, Wendy."

She didn't stop this time, didn't turn back. Probably better that way, for the both of them.

After she was gone, Joe lay down on the couch and swore silently. He shouldn't have told her about Gomez. That was his burden to bear.

He shouldn't be wishing that he could go upstairs with her either.

He shouldn't be thinking every five minutes about the night they'd spent together. He seriously needed to quit doing that.

They'd slept together *once*. Barely knew each other. She'd gone out of her way, on multiple occasions, to let him know that she was less than impressed with him. She had a kid and an asshole of an ex—the very opposite of uncomplicated. Joe didn't understand his fascination with her. Normally, he wasn't a masochist.

She was a good mother; that was obvious from watching her for five minutes. But since when was that sexy? Yet he wanted her. He'd wanted her from the moment he'd laid eyes on her.

She was a city girl. Too tall. She had no rack, he reminded himself, hoping that would save him from making a complete fool of himself. But, nope, his hard-on didn't budge any.

Oh hell. Who was he kidding?

———

Wendy had one of those dreams where you're aware that you're dreaming. She could have fought to come awake, but she didn't.

She was in Philly, heading back into the Ritz Carlton to have the concierge call her a cab after she hadn't been able to find one by the curb. She was halfway across the foyer when Joe Kessler walked out of the grand ballroom, the after-party still in full swing behind him.

In a sharp tux, he looked good enough for the runway. Or the movies. He had those wide shoulders, that easy cop walk of his, that athlete's body. He looked good enough for a spy-thriller blockbuster. The zing she'd felt the first time they'd met was still there, which annoyed her to no end.

"Can I give you a ride home?" He had a smile that could turn from cocky to seductive to disarming in a second. He was the type of man a woman should simply turn away from unless heartache was her hobby.

Wendy's life was plenty complicated already. She put on her coolest, most unaffected expression that she'd perfected for modeling. "I'm not going to sleep with you."

"There's always next season."

"Is that some clever football expression?"

He shoved his hands into his pockets and checked her out, took his time, missing no detail of her floor-length gown, not the slit over her thigh or the neckline's dangerously low dip. His gaze had a life of its own, leaving tingles on her skin.

"Odd how sex is the first thing you think of when you look at me," he said.

She managed to keep her unaffected smile, but only just.

"A ride?" he offered again. "Nothing implied."

She glanced at the concierge, where people waited ten deep. Somewhere in the ballroom, Keith was searching for her. He'd shown up unexpectedly. Hadn't seen her yet, thank God. She'd seen him first.

"Fine. But I'm not inviting you in for a nightcap."

She half expected a police cruiser, but the car the valet brought up was a souped-up black Camaro with red racing stripes, the engine a throaty rumble. The car fit him. When he opened the door for her, she slipped into the black leather bucket seat with appreciation.

"You attend charity balls a lot?" she asked after she gave him her address.

His lips stretched into a playful, mysterious smile. "Maybe I came just to see you."

She refused to acknowledge the tingles. The guy had BIG MISTAKE stamped all over him. She'd already made her big mistake with Keith. She had to be *a lot* smarter going forward.

"Listen, it's flattering, and maybe there's an attraction here..." She flashed Joe an apologetic smile. "I'm not going to pretend there isn't. But I'm not going to go with it. Under any circumstances. So pursuing it is just a waste of your time."

The glint in his eyes turned devilish. "You admitted to being attracted to me. And you care. Otherwise, why worry about wasting my time? Attraction and caring." His amused smile was ridiculously sexy. "Sounds like you're half in love with me. You might be going too fast. I don't want you to get hurt."

She'd responded with some travel advice, recommending a hot, dry climate.

"I won't take offense," he told her casually. "I know city girls can be a little brash. They lack that sweet hospitality of a good country woman."

"Maybe you should stick with those country women. Could be you're out of your league here."

"Could be," he agreed, but didn't look the least disturbed.

In the end, she did invite him in. For a cup of coffee, because it was two in the morning and he still had a long drive ahead of him back home to Broslin. And then there was the fact that he'd walked her to her door to make sure she was safe, then pulled a tiny toy police car from his pocket. "For Justin."

Really, she couldn't just say, *Go away*.

She'd been rude to him, presumptuous too, and she wasn't normally like that. So she made him coffee, but poured it into a travel mug. She wanted him gone and her equilibrium back.

As she handed him the mug, he gently folded his long fingers around her wrist, pulled her to him, and brushed his lips against hers. "Thank you. Good night, Wendy."

His gentle touch had been a whisper against her skin. He was steady and calm, a sharp contrast to Keith, who'd dragged her across the apartment by her hair that morning, threatening to take Justin away from her.

"I'd like to give you a proper good-night kiss," Joe had said, asking for permission, and then he waited patiently for her answer.

No. The word had been on the tip of Wendy's tongue. She didn't want a kiss. She didn't want sex. She'd managed to avoid Keith's advances for months. She didn't even like sex anymore. She couldn't remember the last time intimacy hadn't hurt.

She wasn't sure anymore if she believed that a relationship could be different. Yet part of her desperately wanted Joe to show her that it could be.

The next thing she knew, she was kissing him. "I'm on the pill."

"I'm going to use protection anyway."

"Yes, you will."

And then they were naked, and he was carrying her to bed. Within five minutes, she was flying among the stars, the orgasm ripping through her so thorough and powerful that it scared her. Everything felt good. All of it. So incredibly good that it made her want to cry. She'd wanted him to stay, so as soon as she caught her breath, she'd sent him away.

In her dream, Wendy was back there again, exactly as she had been that night, spent, lying naked on top of the tangled covers, staring at the ceiling as her heart raced, wondering what had just happened, swearing it was never going to happen again.

When she woke from the dream, she spent a moment appreciating the irony that she was now *living* with Joe Kessler.

God, if Keith found out, he was going to kill them.

CHAPTER EIGHT

OUTSIDE WENDY'S APARTMENT BUILDING, KEITH KLINE TOSSED THE last of his morning coffee into the garbage.

Wendy was at Sophie's house in Broslin. With a man who'd better be Sophie's brother on a family visit. Did Sophie have a brother? Hell if Keith knew. He hadn't gotten a good look at the guy's face through the curtains last night. He hadn't seen Sophie either, but it'd been late. Maybe Sophie had been in bed already. He'd watched Wendy go up to sleep. The man, the stranger, had stayed downstairs. Which was why they were all still alive, even though Keith had a mind to set the whole damn place on fire and watch them burn.

In the bright light of the morning, Keith felt calmer. Wendy was too stupid to outsmart him. If he wanted her, he'd get her back. End of story.

He walked into the apartment building and across the lobby, over the worn carpet, past the scuffed walls. Management was sprucing up the place, working from the top down. Their method had a certain logic to it. This way, they wouldn't damage newly-painted hallways while carrying equipment, wouldn't spill paint on newly-installed flooring. They were almost done on Wendy's floor, but Keith couldn't say the "upgrade" made much of an improvement. The building was a shithole, no doorman, no amenities. That Wendy would choose *this* over his penthouse in the best apartment complex in town filled him with dark fury.

He rode the elevator up to the sixth floor, to Ginny's apartment. He'd seen Wendy's schedule stuck on her fridge, the last time he'd stopped in to check on her. She'd be at a shoot this morning, which meant Justin would be with the babysitter.

Justin was Keith's son. Wendy had no right taking off with him. She needed to be taught a lesson. And Keith was ready to deliver it.

He knocked.

Ginny opened the door, a twenty-year-old single mother of twins. She wore faded jeans and an even more faded T-shirt, size large. She'd never lost the baby weight. Keith tried not to look at her body. Fat women disgusted him.

"Nice haircut." He turned on the charm anyway. "I'm supposed to pick up Justin. Have the day off. I figured we'd hang out and do a father-son day."

The confusion on the woman's pudgy face was instant and seemed sincere. "I don't have Justin."

In the living room behind her, her two little girls were watching cartoons. No other kid.

Keith rubbed his thumb over his eyebrow. "Oh man. I'm an idiot. I bet Wendy said she was dropping him off at Sophie's. I was in the parking garage when she called. The phone was cutting in and out. Sorry."

"No problem." Ginny's chubby-cheeked smile was grotesque.

She looked like a happy pig. Biggest favor someone could do for her would be to lock her in a room with a bowl of vegetables for a week. Keith almost told her that, but then again, what did he care? Ginny was nothing to him. She wasn't his. Wendy was, the only one who mattered. Even if she didn't always appreciate the amount of energy he spent on carving her to perfection.

Keith strode back to the elevator. Maybe Sophie did have the kid. Were they home alone? Likely not. If the guy Keith had seen was a visiting brother, he might still be there.

For how long?

Keith stabbed at the elevator button. He could be patient. He'd wait until the time was right. Then he'd pay those bitches a visit.

He already had a gift in the mail for Wendy, to make sure that in the meanwhile she didn't forget him.

Keith rode down one floor, then got off the elevator again and let himself into Wendy's apartment. He wanted to leave a backup message there, something that would make his fury unmistakable.

In case his gift in the mail didn't prove to be sufficient.

———

Joe's presence at the photo shoot, and the zing Wendy felt every time their eyes met, threw her off stride. He was so not the man she needed in her life right now. She had her son to think about.

Justin had the time of his little life, of course, with the models fussing over him. Nobody had an issue with him being there. Joe kept him busy. He read a couple of pop-up books he'd grabbed from the house, then did magic tricks.

He could pull coins and candy out of people's ears, apparently. Of course, Wendy *had* already known that he had clever fingers. She tried not to think about that as she worked.

The other models were nothing but smiles around him. He was good-looking, and not in the androgynous way of some male models. He was all testosterone, hot cop. The scar didn't hurt. *Everybody* had to take a closer look. Not that Wendy was jealous. The girls were welcome to him. She had no romantic interest in Joe Kessler whatsoever.

On the way home, she asked him to swing by the post office on their way home. "If that's okay."

He nodded, as if it didn't even occur to him to mind the imposition. *Keith would have exploded.*

"Need to mail something?"

"Just want to check my PO box." She'd set one up when she'd realized that Keith went through her mail.

Joe turned at the next light, adjusting their course. This time, they were all riding in her car, instead of him following her.

He pulled over in front of the post office, and she jumped out. "I'll only be a minute."

The box was full, a good thing she stopped by. She gathered up the stack of envelopes, grabbed the small box wedged in the back, then she hurried back to the car.

Joe was entertaining Justin with dinosaur tales.

"Thank you." She clicked on her seatbelt.

"That was quick."

"I skipped breakfast for the shoot." She tossed the box at her feet. "I don't dilly-dally when I'm hungry for lunch." She dropped the rest of her mail onto her lap, and began separating bills from junk mail. "Want to look at kitties?" She handed a pet-store flyer to her son, as Joe pulled away from the curb.

When she was done sorting, she put all the important mail on top and went through it one by one.

"My agency is updating their contracts." They sent her a copy of the new one. "Fifteen pages. Jeez."

By the time she read through it, her careful study of legalese interspersed with fending off Justin's entreaties for a cat, they were in Broslin.

"We're not allowed pets in our apartment. I'm sorry, peanut. If someday we move to another place, we'll talk about it, okay?"

"Kitty!"

"How about if I take you over to see Aunt Sophie and you can play with Mango." Mango was Captain Bing's cat.

"Mango! Mango!" Justin laughed with sheer joy.

He was pure and simple, easily delighted to oblivion by the smallest things. He was Wendy's ever-present ray of sunshine, the best part of her life. She loved him so much, sometimes it hurt. Never would Keith *ever* have custody of him.

Wendy gathered her pile of mail from her lap and relocated it to the backseat, then she picked up the package that waited at her feet. Plain cardboard box, no return address. "Wonder what this is."

Joe glanced at her. "Ordered anything online lately?"

"Not that I can remember. Might be makeup samples. I'm on the list for a couple of cosmetics companies."

She ran her fingernail under the tape and popped the box open, screamed before she could stop herself, and shoved the package off her lap. "Oh God."

Her feet were up on her seat, her heart pounding hard, hard, hard. Joe pulled over. "Are you all right?"

"I have to get out for a sec." She jumped to the sidewalk before the car fully stopped. Then her son was in her arms. She was shaking as she walked away, holding him tightly. "Hey, want to go into the bookstore?"

There'd been something furry in the box. And blood.

Dammit, Keith.

Justin pointed at the diner ahead, at the colorful posters in the window. "Cookies."

"Which one would you like?" Wendy glanced back at Joe. She drew a deep breath. She had to stop freaking out. For Justin's sake.

"Cookie! Cookie! Cookie!"

Joe was using a tissue to extract the box from the car. He checked inside, the muscles in his face snapping tight. "I'll have someone from the station come and pick this up. Why don't you and Justin pick us up dessert for tonight? My treat. Tell Eileen to put it on my tab." He shook his head. "Actually, we might be here for a while. Why don't you two grab lunch?"

"Sure." She didn't want to fall apart on the sidewalk. "What is it?"

"Just a wig."

Not a dead animal. Thank God. She was awash in relief as she shifted Justin on her hip. Made herself smile. "Let's go in."

"Yay!" Justin clapped his hands, oblivious to anything else but the promise of sweets.

The lunch rush was over, most of the tables stood empty. Her knees still shaking, Wendy slipped into the nearest booth.

"Look." She pointed at the place mat set up for coloring. "Dancing sheep." Better distract Justin so he wouldn't start asking why Joe wasn't coming in with them.

The diner was clean and bright, nothing fancy. Gleaming glass cases displayed pies and other goodies, the mouthwatering aroma of homemade food mixed with the scent of freshly brewed coffee.

A waitress hurried over, pulled a box of crayons from her pocket, then set it in front of Justin with a wink. "There you go, big boy." She was older and had the kind of ageless beauty Wendy envied, salt-and-pepper hair in a French braid, a warm smile on her face. "Welcome. I'm Eileen. Can I get you anything to drink?"

"Thank you. A glass of water and a glass of apple juice, please."

While her son colored, Wendy looked through the menu. *To count calories or not to count calories?* To hell with it. She needed comfort food.

Eileen served their drinks. "Here you go."

"Thank you. We'd like to share one of your famous meat pies." Wendy pointed at the picture of the one stuffed with chicken, broccoli, corn, peas, mushrooms, and cheese. Thank goodness, Justin wasn't a picky eater.

Eileen didn't write the order down. She just smiled at them the way a mother would when serving food in her own kitchen. "You bet. Let me know if you need anything else."

A police cruiser pulling up behind Wendy's car outside drew their attention to the window.

"Everything all right?" Eileen asked.

Nothing was all right at the moment, but Wendy forced a smile.

"We're good. Joe will take care of it."

"He's a good friend to have. Used to be a hell of a football player." As Eileen walked away, she pointed behind the counter to a photograph.

The picture showed a bunch of waitresses posing with Joe. He wore a football jersey and was grinning from ear to ear, holding up a golden trophy. He had the kind of charisma that would shine through a ten-year-old picture.

A knock on the window kept Wendy from staring longer than was safe. Bing waved hello to Justin from outside. Joe gestured her to stay where she was. So she did and had lunch with her son—what little she could eat with her stomach clenched into a ball of misery.

After lunch, to distract herself, she pulled her camera and took Justin up to the display case. "Ready for that cookie?"

"Everything was baked fresh this morning," Eileen said, back behind the counter.

"I want the green one," Justin piped up, pointing at a cupcake instead. "It's a dinosaur."

Eileen set one on a plate then handed it to Wendy, since Justin couldn't reach that high. "Pistachio frosting with licorice buttons for eyes. Do you like black licorice?"

Wendy passed on the treat and smiled at Eileen. "I guess we will find out."

She watched Justin scramble back to their table with his prize. "Would you mind if I took some pictures?"

"Click away." Eileen beamed, proud of her baked goods and with good reason. "Want me to step out of the frame?"

"Stay, please."

Wendy snapped photo after photo of pies of every variety, from dessert to meat pies, shepherd pies, the works. If only the lattice pies weren't stuck in the corner....

Eileen caught her hesitating. "Anything wrong?"

"Sorry. I'm rearranging things in my mind. Occupational hazard. Just matching color against color and shape against shape, looking for the most interesting combination. In a good photo, like in a good painting, composition is everything."

Eileen squinted at the case then shrugged. "Color and composition are not my thing. But you're welcome to move anything around you'd like."

"Are you sure?"

Eileen grabbed a pair of new rubber gloves from under the counter and handed them over. "Go for it."

The bigger pies went to the back, the smaller ones to the front for visibility, the most vibrant, lattice-top strawberry-rhubarb pies distributed throughout as highlights to draw the gaze. Then Wendy adjusted for scale and movement of color. By the time she finished, the display case looked good enough to paint.

"Like a picture in a magazine." Eileen stared, as if she'd just witnessed magic. "Is this what you do for a living?"

Wendy snapped more pictures. "I wish."

When she was finished, she thanked Eileen profusely for putting up with her.

"Gosh, it's almost too pretty to mess up by selling something." The woman laughed. "I suppose I'll have to bring myself to do it."

By the time Wendy walked outside with Justin, Bing was gone.

Justin proudly showed Joe the sheet of animal stickers he'd received as a parting gift. "Puppies and piggies!"

"Sweet deal, bro." Joe opened the back door of the car so Wendy could put Justin into his car seat. He nodded at the white Styrofoam box she was carrying. "Leftovers?"

"Eileen sent you lunch. A Portobello and Bacon Extravaganza Burger with spicy fries."

He took it from her so she could strap Justin in. "I don't suppose you know who I'd need to call at the Vatican to have her sainted?"

"Not something that comes up in the course of my average day. Sorry."

Joe set his lunch on the dashboard. "I'll eat at the house. Bing said he's coming by to talk to you. He took your package to dust it for prints. He's *officially* assigning you a protection detail. I'll be staying with you all of today and tonight. Mike will spell me in the morning. Officer Mike McMorris."

Wendy's first instinct was to protest that she didn't need all this fuss made over her. Then she decided that was stupid. Maybe she could handle Keith if he showed up; maybe she couldn't. She might have taken the risk for herself, but she wasn't willing to take it for Justin. "Thank you."

"How was lunch?" Joe asked as they got into the car, Justin happy with his stickers in the back.

"Perfect. Eileen spoiled us rotten. She's a great waitress."

"She's the owner," Joe said.

"Really? Wow." Owning an entire diner with customers and employees, delivery schedules... And here Wendy was, nervous about snapping some photos and trying to sell them. "She's pretty impressive. I'd like to be her when I grow up." Maybe she could start with facing her problems. "What did the wig look like?"

A muscle ticked in Joe's face as he drove. "Dark. Short. You own anything like that?"

"I have a dark, short wig that I used for a photo shoot a couple of weeks ago." Cold snaked down her spine. Last she'd seen the wig, it'd been hanging in her bathroom at home. She glanced at Justin who was still absorbed in his stickers. "Keith might have been to the apartment," she whispered to Joe.

"He has a key?"

"He pocketed my spare when I wasn't looking. It's no big deal. When I'm home, I keep the dead bolt turned."

"Has he ever used the key before when you weren't home?"

"No." She paused. "I've come home a few times and thought that maybe things had been moved, but I couldn't be sure."

"What things?"

"Sticky notes, where I jotted down appointments, went missing from my desk. Food missing from the fridge and ending up in the garbage, but I didn't remember tossing it. My clothes hanging differently in the closet. But I might have done that and I just didn't remember."

"You need to change the lock."

"Can't, according to the rental contract. Property management has to be able to get in with their master key."

He looked like he was about to argue, but then, instead, he said, "I'll swing by your place later and check on that wig. You and Justin could visit with Sophie at the farm while I'm out."

"Thank you. Okay." She glanced back at Justin again. He was playing with a black travel mug. "I need that, sweetie. That belongs to your dad." She took the designer brand mug away from him. Too late. The side was dotted with animal stickers. Keith was going to blow a gasket.

"Hey, it looks nicer that way." Joe winked at Justin.

Justin ignored both of them. His eyes were slowly closing. Post-lunch car ride equaled a nap.

Keith hated when Justin messed up his things. He'd be mad at Justin for doing it, and mad at Wendy for letting it happen. She should have noticed the mug sooner. Must have been under the little blue blanket she kept in the car for Justin. She scraped off as many stickers as she could, then stashed the mug in the glove compartment. It was a problem, but not her biggest problem by far.

If Keith was now sending her hate mail, it meant he was really, *really* angry. She shouldn't have moved out. She shouldn't have listened to Sophie. Everybody was trying to help, but... Wendy clenched her hands on her lap. They didn't understand that they were making things worse for her. She'd made Keith mad, and now there'd be consequences.

Justin didn't wake up when Joe pulled into Sophie's driveway. Wendy carried him upstairs to bed. Used the bathroom. Changed her shirt. Realized she was stalling, so she returned downstairs.

Joe was eating in the kitchen. Bing was with him.

"Wendy. How are you?" The police captain pulled his notebook. "I have a couple of questions."

Joe popped his last fry into his mouth, then carried his plate to the sink. "While you have the captain here, I'll go and see if Keith lifted that wig from your apartment. Maybe we can get him on breaking and entering."

Bing didn't comment. The two men must have already discussed it.

"Okay." Wendy handed her keys to Joe.

Then Joe was gone, and Wendy was alone with Bing.

"He's a good friend to have." The captain echoed Eileen's words.

"Yes." Truth was, Joe Kessler did make a good friend.

He listened to Wendy, played with her son, protected them. And Wendy was grateful for all of that. God knew, she didn't have many friends.

Too bad their tenuous friendship was going to end once she told him her secret.

CHAPTER NINE

THE FIRST TIME JOE HAD BEEN IN WENDY'S APARTMENT, HE'D BEEN so focused on her he'd barely noticed the details. And now the details were obliterated.

Smashed pictures. Broken furniture. A cracked high chair lay at his feet, antique tiger maple, probably a family heirloom. Joe pulled his cell phone from his pocket, dialed 911, and gave them the address, anger shimmering through him.

He reported the break-in then called Wendy, hating to give her the news. At least his Philly undercover gig was over. He could stick close to her as long as necessary.

"Hey," he said when she picked up. "I'm at your place. Looks like Keith has been here."

The small sound of her catching her breath came through the line. She knew it was bad.

"What did he do?"

"Made a mess." Joe catalogued the broken furniture and the couch that had been sliced open. "Couple of thousand dollars' worth of damage. I can help you clean up. I have an old pickup I use to haul things. There's a great furniture consignment shop in Broslin, if you want to replace anything on the cheap. I can take you and transport whatever you buy, bring it up, set it up, anything you need."

"Thank you." Her voice was watery. "I'll be right over."

"You don't have to rush. Police are on their way. I can deal with them, if you'd like."

"I should be there. It's my place. Bing is still here at the house. Sophie popped in too. Let me see if I can leave Justin with them."

"Okay." Maybe she needed to deal with the situation herself, take back some of the control that had been stolen from her. And maybe she needed to see the aftermath of Keith's violence. Maybe it would help her decide to walk away from her ex for good. Maybe she'd finally press charges. "I'll hold down the fort until you get here."

They ended the call, and Joe stepped back out into the hallway so he wouldn't contaminate the crime scene. While he waited for Wilmington's finest, he called Captain Bing. "Wendy said you were still over there."

"I was just about to call you. She told me her place was broken into." The captain's ominous tone promised hardcore ass kicking. "Keith."

"Knowing it and proving it are two different things." Joe was too tightly wound to stand still. He walked a dozen steps toward the end of the hallway, then a dozen steps back, careful not to brush against the freshly painted walls. "Do we know if Keith Kline has a record? A documented history of violent behavior?"

"Not so much as a parking ticket. He's canny. Knows how to keep up a good front."

"Most chronic abusers do. That's how they get away with it for so long."

"But not forever. Hold on. Harper's calling in." The line went silent for a couple of minutes. Then Bing came back. "Harper's got a new lead in the Brogevich case. The wife remembered something. About a month ago, a schizophrenic patient threatened Phil. The patient accused Phil of working for the government and giving him drugs to make him crazy. Harper is trying to track the guy down, but he's paranoid, doesn't like to stay long in one place, bunks with a family member or friend for a few days then moves on."

"Marie deserves closure. Knowing who and why won't erase the grief, but having to wonder makes everything that much worse. What can I do to help?"

"Harper will bring the guy in. You stick with Wendy for now."

The captain was right. Joe couldn't be at two places at the same time. "When Harper brings in the suspect, I'd like to be there for the interview."

"I'll tell him to give you a call."

"I appreciate it." The elevator dinged behind him, making him turn. "Wilmington PD is here. I'll call you later with an update."

He clicked off, then strode down the hallway to meet the officers. "Officer Joe Kessler, Broslin PD. I called 911."

"Officer Conti." The man, close to fifty, short, sported a potbelly. His sharp green eyes scanned Joe before cutting to the open apartment door. "Your place?"

"A friend's. Her name is Wendy Belle."

"Officer Tuchman," the female officer with Conti introduced herself but didn't offer a hand. She stood an inch or two taller than Conti, her red hair in a ponytail. She didn't look older than thirty, no makeup, seemed like a no-nonsense type of woman. Her gaze hesitated on the scar on Joe's face. "You have your badge?"

"Off duty. On sick leave." Joe gave them his badge number as he led them to the apartment. "I have a pretty good idea who did it. Keith Kline. Ex-boyfriend. He's been harassing Miss Belle lately."

Conti shot Joe an I'll-be-the-judge-of-that look and stepped inside. "You stay out there." He strolled to the middle of the kitchen. "Did you walk in when you got here?"

"Just to the edge of the carpet."

Tuchman walked by him too. "Touch anything?"

"The doorknob."

The two looked around, then Conti ran down for the crime-scene kit, and they snapped pictures and dusted for fingerprints. They did a thorough job. Joe was prepared to push if they didn't.

They were about done when Wendy rushed down the hallway. "I tried to get here as fast as I could. Why is there always more traffic when you're in a hurry?"

She managed to stay graceful and poised even under the circumstances, still wearing the same sleek slacks and formfitting tan sweater
that she'd worn to the photo shoot. Her cream-colored coat was
cinched at her waist, fresh and crisp. Come to think of it, Joe had
never seen a smudge of dirt on her, not even when she was cleaning up
after Justin. Must be a model thing.

Only the turbulence in her gray eyes betrayed that she was stressed.
"Let me see."

She would have sailed right in, but Joe caught her by the wrist and
held her back.

The distress in her eyes switched to naked alarm in a blink.

He immediately let her go. *No grabbing.* He knew better, dammit.
"We have to stay out here until they're finished. Hey," he added quietly.
"It's going to be okay." He reached out slowly and took her hand, ran
the pad of his thumb over her fingers.

No alarm this time. She let him. For a few seconds, at least. Then
she stepped away. She stuck her head inside the apartment for a better
look, and for a moment she looked as if she might cry. "That high chair
was my mom's. My grandfather made it. It was supposed to be handed
down in the family."

Joe resisted the impulse to pull her into his arms. They'd had one
wild night. One wild hour and a half, really. She wasn't his.

Officer Conti shuffled over. "Ma'am, are you the tenant?"

"Yes. Wendy Belle."

He introduced himself and his partner. "Can you tell me when you
left home, Miss Belle?"

"Yesterday morning. I'm staying at a friend's place."

"Does anyone else have a key to the apartment?"

"My ex-boyfriend, Keith Kline."

The man's gaze cut to Joe. "And Officer Kessler here?"

"I gave him my key to check on something." Wendy rubbed the
heel of her hand over the side seam of her coat. "I received a bloody
wig in the mail today. I thought it might be mine. Joe offered to come
over to see if it's missing."

"Is it?"

"I don't know." Wendy's gaze darted past the man. "Is there a short, dark wig on the peg on the back of the bathroom door?"

Conti called out the question to his partner. Officer Tuchman checked the back of the door, then the rest of the bathroom. "Not here."

"Can you tell if anything else was taken?" Conti asked Wendy next.

She looked around from the threshold. "Hard to say from here."

"The TV and the iPad weren't stolen," Joe pointed out. He could see both from where he was standing. "A burglar would have gone after the electronics."

Officer Conti nodded. "Do you have contact information for—" He checked his notes. "Keith Kline?"

Wendy rattled off the address and phone number.

The man jotted them down. "I'm also going to need your number, and the address where I can reach you in the next couple of days, if you don't feel comfortable staying here."

After the officer wrote all that down, he turned to Joe. "I'd like your information too. You were first on the crime scene."

When Joe listed the same address, the officer raised an eyebrow, but he didn't comment.

Tuchman finished cataloguing the damage and gave the all clear, and they finally let Wendy in.

Joe went with her, staying two steps behind, giving her space. "Take your time."

She walked through, her face tight as she checked the damage. She didn't cry or throw a fit. She kept her expression schooled, although she couldn't completely hide the fear and sadness in her eyes. Or the resignation in the set of her shoulders, which was what really got to Joe.

"I can't believe he trashed Justin's room." She stood in the doorway, at the edge of the sea of scattered toys, as if unable to step inside. She shook her head, quick and hard, then hurried into the bathroom. "He took the wig. And..."

She came out with her arms wrapped around herself, looking at anything but the people in the living room.

Tuchman stepped closer to her with a sympathetic expression, not unsensitive to her turmoil. "And?"

"A pregnancy test." Wendy's voice dropped to a whisper.

"Why would he take that?" Tuchman asked.

Wendy hugged herself tighter. "It was positive."

Joe's gaze dipped to her slim waist. The pregnancy had to be fairly early.

He acknowledged the disappointment that hit him. She was still hooking up with Keith. Then his next thought—*might not be by choice*—made him want to strangle the guy. Keith wouldn't be the first violent bastard who forced himself on his partner. Joe kept his anger on a tight leash, but he was definitely going to talk to Wendy about the pregnancy later.

"Is Keith Kline the father?" Tuchman wanted to know.

Wendy shook her head.

She seemed sure. *Good.* Joe wasn't crazy about her seeing someone else, but it was better than Keith forcing her into something she didn't want. Of course, her revelation brought even more questions. Who was she seeing? How serious was it? Why the hell hadn't the guy protected her from Keith?

Joe was more than a little mad at the unnamed father. Maybe more so than he should be. Oh, fine, *jealous.* He could admit it. And of course, any jealousy on his part was stupid beyond stupid. Wendy wasn't his girlfriend. They'd spent an incredible hour and a half together three months ago. She'd let him know right away that there wouldn't be more, that it meant nothing to her. She hadn't led him on, not for a second. And then she met someone she liked better.

Joe had a dozen questions to ask her and no right to be asking.

Tuchman tapped her pen against her notebook. "Your ex didn't know that you were pregnant?"

Wendy kept looking at her feet as she shook her head.

Joe had a feeling more private questions were coming, so he left them and walked down the hallway, then down the stairs. He had to put more money in the parking meter.

He dropped in a few quarters. *Highway robbery.* Couldn't pay him to live in a city. Bad air, traffic, higher crime rates... He catalogued all his grievances. It was easier than thinking about Wendy with another man.

He let the cold air cool him off before he went back upstairs. The officers had moved on to interview Wendy's neighbors.

"I want to pick up some more clothes for Justin," Wendy said when Joe walked in. "Would you mind staying?"

He bristled at the question. "Of course, I'll stay."

Like he would abandon her here? Leave her there alone and risk Keith stopping by again after the police left? Is that what she thought of him?

He didn't argue with her. She had plenty of stress, plenty on her plate already, especially for someone who was pregnant.

The father wasn't in the picture, Joe surmised. Otherwise, Wendy would have gone to his place instead of Sophie's.

Was the baby an accident?

Wendy had told him, during their one night together, that she was on the pill. She might have forgotten to take it one day. Joe didn't have accidents. He wore a condom. Every time. No exceptions, no excuses.

"Done." She walked out of Justin's room with a bulging shoulder bag.

She was pregnant, the father wasn't in the picture, and her ex was harassing her. She was holding up pretty damn well under the circumstances. She might be stressed, but she didn't let any of that touch Justin. She took care of her son; she went to work; she kept everything together.

She was an easy person to admire.

Joe followed her back to Sophie's, annoyed at himself that the thought of another guy in her life bothered him as much as it did.

At the house, Sophie was playing with Justin in the living room when they walked in. The kid ran straight to his mother, and Wendy hugged and kissed him like they'd been apart for a week.

"Is the captain still here?" Joe asked.

"Went home for Peaches. There's no resisting a kid begging for a dog. Never seen a man fold that fast." Sophie laughed. "He should be back any second."

Even as she said that, Bing's pickup was rumbling up the driveway.

Justin was at the window so fast, Joe wasn't sure if he'd seen the kid move. "Doggy, doggy, doggy!"

Peaches, a sweetheart of a Rottweiler, took turns greeting every-body, tongue lolling, tail wagging. After a round of ear scratches, he settled down by Justin.

"I just got off the phone with Wilmington PD," the captain told Wendy. "They grabbed Keith. One of your neighbors saw him go up. With some luck, his prints will match the prints lifted off the broken items. Breaking and entering, destruction of private property. We might be able to get him on stalking and harassment too, with the package he sent, once the prints come back on that."

A look of guarded optimism spread on Wendy's face. "Are they going to keep him?"

"They can hold him for three days on suspicion. By the time that's up, they'll have the prints, and the DA can charge him."

The captain motioned to Joe with his head, so he followed the man out back. They gave the dog a chance to go with them, but he chose Justin, not even tempted by the large, fenced-in yard. Peaches had his priorities straight.

Bing closed the door behind them. "I heard from Chief Gleason too." Regret glinted in his eyes, as if he didn't want to say what he had to say next. "They found Gomez's body washed ashore outside of Phil-adelphia. A jogger called it in."

"Shit." Joe tipped his face up to the sky. *Shit.*

He'd known something like this was coming, but the confirmation hit him hard anyway. *Senseless, avoidable tragedy.* "Gomez was just an impressionable kid. If he'd known better, he could have done better. I hate it that we always see these kids after it's too late."

"We are the police." Bing nodded. "But there are social workers."

"And what the hell are they doing?" Frustration pushed the words from Joe louder than he'd meant to speak.

"We're all doing our best. It's just not always enough."

"Have they identified the driver of the Hummer that pushed us into the river? The bridge cameras should have recorded him."

"Marco Sousa, Racker's right-hand man. Gleason thinks Marco decided to take Gomez out to hurt Ramos. Marco's uncle was recently killed in a shootout with two law enforcement officers. Marco would have considered taking a couple of cops out with Gomez a bonus."

"Does Ramos know yet that the Twentyniners killed his little brother?"

"Apparently. Either someone saw the incident, or Racker has been bragging. A gang war is imminent." The captain reached up and rubbed the back of his neck. "Chief Gleason asked about you. He wants you back."

"For what? Better to let Ramos think I drowned with Gomez."

Joe had wiggled his way into the group posing as a Jersey wise guy. He was supposedly hanging out in Philly to put some distance between himself and the Trenton cops. While in town, he offered money and the bale of weed in the trunk of his Camaro to Ramos's gang to protect him, plus promised delivery of some serious weaponry.

Ramos had run a check on him through his dirty cop, but Chief Gleason had set it up so Joe's organized-crime connections would be confirmed by the police database. The first few weeks had gone fine, buddy-buddy. Then, as Joe had started asking questions, Ramos become suspicious that maybe the Trenton boys wanted to take over his operation in Philly. Joe'd been working on allaying those fears, before he'd ended up in the river.

Still, the op had been a success.

"Chief Gleason has his dirty cop," Joe told Bing. "Ramos and I didn't part on the greatest terms. Last time we talked, he accused me of being a scout for a hostile takeover."

"Water under the—" The captain winced. "Sorry." He shook his head. "Anyway. Word is, Ramos is mourning you like a best friend. You went down with his little brother. Everything else is forgotten. His focus is on Racker now. If you were to turn up...."

"He'd be glad to see me, if for nothing else than for the guns I promised," Joe finished for him. "He'll need some high-end weapons if he means to hit Racker's crew. If I go back now, I could find out how and when he's going after the Twentyniners."

"And figure out where Officer Tropper is."

"Did Chief Gleason lose him?"

"Tropper reported in after the bridge accident, but he's been missing in action since."

Joe glanced over his shoulder, into the living room where Sophie was giving Wendy a hug. He was glad Wendy had friends. She needed the support, especially with a new baby coming. "How long does Chief Gleason need me in Philly?"

"Day or two? Ramos isn't going to wait long with the hit. You go in, figure out when and where, then pass on the intel. Then the chief will call in the SWAT team and have those guys waiting when the cars roll up. Otherwise, this could turn into an all-out gang war."

"More dead bodies."

Bing nodded. "You have a choice here. I don't want you to think you don't. I thought of you for the undercover op because you're an excellent officer. You're going to make an excellent detective someday soon. I don't want to lose you to a skirmish in Philly. You helped Chief Gleason already. You don't owe him anything. It's up to you."

Laughter reached them from inside, a stark contrast to the conversation they were having. Justin was trying to ride Peaches.

"With Keith in custody," Bing said, "Wendy and her boy should be safe for now."

Joe sure as hell hoped so. "You can tell Gleason I'll do it."

The thought of the dirty cop still out there bothered him. And so did the thought of innocent people dying, caught in the crossfire. Neither Ramos's crew nor the Twentyniners cared about bystanders. Saving someone else wasn't going to bring Gomez or Phil back, but if Joe could help, he wanted to help. That was why he'd joined the police in the first place. "When do I go back in?"

"The sooner the better. Where is your undercover car?"

"Probably still parked where Gomez and I got picked up." He'd driven his reconditioned Camaro. Since most of the guys on Ramos's crew were car fanatics, the Camaro—and a couple of midnight drag races—had given Joe some street cred with them.

The captain clapped him on the shoulder. "Why don't you come into the station after dinner? I'll have someone drive you in and drop you off a block or two from your car. Then you can go see Ramos."

"And hope he doesn't blame his little brother's death on me." Because if Ramos decided to hold Joe responsible after all, Joe wasn't going to make it out of South Philly alive.

CHAPTER TEN

WENDY GLANCED OUTSIDE, AT JOE AND BING DEEP IN conversation on the deck.

"How about some raspberry fusion tea?" Sophie asked.

"I'd love a cup." The weather had turned a few degrees warmer finally, but the air still had enough chill in it to make a cup of hot tea pleasant.

When the tea was ready, they carried their cups over to the couch. Wendy kept an eye on Justin, but Peaches kept him busy. They were playing hide and seek around the furniture.

"Now that Keith is behind bars, we can move back home," she told Sophie.

"No rush. Honestly. You are more than welcome to stay for as long as you'd like."

"You've been so fantastic about everything. Thank you." Wendy took a sip of fragrant tea and enjoyed the warmth that spread through her. "But you know how it is. Every time I reach for something I need, it's at the apartment. And Justin will be more settled at home." She drank another sip. "How is the farm? Are you in full farm-girl mode? Any chickens on the horizon?"

Sophie laughed. "No chickens. Yet. But the mares will be foaling soon. You should bring Justin out."

"Sure. And then he'll be begging me to get a horse. How do you like living with Bing?"

"I like it a lot. Like pitifully a lot. He's kind, and he's considerate. He's funny. I'm so much in love with him it's embarrassing. I'm officially, cross-eyed in love." Sophie groaned into her tea. "I turned into one of those women who can't shut up about their men. Kill me now. Where is my pride?"

"Drowned in hot, steamy sex? Maybe you're cross-eyed from that."

Sophie laughed again, and then she sighed with a dreamy smile. "I've never been this happy."

A relationship like Sophie and Bing had seemed so foreign to Wendy, she had trouble believing something like that existed. Yet she was looking at the proof.

"I couldn't be happier for you." She meant it.

"Thanks. Do you need help with cleaning up your apartment?"

Ugh. "I don't even want to think about the mess. I think I'm good, though. It's just carrying down the broken stuff and straightening the rest. I can do that tomorrow."

"You should get a restraining order."

Wendy gripped her cup. "I don't want to make Keith mad."

"I don't think you can get away from him without making him mad."

"Maybe if I'm nice to him, he'll be nice about custody."

"How has that worked out for you so far?"

Okay, so Sophie was the type to call an ace an ace. Or a jerk a jerk.

"Not too well." Wendy lowered her cup to her lap. "You're right. A restraining order is the way to go, in case he gets out. I'll stop by the police station on my way home tomorrow."

"Do you want me to go with you?"

"Thank you, but I'll be fine. I have to be able to handle my own life. Now, on another subject," Wendy said. "I met Terry from down the street. If you want to rent to her, she could have the house. Justin and I'll spend the night, if you don't mind, since it's too late to start cleaning the apartment tonight. But we can head back home in the morning, fix things and have the place back to semi-normal by tomorrow night."

"I don't want you to feel rushed."

"I don't. And you should have seen the desperation on Terry's face."

Sophie sipped her tea. "I'll call her, but only if you're one hundred percent sure."

"I am," Wendy promised. "Terry needs to be saved from a nervous breakdown. And you shouldn't lose out on rent money. The way Bing looks at you, you better start saving for a wedding."

Light spread through Sophie. "He's amazing, isn't he?"

Love looked good on her. Gone were the post-transplant dark circles from under her eyes, and the tired look that had lingered on too long after the last surgery.

Sometimes love gives you a glow, sometimes it gives you bruises. Wendy bit back a groan. She was beginning to sound like a country song. "Bing makes you happy. He's a little scary, though, isn't he? He looks like he could seriously hurt someone if he put his mind to it."

"He's a big teddy bear." Sophie grinned. "Joe too, by the way. He looks tough, but I've never seen him lose his temper." Sophie glanced toward the sliding glass doors to the deck, at the men who were still in a serious discussion. "He's so sexy even his scar is sexy. Did you know he used to be a wide receiver?"

"How could I not? Local businesses have his picture on their walls. I'm surprised the town doesn't have a statue of him in the Main Square."

"Don't give anybody ideas. People like him a lot around here. Bing says he did a lot for the town for the short time that he was in the limelight. Funneled in a ton of charity money. He set up the fund that keeps the no-kill animal shelter going."

"I've always pictured Joe's big-shot football-player years as partying with cheerleaders, not worrying about strays."

Sophie shook her head. "You know he likes you, right?"

"I'm not going there. Wrong guy, wrong time."

"That's what I said about Bing. Turns out I was wrong. I know, shocking."

Wendy lifted her mug in a toast. "I won't tell anyone if you won't."

After Sophie and Bing left, Joe cooked dinner. He insisted that it was his turn and made a mean spaghetti-and-meatball dish. The aroma of tomato sauce and parmesan filled the air, along with oregano and basil. He was whistling as he stood by the stove, shirtsleeves rolled up over sculpted forearms. And if that wasn't enough to make Wendy's heart skip multiple beats, he picked up Justin and let him stir.

He caught her staring. "You look surprised."

"I didn't picture you cooking." More like watching a game on TV while the woman in his life got dinner ready.

"You take me for a total jock. I should be offended."

"No offense."

"None taken, then. You don't like jocks."

"Keith was one. Played football in college. He likes to golf now."

"I see."

She had no idea what he saw, and she didn't ask.

He was preoccupied while they ate an early dinner, but chatted with Justin about dinosaurs. He was a veritable paleontologist and kept Justin completely engaged with his esoteric knowledge.

"Did you know that a Tyrannosaurus Rex's tooth was as long as your arm?"

Justin waved his arms around madly, pretending to bite Joe with them.

"And do you know what the longest dinosaur name is? Micropachy-cephalosaurus."

"Microsaurus!" Justin shouted at him.

"That's an excellent nickname." Joe got up and brought a clove of garlic from the counter and handed it to Justin. "That's about the size of a Stegosaurus' brain. If our brains had the same proportion, it'd be the size of half a pea."

"Pea brain," Wendy muttered.

Joe grinned at her. "Exactly."

"Dinosaurs are big," Justin put in.

"Actually, most were about human size," Joe told him.

"For some reason," Wendy paused with her fork in the air, "that strikes me as really creepy. A predator that can look you right in the eye."

"Most dinosaurs were vegetarian." Joe sounded like he could go on all night.

"Hear that?" Wendy ruffled her son's hair. "Eat your carrots."

Their rule was that every meal had to include a raw vegetable, so two baby carrots waited for their turn on Justin's plate, now that his spaghetti was mostly gone.

"Chomp, chomp," Joe encouraged.

And, of course, because Joe said it, Justin put down the garlic, picked up a carrot, and ate it.

Joe turned to Wendy. "I have to go out tonight," he said quietly. "Police business. Are you going to be okay alone?"

The instant unease she felt was just stupid reflex, she told herself. "Keith is in custody. We're going home in the morning. I'd better get used to living without a bodyguard."

Joe looked like he might protest, but instead, he picked up his empty plate and walked it over to the sink.

A man who cleaned up after himself. Would miracles never cease?

As much as Wendy hadn't liked the idea of Joe moving in, she did appreciate him. It *was* nice of him to take time out of his schedule. He'd been kind to watch Justin while she'd worked. And she *was* glad that he'd been with her when she'd found the bloody wig. That had freaked her out badly.

She carried her own dishes to the sink, along with Justin's. "Thank you for watching over us."

"Anytime." Joe rinsed his plate, put it into the dishwasher, then walked to the coatrack in the foyer. "I'm not sure when I'll be back."

If he wasn't back by morning, they'd be gone. She'd miss him. Wendy squashed that thought. "Stay safe."

"You too. And lock up behind me."

She did, then she picked up Justin. "Bath time!"

"Nooooo!"

"You can come back down and play some more afterwards."

On their way up the stairs, her cell phone rang, a number she didn't recognize. She picked it up in case it was a last-minute booking.

"Hey," a strange voice said. "Keith used his one phone call already to call his lawyer, and he promised me money to call you. He said don't worry about anythin'. He'll be home soon. He'll be takin' care of you and the kid. He says that's a promise."

The man on the other end put the phone down, the cold click ringing in Wendy's ear. She held on to her baby and carried him into the bathroom upstairs, shaking, as much from anger as fear.

You'll never be out of my reach. That was the message Keith had intended.

"All right. Clothes off!" Her voice was tight, brittle, but thank God, Justin didn't notice. He was stripping already.

She started the water in the tub, while her brain replayed the brief call over and over again.

"He'll be takin' care of you and the kid."

She knew what Keith meant by *taking care* of her. But Justin? Would Keith file for custody to teach her a lesson? He'd had no interest in taking care of his son in the past. And now? Maybe he was mad at her enough to do anything to hurt her.

She tested the water. She hadn't brought their baby bubble bath, but Sophie had an ample selection. Wendy chose lavender. "You can hop in, if you want."

Justin raised his chubby little arms for a lift. Wendy picked him up and held him for a few seconds before lowering him into the bubbles. "I love you. You're the best kid in the universe, and I'm glad you're mine."

"I love you too, Mommy."

She let go of him, reluctantly, but she didn't step back to sit on the closed toilet. She sat on a folded towel next to the tub instead.

Keith would *not* get full custody of Justin. He wouldn't get any kind of custody for years. He was going to prison. Breaking and entering, along with destruction of private property, should earn him a couple of years, at least. And during that time, Wendy would figure out how to be free of him forever. She would save every penny she made and hire the best lawyer. Or move far away with Justin, someplace where Keith would never find them.

Just moving into her own apartment obviously hadn't worked. And staying friends hadn't worked either. She'd made a mistake there. Keith wasn't going to let her go easily, no matter how nice she played it. She was going to have to fight him.

CHAPTER ELEVEN

KEITH WAS IN JAIL, BUT JOE STILL HATED TO LEAVE WENDY. HE strode into the station in a foul mood, had half a mind to turn around and go home to her.

"Bing here?" he asked Leila behind the reception desk.

In her mid-forties, the Broslin PD's den mother was trim, with short dark hair, a no-nonsense style and attitude. "Captain's in his office, but he has Jack Sullivan with him." She squinted at Joe's under-cover gear: expensive sneakers, loose pants, black shirt. "That's a new style for you."

Joe shrugged. "It's good to switch things up now and again."

He'd gone undercover as an up-and-coming Jersey wise guy, wearing an Italian suit when he'd first approached Ramos, then he'd changed little by little to fit in with the crew. In Ramos's neighborhood it was better not to stick out too much on the street. Especially since Joe was supposedly *hiding* in Philly. Gomez had had a lot of fun advising him on how to blend, then mocking him when he'd been slow on the uptake.

The more he looked like one of the guys, the more they treated him as such. His skills with the ball didn't hurt either. Gomez and the others tossed a football around most days. They were just kids. Ramos was the oldest at twenty-three.

Leila shook her head as her gaze settled on Joe's feet. "I don't know if I can trust a man who has fancier shoes than I do."

A person was well advised not to ask her how many pairs of shoes she had. Footwear was her one weakness.

"You're jealous, and you know it." Joe grinned. "Working late?" Something sparkly on the bulletin board behind Leila caught his gaze. The...*ornament?*...hung from a long piece of red yarn and threw a rainbow over the paperwork. "What's that?"

"A crystal." Her tone would have gone better with *dog turd.* "Something to do with breaking up bad energy." She rolled her eyes. "Robin. She'll be in later. She's having plumbing issues."

Joe nodded, noticing the lucky bamboo on the counter.

Leila followed his gaze. "Don't ask."

Leila was a no-nonsense woman, likely a drill sergeant in a previous life. The front desk, the break room, the files, the entire station, in fact, were organized within an inch of their lives. She made life easier for everyone. They had more time to spend on fighting crime if they didn't spend half their lives looking for something.

Robin Combs, the new part-time dispatcher, was a hippie in her mid-sixties, a self-professed psychic.

"She wants to paint the front door red." Leila's lips flattened. "It brings good luck in feng shui."

"Isn't that Chinese?" Joe had heard about it on the radio once. He usually had NPR on in his cruiser.

Leila's nostrils flared. "She's one with the universe."

Joe made a mental note to suggest to the captain to always have someone at the station around shift change. It'd be bad press for the PD if the two dispatchers strangled each other.

Come to think of it, it wasn't like Leila to get upset over every little thing. This went beyond crystals and feng shui. About to walk off, Joe pulled back. "What did Robin really say?"

Leila huffed. "She said I'll fall in love again. That I'm going to get *married.*" The last word was uttered in a tone so cold it could have frozen the leaves off the lucky bamboo. "As if I didn't love my Billy."

Joe clamped his lips closed. In fact, he grabbed an oatmeal cookie from the counter and shoved it into his mouth. "Mhm. Uhm." He made sympathetic noises, then took the coward's way out and slinked off for coffee.

Harper stepped from the interrogation room. "Hey Joe. The captain said you'd be coming in. I'm interviewing the suspect in the Brogevich case."

"The schizophrenic patient? Lewis Brown?"

"He's not saying much."

"Can I give it a go?"

Harper moved aside. "No problem. He's all we got for now. Judge's dragging his feet on the warrant for patient records. Touchy subject, since the victim was a psychiatrist. He could have prominent people among his clients."

"Like who?"

"The mayor?" Harper shrugged. "I'm sure he wouldn't want us to know if he gets turned on by wearing a diaper."

"A what?" Joe shook his head at him, laughing. "Where do you get this stuff?"

"It's a thing. I saw it on TV," Harper said, dead serious. "Anyway, the captain put a call in. We'll get a warrant, but it might take a while."

"Once you get the patient records, I can help you go through them."

"That'd be great."

They exchanged a look of we'll-get-this-done, then Joe stepped into the interview room, while Harper went to the observation room to watch.

The man at the small table in handcuffs was in his mid-twenties, average height, skinny, wearing faded jeans and a wrinkled yellow shirt. His wild black hair stuck up in every direction. He fidgeted in the chair, clasping and unclasping his hands on the table, clearly agitated.

He started with, "They want to frame me."

"Hi, Lewis. I'm Officer Kessler. I'm here to help you." Joe took the empty seat across from the guy. "Who wants to frame you?"

"The government."

"Why is that?"

"I don't trust them. I don't trust you either. First, they used my doctor to make me crazy, now they're using you." Lewis dropped his hands into his lap. "You're here to kill me, aren't you?" He shrunk back in his chair, sweat beading above his lips.

Joe kept his posture relaxed. "I'm here to help. I promise. Where's your doctor now?"

"Dead. They killed him. They killed him because he failed with me."

"Were you mad at Doctor Brogevich?"

Lewis wouldn't meet Joe's eyes. "He set me up. He was a bad man."

"Bad men have to be punished. That's what I do. Did you punish the doctor, Lewis?"

"The government did. Not me."

Joe went a few rounds with him, getting nowhere, before his lawyer arrived. And then, with the lawyer came the alibi. Lewis had been with his attorney at the time of the murder. He was suing his parents for trying to force him to take his pills.

"Hitting jackpot on the first try would have been too easy," Harper remarked once he released Lewis to his attorney.

"Maybe we'll get a better lead from the patient records. We'll keep going until we get there," Joe told him.

"I'll call you when the warrant comes in, In the meanwhile, lab reports are back on the murder weapon. All the blood on the phone is from the victim, but there are also traces of fresh paint."

"The railings outside were painted the day before the murder."

"Right. That paint might have preserved the killer's fingerprints before it dried. I'm heading out there to see about that." Harper hurried away.

Then the captain spotted Joe through the window of his office and waved him in. Jack was still with him.

"Jack will drive you into the city. He's heading in to pick up Maddie from her grandfather."

"Thanks." Joe followed Jack out. "How is Maddie doing?"

Maddie belonged to Jack's girlfriend, Ashley. The seven-year-old cutie-pie pretty much had Jack and the entire station wrapped around her little finger. Looked like an angel on the outside. On the inside.... *Inventive.* The week before, she'd jammed a chocolate chip cookie into the copy machine, since her mother had said she could take only one cookie from the jar at reception.

"She spent the day with her grandfather." Jack rolled his shoulders. "I'm preparing myself for the sugar high."

They barely reached reception when the captain called after them. "We'll be here, if you change your mind."

Jack nodded, then he glanced at Leila who was on the phone, staring balefully at the rainbow the crystal cast over her paperwork. Jack raised an eyebrow at Joe. Joe shook his head. He wasn't going there.

"Change your mind about what?" he asked as they strode out of the station.

"I handed in my resignation."

Joe stopped in his tracks. "What are you talking about?"

Jack smiled, which would have been unheard of a year ago. He'd been a morose bastard and then some, obsessed with tracking down the serial killer who'd murdered his sister. He did get his man—and saved Ashley and Maddie in the process. And he'd found love.

Love was a pest, no doubt about it. Joe had tried it once. It'd ripped his guts out. No sane man would go back.

Yet not only did Jack's smile not fade, but his lips stretched even wider. "Ashley's expecting."

Joe almost asked, *Are you sure?* Quitting a job because a woman said she was pregnant didn't seem like the best idea. Okay, Ashley wasn't Erika. All women didn't make up pregnancies to trap men. But some did. Erika had done it to Joe. And these days, a woman could buy a positive pregnancy test for fifty bucks online to drive her boyfriend crazy.

None of which had anything to do with Jack, so Joe reached out to shake his hand. "Congratulations. Man, that's huge."

"Yeah. I can't wait."

"We're going to miss you at the station."

They were out of the parking lot by the time Jack gave further explanation. "I became a cop for one reason only, to catch the man who took my sister. All my adult life, all I've done was look for a murderer. I want to try something else."

Okay, that made sense. "What do you think you'll do next?"

"Private security? I'm going to take a few months off, be there for Ashley when the baby is born. After that...." He shrugged. "I'll figure something out."

"How did the captain take it?"

"He's not happy that I'm leaving, but I think he's happy for me."

That made sense too. "When are you leaving?"

"I'm going to close out my current cases, but I won't take any new ones. Once my desk is clear, I'm good to go."

"You need help with anything?"

"Thanks, but I think I'm all right. You?" He checked over Joe's unusual clothes and narrowed his eyes. "I guess you're in some kind of undercover gig. Bing wouldn't say." He waved off his last words. "Never mind. It's on a need-to-know basis, and I don't need to know. Be careful."

"I promise not to go out of my way to get myself shot."

On the drive into Philly, they talked about Jack's current caseload. Then Jack dropped Joe off two blocks from his car and drove away.

The black Camaro was where Joe had left it. He hadn't even gotten a ticket or his hubcaps stolen. *Sweet.*

He drove down dirty streets, past an abandoned factory that had all its windows broken out, then down Brant Street to Ramos's aunt's house.

The neighborhood was poor, with a mix of ethnicities. The kids in the hood grew up together, joined the gang together, replacing members who were killed. Black, white, Hispanic, Asian—color didn't matter. Their common link was the bone-deep poverty they'd been born into and their burning desire to conquer it.

The four-bedroom row house belonged to Ramos's aunt who was in a wheelchair, restricted to the upstairs. The downstairs belonged to Ramos and his crew, their headquarters. He liked to keep the "family" together.

Trigger, a Pitbull recently retired from fighting, guarded the property. Paco, Will, and DeShawn lounged on the derelict front porch. Trigger recognized Joe first, running to him. The dog was missing most of his left ear, his muzzle crisscrossed with scars. He had a limp, but he didn't let that slow him down any.

He greeted Joe, his whole body wiggling, as sweet as a lapdog. When Joe squatted to give him a treat, the Pitbull swallowed it in one gulp, then licked Joe's face with enthusiasm. Trigger loved people. Sadly, he'd been trained to hate other dogs, and he did that with a burning passion. Letting him run free outside was beyond stupid.

"Hey. Better take this bad boy inside before he eats a Chihuahua," Joe called to the men as he straightened. "Ramos needs no police around here."

Paco and DeShawn pushed to their feet, swearing after the dog and calling him back, staring wide-eyed at Joe.

"What the hell?" DeShawn bumped fists with him. "We thought you were dead, bro."

Joe put on a miserable expression. "Freaking concussion. Got my face busted. I had to go to the hospital, then just laid low, whacked out on painkillers. My phone's on the bottom of the river." He gave an aggravated grunt. "S'up here?"

Paco and Will came to clap him on the back. They escorted him in, and he made sure the dog went inside with them.

"Going to war." An excited grin busted free on Paco's face.

Ramos and six others sat in the sixties style kitchen in the back, sorting ammo on the scarred, yellow Formica table.

Ramos was as badass as they came, would shoot a guy for looking at him the wrong way. Joe had studied his file, done some of his own research too, before he'd gone undercover. And he'd been collecting every snippet of information he could find on the gang leader since.

Ramos had been born to a drug-addict single mother. He had other brothers and sisters, but they were taken by Social Services. By the time he was six, he was buying his mother drugs on the street. By the time he was eight, stealing their daily food was his responsibility. He killed his first man when he was ten, his mother's dealer who'd come to their house to harass her for money, then proceeded to rape her.

They had one semi-good year after that, at the end of which she gave birth to another child, Gomez. She overdosed the day she got home from the hospital with the baby. That was when Ramos and

Gomez, a crack baby no one ever gave much of a chance for making it, came to live with their aunt.

The brothers stuck around, even after their aunt had been relegated to a wheelchair, even after her mind gave out to Alzheimer's. She wasn't much trouble. She spent her time watching TV upstairs. She was happy as long as she was fed three times a day. She didn't interfere with any of the business going on downstairs.

Ramos loved three things: the gang, his aunt, and his brother Gomez.

When the crew around the table spotted Joe, a cheer rose. They all got up to punch him in the shoulder or whack him on the back.

"Hey." Joe stepped forward, keeping his eyes on Ramos.

"Yo, bro." Ramos stayed in his seat. "Back from the dead, man?"

"Fucking Hummer pushed us right off the bridge."

"We gonna take care of that." Ramos's eyes narrowed to slits as he looked Joe over. "Where you been?"

"Got a concussion when the car crashed into the river. Wasn't sure who pushed us over. I thought I'd better lay low for a couple of days."

Ramos's expression tightened. "Word on the street is J.T.'s guy did it."

"Where's Gomez?" Joe made a show of looking around. "Last I saw him he was hanging on to a log."

"He couldn't swim," Ramos said darkly. "Those fuckers killed my brother."

Joe swore. "What do you want me to do?"

He didn't normally join the gang when they did business, but he had a perfect excuse this time. He'd been personally affected.

"You got those guns you promised?"

"Can't get them out of Trenton. Maybe in a day or two. I'm trying, man. The cops are watching my cousin."

Ramos cracked his knuckles. "I sent a couple of boys to check out the situation at J.T.'s place. I'll let you know when we're ready." His hard gaze held Joe's. "No bastard that goes against me's gonna live long enough to regret it."

"I'm ready. You let me know what you want me to do and when."

Joe pulled out his new phone. "Old one sank in the stupid river. I'm texting you the number."

"It's good that you made it out."

There was something in Ramos's eyes beyond grief, beyond murderous anger for his enemies. Joe couldn't see past the curtain of ice that had been drawn. He didn't know what it meant.

All he knew was he'd better watch his back.

CHAPTER TWELVE

JOE HUNG WITH THE CREW FOR A WHILE, HIS THOUGHTS SKIPPING TO Wendy every five minutes. When it looked like he wasn't going to gain more information from Ramos, he took off. Wendy was back in her apartment, so Joe didn't return to Sophie's place. He went home, put on the uniform, then reported for duty. He could still work what was left of the second shift.

Robin was sitting behind the reception desk, dressed in pink, her pixie haircut styled with sparkling hair gel, her angel earrings catching the light every time she moved.

"How is it going?" Joe stopped to check through the stack of yellow message slips.

"Love this job." The smile widened. "A lot more interesting than post office work. And I don't have to fight traffic."

She'd been a mail carrier in Broslin for twenty years, then retired to help her sister battle cancer in Upstate New York. That successfully completed, she'd returned and taken a part-time job at the PD.

Leila usually worked a full first shift, then Robin, as a part-timer, carried half of the second shift. It gave the station front-desk coverage for most of the day. At night, the officers on duty fielded calls themselves.

"This whole desk is so severe." She clucked her tongue and reposi-
tioned the in-bin. "Very regimented. That's not good for creativity. We
need to bring some color and fun in here. Leila has been so stressed
out lately. Have you noticed? She has such a beautiful future waiting
for her. If only she could open up and take it. I think she needs her
chakras aligned."

Joe coughed, choking on his own saliva. "Yeah. Hey, do me a favor
and don't mention that to her right now. Maybe next week."

He strode over to the captain's office, and the captain waved him
in. Joe made his report to Chief Gleason from there, with the captain
listening in.

"You can go home," Bing said afterwards. "It's a slow day. Chase
and Harper have everything under control."

Joe wasn't about to argue with having time off. "Would you mind if
I drove over to Wilmington? I'd like to check on something."

"I assume it has to do with Wendy? Go ahead. But if you're planning on stopping in to see her, she's decided to stay another night at
Sophie's place."

Joe drove to Wilmington and went straight to the jail that held
Keith Kline, asked to have a word with him.

The officer on duty, a matronly woman with strict eyes and short
orange hair, took in his Broslin badge. "It's pretty late for a visit. Official business?"

"I want to ask him a couple of questions regarding a harassment
case that took place in my town. Hate mail. It's related to the
vandalism charge here. Same victim."

"Let me check." She called the arresting officer. After she hung up,
she said, "All right, I'll take you back."

Joe followed her to an interview room and waited inside the
cramped space that held nothing but a stainless-steel table and two
chairs. The cement floor was stained, the white walls scuffed and splat-
tered with all kinds of bodily fluids.

An older officer brought in Keith.

"Here you go." He nodded to Joe, then left, closing the door
behind him.

Keith wore an orange jumpsuit and white sneakers without laces.

He was cuffed, but the look he shot to Joe was pure superiority. He was roughly the same height as Joe, built like a linebacker. Blond hair, cold blue eyes, an arrogant set to his jaw. Had to weigh close to twice as much as Wendy. The thought of the guy hurting Wendy filled Joe with a cold rage.

He pointed to the empty chair. "Mr. Kline. I'm Officer Kessler. I'm here to ask you a couple of questions.

"I've seen you at Sophie's." Keith's square jaw twitched as his chin came up. "I demand to be released immediately. I'm suing this entire department. Your incompetence is criminal."

"I'm here to talk about Wendy Belle."

"I already told the other officers. I didn't touch her apartment. She is my girlfriend. She's the mother of my child, for heaven's sake. Why would I want to harm her?"

Why indeed? "I'm here about the package you sent her in the mail."

The man's eyes barely flickered. "What package?"

"The one with the bloody wig."

Keith's superior air switched to a slightly overplayed look of concern. "Is someone harassing her?" He sank into the empty chair at last. "Listen, you have to let me out. I need to be with her to protect her."

An officer with less experience with abusers might have bought the performance. Joe didn't. He kept his expression neutral. "You haven't sent Miss Belle a package recently?"

"Why would I send a package? If I want to give her something, I just take it over to her. I see her all the time."

"When was the last time you were in her apartment?"

"I stopped by the day before yesterday."

"And not since?"

Keith shook his head with what looked like sincere regret. "I have a demanding job. I don't get to spend as much time with my family as I'd like." He offered a flat smile. "I suppose people who provide for their loved ones often have that problem. I'm sure you understand, Officer."

Joe flashed him a dispassionate look. If Keith thought they were going to bond over work schedules, he had another think coming.

"I'm sorry for my impatience." Keith tested a different approach. "I understand that when women are harassed, more often than not, it's by the men in their lives. But that's not the case here. I love Wendy and my son. I would do anything for them. Me being locked up just makes them that much less safe. I need to be with my family. I want to see my lawyer."

Joe stood. "I'll pass that on, on my way out."

He'd come to get the measure of the man, and he got it—cold, calculating, a manipulator.

Joe had Keith taken back to his cell, then he drove back to Broslin.

He drove by Sophie's place.

With all the trees and bushes up front, the house looked like a fairy cottage in the woods. The windows were dark, Wendy and Justin probably sleeping. A light by the door shined its warm glow over the front stoop.

A quick smile ghosted over Joe's lips. She'd left the light on for him.

The gesture caught him off guard. He'd never had anyone leaving the lights on for him before. Well, duh, he lived alone. And he wasn't scared of the dark. Yet, the stupid light, the thought that someone was waiting for him, made him feel good, made him think, for a moment, about what life would be like with a partner.

The captain had that now, and Jack too. And Murph. One by one, Joe's friends were getting involved, getting tied down.

He glanced at the dashboard clock. The diner wasn't open yet, but in an hour Eileen would be there, getting ready to bake up a storm. If he knocked on the door, she'd let him in.

Wendy and Justin were asleep. No sense in making noise and waking them up. Better to grab breakfast, then come back when they were ready to start their day.

CHAPTER THIRTEEN

WENDY WAS GLAD TO BE BACK HOME IN HER OWN APARTMENT, despite the enormous mess. She enjoyed having her own place. Especially now that she didn't have to worry that Keith would show up unexpectedly. *Safe.* She could get used to the feeling.

She dropped the last bag of garbage down the disposal chute at the end of her hallway, then grinned at Justin. "Race!"

"I win! I win! I win!" Justin yelled as he ran ahead of her. He reached their door first, smiling from ear to little ear.

"You won! Good job, buddy."

"Big mess," he said once they were back inside.

She locked and dead-bolted the door behind them. "Good thing you have big, strong muscles. Can we clean this up? Yes, we can!"

"Yes, we can! Yes, we can!"

The broken dishes and chairs were already disposed of, Wendy just had to straighten up the rest. She flipped the ripped couch cushion over. That would have to do for now. Later, while Justin napped, she would sew up the tear. With the cushion flipped upside down, nobody would guess the damage. Everything didn't have to be perfect.

She gathered the throw pillows, then picked up the toys Keith had dumped from the toy chest. The ones he'd stomped on, she'd already discarded, but there were plenty of toy cars and balls and stuffed animals left.

Justin settled in next to a pile of wooden blocks that had been a castle before Keith had kicked it over. "Did a dinosaur sitted on it?"

"He did."

"Where is he?"

"He got grounded. He's not coming back. You don't have to worry about him."

Not that Justin looked worried. If anything, he looked disappointed that he missed a dinosaur nesting in their living room. He set aside that disappointment pretty quickly, though, and began throwing his wooden blocks into his blue, car-shaped toy bin, helping to tidy up.

Wendy headed to the kitchen. "Are you hungry?"

"Cookies!"

"Not for cookies. How about lunch?"

Joe had brought them breakfast, just as they were getting up at Sophie's. Afterwards, he insisted on going with her to Wilmington PD to file the restraining order. Then he followed them to the apartment and carried the larger pieces of broken furniture to the dumpster behind the building before he left, telling her to call him if she needed help with anything else.

"Where's Joe?" Justin asked, finished with his blocks.

"He's at work."

"Is he coming back?"

"I don't know. He hasn't said." Did she want him to? *Maybe.*

Joe treated her with respect. He played with her son. He was there when she needed help. But even if deep down Wendy knew he was nothing like Keith, she still had trouble trusting him. He was strong, and she was wary of masculine strength, wary of the moment when a man might turn his muscles against her.

Even Joe's kindness and protectiveness freaked her out sometimes. Keith had started out kind and protective. Now and then, when Wendy was with Joe, enjoying herself, she caught herself mentally holding her breath, waiting for the blow.

Yet she had to find a way to trust Joe enough to tell him what she needed to tell him. Just the thought of that conversation made her feel like the walls were closing in on her.

"Cookie!"

"No cookies before lunch."

"Not hungry."

"Fine. Want to go to the park first?"

She was safe from Keith for the moment. She was not going to waste a perfectly good day by obsessing over Joe. A walk in the park, in fresh air, might be just the thing to work up Justin's appetite.

"Park!" He clapped with glee. "Doggies!"

Wendy picked him up and swung him around. "All right. Let's get bundled up."

She helped him with his favorite red jacket, then she picked up her camera that had been safe at Sophie's house during the rampage at the apartment, thank God. She shrugged into her own coat then locked the door behind them. For added exercise, they took the stairs, jumping from step to step like a pair of grasshoppers.

"Cookie!" Justin demanded as soon as they reached the bottom landing.

"You can have a treat when you're in your car seat."

She'd learned that trick from a makeup artist she'd worked with, an experienced mother of three. Give the kid a treat each time he goes into the car seat, so he'll cooperate instead of fighting the straps.

Wendy's Prius was parked by the curb. Once she secured Justin in the back, she handed him a small bag of animal crackers from her pocket.

"Want to listen to the puppy song?" she asked as they drove off.

"Puppies! Happy puppy, jump, jump, jump!" He was singing in the backseat.

She sang with him. Traffic was sparse. Then sparser yet as they left the city, heading to the State Park instead of the small nearby play-ground—a spur of the moment decision. Justin loved throwing rocks into the creek.

They were on the old nursery rhyme Humpty-Dumpty, by the time Wendy rounded the steep curve of the off-ramp, nearly at their destination.

"And all the king's horses—" She tapped the brake pedal, then tapped it again with more force.

Nothing.

"Nonononono." She was the only car on the ramp for the moment, so she wasn't worried about plowing into anyone else, but she couldn't take the curve as fast as she was going. "Hold on!"

She had half a second to panic before the car crashed through the guardrail with a sickening lurch. They spent a split second in the air, then they were crashing down a steep embankment, until a sudden stop rattled her brain. Her car was caught between two trees, perilously balanced, creaking as if thinking out loud about whether or not to fall the rest of the way.

Do not fall. Wendy sat frozen, too scared to breathe.

The bottom of the rocky ravine waited about a hundred feet below them.

"Justin?" She looked back at her son as the car swayed precariously. "Are you hurt, honey?"

He burst into tears.

"Where does it hurt, sweetie?" He had no injury anywhere she could see. The car seat had kept him safe, thank God.

"I'm scared, Mommy." He squirmed. "Out!"

"You have to stay still, okay? People are coming to help us." Somebody had to have witnessed the accident. And if nobody had... "At the very least, people will see the broken guardrail," she told Justin. "Just stay as still as you can, okay?"

He kicked his feet forcefully and reached his arms toward her. "Out!"

"We have to wait for help. Somebody will come."

Unless, people looked at the damaged guardrail and thought it was the result of an earlier accident, days or even weeks ago.

Wendy looked for her cell phone that she'd dropped onto the passenger seat when she'd gotten into the car, but the phone had bounced off in the crash, nowhere to be seen.

Panic choked her.

Think.

She turned off the engine. There could be a fuel leak. A fire was the last thing they needed. Being proactive made her feel less helpless, more in control, even as Justin wailed in the back.

She rolled down her window. "Help!" Then again, louder, putting everything she had into the shout. "Help! We're down here!"

She heard a car rush by above. It didn't slow. She stopped yelling. With windows rolled up against the cold and engines rumbling, other drivers wouldn't hear her, and there'd be no pedestrians on the ramp of a major highway.

She was on her own with Justin. If they were to be saved, she had to do it.

Since the car was chilling fast, she rolled the window back up. Then she couldn't think what else she might do, so she panicked again.

"God, you're helpless. You're weak. You're stupid." Keith's words rose from the past to attack her anew. *"You need me. You need someone to take care of you. Women like you don't make it on their own."*

She stared down at the jagged rocks at the bottom of the ravine. If she was stupid and weak, then she was going to die here today with Justin. If she made a mistake, if she upset the car's precarious balance...

"Mommy?"

She filled her lungs and looked into her son's trusting blue eyes. Justin expected her to fix this current crisis like she fixed spilled juice and broken toys.

"I'm here, honey." Even weak and stupid people could have one moment of heroism now and then, couldn't they? Today had to be her day.

As soon as she made that decision, an idea popped into her head. *The horn.* She'd been too shaken to think of it before. That her brain was working again must mean that she was past the shock. *Good. One step forward.*

She pressed the heel of her hand against the middle of the steering wheel, beeped long and hard.

Waited.

Nothing.

She beeped again.

Cars rushed on above them. Nobody stopped. The drivers had no way of knowing the sound was coming from the ravine.

She swallowed her disappointment. "Mommy is going to get us out of here in a minute, okay?"

She opened the window again and shifted her weight carefully, then she stuck her head out, but she couldn't see so much as a foothold outside her door, just the steep embankment. As soon as she released her seat belt and opened her door, she'd fall.

She pulled back in.

"Can you see Mommy's phone?" She scanned the car again, and this time she caught sight of the plastic case wedged between the passenger seat and the door.

Too far to reach.

If she released her seat belt and moved that way, she'd upset the car's balance and they might tumble into the ravine. Yet reaching the phone was their only chance for rescue.

Move slowly. Move carefully.

Justin started crying again, louder and louder, his voice amplified in the small space.

"Hang in there, sweetie. Mommy's going to fix this." Wendy had said those words a hundred times in the past two years, but never under more dire circumstances.

She said a brief prayer, braced herself on the dashboard with her left hand, then reached for the release latch of the seatbelt with her right, and set herself free. She slid against the door, twisting her body to make sure she didn't hit her belly.

She held her breath. Even Justin stopped crying. The car creaked and swayed but didn't plummet below.

"See? We can do this." She *would* do this. Because she wasn't going to let anything happen to her babies.

She shifted her weight and braced her right knee on the gear shift, then she leaned forward as far as she could without transferring her body weight.

Then the tip of her finger finally reached the phone. *One more inch.* She prayed out loud as she went for it.

Yes! "I've got it."

She held still, her heart clamoring. The car didn't shift. She retreated slowly, no sudden movements, no upsetting the applecart. They'd made it so far. No making mistakes now.

"I'm going to call for help."

She touched the screen. The battery icon flashed red in the top right corner. She hit the speed dial for Joe. She couldn't risk 911 and have them put her on hold. If Joe saw her name flash onto his screen, he'd pick up.

"Hey."

Her heart leapt at his voice. "We went off the ramp." She quickly rattled off their location. "Nobody can see us from the road. Nobody knows we're here. I don't know how long the car can hang on. We're stuck between two trees, dangling over a long drop to the bottom. We can't get out."

"I'll call 911. I'm on my way. You stay put, okay? Did you shut off the engine?"

"Yes."

"I'll be there in a minute." He sounded sure and steady, as clear as if he was standing next to her.

"Hurry."

She didn't get to say more. The battery went dead, and the screen turned dark with a last beep. She slipped the phone into the cup holder and carefully turned to Justin. "Joe is coming. Do you want to sing some more songs?"

"No."

"Okay." At least he was no longer crying. "Then we'll just sit here and look at the birds in the trees."

He looked out the window, immediately distracted.

They didn't have to wait long. A horn beeped above them fifteen minutes later.

She beeped her own horn, then cracked her window again. "Down here! We're here."

"I'm coming down," Joe called back. "Don't move!"

"Joe!" Justin shouted with perfect faith and trust on his tear-streaked face.

Wendy watched the rescue unfold in her side mirror.

Two coils of rope rolled down, then Joe's dark form appeared. He rappelled down barehanded, no security line, just holding on to the rope, walking down the steep embankment to them.

His face betrayed no fear. He kept coming, slowly but steadily, with determination, as if nothing in this world could stop him.

"Hey." He stopped behind her car. "I'm here."

She shifted her gaze to the rearview mirror to see what he was doing next. "Be careful!"

He bent down. Looked like he was tying the second rope to the trailer hitch that had come with the car when she'd bought it from the previous owner.

"Are you two, okay?" he called over as he straightened.

"We're fine."

Her throat was so tight she could barely swallow. Could a single rope hold the full weight of the car if it slipped?

Joe lowered himself in-line with her and looked in her open window, checking her over first, then checking out Justin. "Hey, buddy. Look how brave you are. Did you keep your mom calm?"

Justin smiled as he nodded.

Tears burned Wendy's eyes. "Did you call 911?"

"Rescue should be here any minute. The rope should hold until then."

Would it?

The chassis creaked and popped around her. The car slid forward a couple of inches before it stopped. She hung on to the steering wheel for dear life, not that it would help her if they crashed.

Justin started crying again. He stretched his little arms forward. "Out!"

There was no worse feeling in the world for a mother than her child asking for help and not being able to help him.

"If I get him out of the car seat," Wendy asked Joe, "and hand him out to you through the window, could you take him?"

"The car isn't going anywhere."

"Please get him out. Please?"

"Okay." He seemed to understand that she couldn't think past her panic. "I'll go around and lift him out on his side." And then he leaned in and kissed her, before she could fully regain her bearings.

Now he was kissing her? *Now?* "Why did you do that?"

He flashed a devilish smile. "Could be my last chance. I mean if you do fall to a fiery death."

He went back up, then around to the other side of the car.

"You're such a freaking jerk!" she yelled after him, but she was smiling. He managed to take her fear away, even if for only a few seconds.

Joe shrugged out of his jacket one sleeve at a time while hanging on to the rope with his other hand, then he made a harness across his chest. "Roll the back window down."

She did, then held her breath as Joe reached in and unsnapped the car seat's harness.

He was smiling at Justin, as if what they were doing was no big deal. "I'm going to pull you out, and you'll sit inside my jacket, okay?"

"Out!" Justin scrambled toward safety.

Joe eased him through the window, placed him into the harness one-handed, then tightened the jacket around Justin's small body. "Can you put your hands around my neck and hang on?"

"Piggyback ride."

"Almost. We'll do piggyback ride on the front." Joe tucked him in securely, and Justin clamped on.

"Want to play *freeze and wiggle?*" Joe asked next. "When I say freeze, you have to stay still. Can't move a muscle. Then when I say, wiggle, you wiggle and jiggle as hard as you can."

"I want to play!"

Joe's eyes met Wendy's over her son's head. "I'll put him in my car, then come back for you."

"No. Stay with him. I'm fine."

"Okay. I'm not going to let anything happen to him. I'm not going to let anything happen to either of you." He checked to make sure he had Justin tied to him securely. "Ready? Freeze!"

Wendy watched every step of their climb in the rearview mirror, praying. They were halfway up when she heard sirens, the sound getting closer and closer. Cars screeched to a halt. And then firefighters were stepping over the guardrail and helping Joe up and over.

More ropes were dropped, with proper security lines this time. Two firefighters came for her, descending side by side.

The rescue lasted another twenty minutes. In full gear, the fire-fighters moved slower than Joe had.

Wendy's legs were limp noodles by the time she was on safe ground, standing on her own.

Joe was right there, holding her son who was wiggling like a drunken worm. "I want Mommy!"

Joe smiled at her.

He'd come and saved them. She didn't care about anything else. Even as the rescue personnel tried to talk her into lying down on the waiting stretcher, Wendy threw her arms around Joe and Justin with a sob of relief. "Thank you."

Justin wiggled over to be held by her, threw his little arms around her and held tight, burying his face into her neck. His soft puffs of breath on her skin were the most wonderful thing she'd ever felt. She had him.

She turned her head toward Joe to thank him again. "I—"

"Freeze," he ordered, and his lips closed over hers in a soft kiss. And this time, he wasn't satisfied with a quick peck. He lingered and drank his fill.

Liquid need shot through Wendy so strongly that it buckled her already weak knees. And for a second, just for a second, she let Joe hold her up, let her lips relax against his before she pulled away.

———

Joe went with them in the back of the ambulance. Couldn't let Wendy and her son out of his sight. Just needed to make sure they were all right. He made himself useful by entertaining Justin, who wasn't thrilled with the prodding and poking of the medics.

The space was tight, Wendy on a stretcher as a precaution. Joe held Justin. The kid wouldn't let himself be tied down, and screamed bloody murder. He didn't like anything about the trip, including the smell of disinfectant.

"Stinks!"

Joe started into a tall tale about a giraffe to keep him busy, only half hearing as Wendy answered a list of questions.

"I'm three months pregnant," she told the medic taking care of her. *That* got Joe's attention in a hurry.

Okay, what?

He'd assumed the pregnancy was a more recent thing. Three months was.... Their wild night had happened three months ago.

He cleared his throat. "Wendy?"

She looked at him at last, a sea of trepidation in her eyes. "I was waiting for the right time to tell you. It's—" She swallowed. "I'm having your baby."

The stainless-steel interior spun around Joe, along with all the supplies and instruments tucked neatly into every nook.

He handed Justin to the medic next to him and called up to the driver. "Stop the ambulance, please!"

Joe moved past the stunned emergency personnel to the back door, opened it, and stepped out right in the middle of downtown traffic. People might have beeped their horns around him. He couldn't hear a thing.

CHAPTER FOURTEEN

"Joe will come around." Wendy reached over from the hospital bed and patted Justin's little fingers grabbing the crib they'd been provided. The nurse had been nice enough to put them close enough to each other to touch.

"Hey." Sophie sailed in, breathless, her red curls messy as if she'd run all the way from Broslin. "Are you okay? Is Justin okay? What happened?"

"We're fine. I lost control of the car."

"Aunt Sophie!" Justin bounced in the crib, demanding to be released.

Sophie hugged Wendy, then kissed the top of Justin's head before lifting him into her arms. "Here you go, big boy." She turned back to Wendy. "If you're fine, why did they keep you?"

"For observation." Time to come clean. "I'm pregnant."

"What?" Sophie dropped into the nearest chair. "How?"

"I'm immune to contraception, apparently. Fertility researchers should study me. I have the super-fertile gene. I'm not kidding."

"Who? When? Oh God. Please tell me Keith is not the father."

"It's Joe." And, to be fair, he *had* taken the news better than Keith had, back in the day. At least Joe hadn't screamed at her and threatened her if she didn't get an abortion.

Sophie's eyebrows shot up. "But you only spent a day together. Like yesterday." She stared. "I mean, the man has a reputation for being quick, but how quick can he be?"

Wendy closed her eyes, halfway between laughing and crying, her emotions a tangled mess. "Three months ago, he came to a fund-raiser where I was modeling."

Justin tugged on Sophie's hair.

On autopilot, Sophie reached into her purse and handed him a lollipop. "Okay. Obviously, you did more than fundraise."

Wendy groaned.

Sophie helped Justin with the wrapper. "Why didn't you tell me?"

"I thought I should tell him first, but then I could never find the right time."

Sophie didn't complain. That was the kind of friend she was—always there, always supportive. "How do you feel about it?"

"If I lived in a village, I'd be the village idiot. I mean, I'm okay with the baby. I just wish I could have planned for him or her. I was on the pill. And Joe used protection. What's wrong with me?"

"You have to give my brain a second here to catch up with all this." Sophie's gaze flitted to Wendy's midriff, then back to her face. "Have you told him?"

Wendy nodded.

"And?"

"He ran. He actually jumped from a moving ambulance."

"Wow."

"Yeah."

They looked at each other in stunned silence.

Sophie gathered herself first. "He'll come around. He's a good guy. Bing wouldn't have hired someone who doesn't have moral integrity."

"He's a womanizer."

"It doesn't mean he's going to shirk his responsibilities. If he does, I can have Bing arrest him."

"You're a good friend."

"I know."

"He saved our lives."

"There's that." Sophie patted Wendy's knee. "I can see the attraction. Those worn jeans." Sigh. "And the way he wears them."

"It's that laid-back, lazy smile," Wendy said miserably. "It gets to you. That big smile, those big hands...."

"Big feet?" Sophie added helpfully.

Wendy couldn't hold back a smile. "What are we, juveniles?" She groaned. "Yes, big...feet." She closed her eyes for a long second. "Why is life so complicated? I just want a normal guy who's nice, who will love us and stick by us. When I'm ready for a relationship," she added. "I'm so not even ready."

"It could be Joe," Sophie said carefully.

"What are the chances?"

Sophie looked away to examine the wallpaper.

Wendy sat up. "What is it?"

"I'm not sure I should tell you. Probably shouldn't. It's Joe's private business."

"But you're *my* best friend."

Sophie hesitated. She blew out a soft breath. "Okay, so you know he used to be this great local football star, and he got to go away on a football scholarship?"

"I think everybody who's ever been to Broslin knows that. I'm surprised they haven't renamed Route 1 the Joe Kessler Highway."

"He was being recruited to turn pro, but he left everything and came back to town." Sophie's fingers fidgeted on Justin. "There's a rumor about why he quit just when he was making it big."

"Why?"

"It's only a rumor."

"Sophie!"

"I heard that he hooked up with someone when he was back in town for a visit. And then a month later, she tracked him down and told him she was pregnant. He left everything for her. Then, a few months into their rushed engagement, she told him she lost the baby. Only she faked the whole pregnancy." Sophie scrunched up her nose.

"The woman was trying to get him on the hook before somebody else did," Wendy finished the story for her. "Before he hit it big in the NFL. That's terrible." Pregnancy was a blessing, not a weapon.

To know that you had a baby on the way, be all excited about it, then have that beautiful hope crushed—she couldn't even begin to imagine how much that would hurt. And to find out it'd all been a lie, getting fooled like that... Okay, that could make a man jump out of a perfectly good ambulance, if he thought he was being set up again.

Sophie bounced Justin on her lap. "He hasn't taken a woman seriously since."

Wendy clasped her hands. "And here I am with more baggage than a socialite on a world tour. A toddler, another child on the way, and a violent ex." No wonder Joe ran in the opposite direction.

"He just needs to get used to the idea."

Wendy had held it together during the accident and its aftermath, but now tears clouded her eyes. "He's been burned before. He isn't going to stick his hand into the fire again. Not that I expected him to. I was just hoping for a civilized arrangement."

She hadn't been foolish enough to think that he would suddenly turn into the perfect guy for her and they'd create the perfect family. Or had she? After they'd spent time together in Broslin, was part of her beginning to hope?

Didn't matter now. "God, I really am stupid."

"You're not only smart but you're a beautiful person, inside and out." Sophie reached over and squeezed her hand. "Any guy would be lucky to have you."

Wendy swallowed her tears. "I'm going to have two children from two different men, married to neither. I should go straight to a tattoo parlor from here, get my tramp stamp, and get it over with."

"How many men have you slept with? Grand total?" Sophie demanded.

"Three. Including Joe. But I went out a lot pre-Keith. I was a model and super tall for my age. I never got ID'd. I partied."

"You were young. It's not a sin. Some partying a tramp does not make."

Bing popped his head in the door. "Hey there. Can I come in? Is everybody okay?"

"Bi-bi!" Justin squealed.

The police captain didn't look the least put out by the indignity of a baby name. He loved Justin, and Justin loved him right back. The kid couldn't wait to go out to the farmhouse, where there were horses and his favorite dog in the world, Peaches. Not to mention Mango, the cat.

"Hey, little trooper." Bing plucked Justin from Sophie. "How do you feel about an oatmeal cookie? If that's okay with your mom?"

Wendy nodded. "We've missed lunch."

Justin smacked his lips.

Bing pulled a giant cookie from his shirt pocket, unwrapped the clear plastic, and handed over the treat.

The look of longing on Sophie's face caught Wendy by surprise. Were they trying for a baby? A proposal from Bing was just a matter of time. Theirs was the kind of fairy-tale, all-out love story movies were made of: danger and passion, unimaginable setbacks, then love conquering everything.

Then again, since Sophie was a heart-transplant patient, maybe she was advised not to have a child. She was supposed to avoid physical stress as much as possible.

Wendy watched her friend's wistful expression, and her heart twisted. She placed her hand over her belly and smiled at her son. If she could have another baby as healthy and happy as her firstborn was, she would count herself extremely lucky. She'd been an only child of older parents who didn't have the energy to drag her around to play-dates. She'd been a lonely kid. She didn't want that for Justin.

Sophie caught the hand on Wendy's barely-there baby bump. "Did everything check out?"

"Yes. No harm done. We're all healthy." All three of them. "As soon as the doctor comes and signs the discharge papers, we're good to leave."

"Bing can drive you home. I'll swing by the grocery store and bring you enough food to fill your fridge so you won't have to leave the apartment for a couple of days. And if your car isn't fixed by then, I'll bring you more."

"I just hope it's not totaled." Wendy had no idea where she was going to get the money for repairs. All she could do was pray that her insurance would pay. "Thank you. Both of you."

"Good thing we came separately," Bing said. "I was at the station."

Sophie stood. "Do you want to get dressed while we're waiting for you to be discharged? I'll help. Bing can take Justin out to the hallway."

Wendy ran her fingers over her green hospital gown. The split in the back would make undressing easy, even if her entire body ached. On the other hand, dragging on pants and tying her shoes might be more difficult. "Yes, please."

By the time she was dressed, the doctor was there to discharge them. Within an hour, they were home, her fridge stocked, and Bing and Sophie gone with reassurances that they were only a phone call away. Justin was sleeping in his room, tuckered out from all the excitement.

Wendy watched him sleep. "I love you," she whispered. "I love you most in the whole world."

They could have *died* in that ravine. She shuddered. Then she drew a deep breath and shook off her dark thoughts.

She'd received a second chance with her babies. She wasn't going to waste it. She wasn't going to live in fear. She was going to make some-thing of herself. She was going to create a good life for her little family. She was going to make her fledgling photography business work.

Since she'd moved to Wilmington, she'd been modeling for weekly circulars, corporate commercials, charity fashion shows, and even received regular calls from a home shopping channel that filmed its shows in West Chester.

She'd lost a lot of that during her first pregnancy, but her needs had been minimal at the time. She'd been living with Keith. She didn't have to worry about rent.

After Justin was born, she shed the weight quickly and returned to work full-time. But a lot of that work would stop again once she started showing with this baby. And even if her agency still wanted her after the pregnancy, the income simply wouldn't be enough to support her and two children.

She was twenty-six, soon to be the single mother of two, with no formal education, and no marketable skills. But the good thing about making bad decisions was that anyone could stop at any time and march off in the opposite direction.

Keith had always said that if she ever left him, she'd starve to death. He'd taunted her with predictions of how fast her life would fall apart on her own.

Wendy refused to prove him right. That wasn't the kind of role model she wanted to be for her children.

She thought of Sophie, the strongest woman she knew. What would Sophie do?

She'd have some inspirational quote handy, for starters. Like CREATE THE LIFE YOU WANT TO LIVE or something similar.

Then she would probably write a list and make a plan.

"Time to stop letting others define me, figure out who I am, and make life work for me," Wendy said aloud as she pressed a light kiss onto her son's head. "You deserve a mother who has her stuff together." The words felt good as they left her lips. They felt right.

Sophie always said you had to state your intention clearly to the universe.

Joe knew who he was: hot jock, football hero, officer of the law. He was cocky and self-assured and sometimes full of hot air. She didn't necessarily like everything about him, but the man knew exactly who he was, and that was something.

Wendy bit her lip. Everybody was who they made themselves, her agent was fond of saying.

"Time for a change."

CHAPTER FIFTEEN

Joe was done thinking about Wendy and why she might be claiming to be pregnant with his baby. All afternoon, her words kept popping into his head at work. What on earth was he supposed to do with them? She was a lovely woman with a great kid, in a bad situation. Joe wanted to help her, he really did. But he kept getting hung up on the pregnancy claim.

He needed to focus on the Brogevich case.

The warrant for the patient records had finally come in. Harper had the boxes taken straight to the conference room. Joe went to assist.

A dozen folders were laid out on the long table already. The rest waited for unpacking.

"That looks like a lot of work."

"Over two hundred files to go through." Harper grunted at the prospect. "And these are just the active patients. Some saw the doc a few times a week, some once a week, some once a month, some only once every three months."

"Maintenance." Joe nodded.

"Let's hope we find what we're looking for here," Harper said.

"Because if we don't, I'll have to get a warrant for the data storage vendor who has the files for all the inactive patients."

"The sooner we start, the sooner we'll know." Joe stepped forward. "We could separate out patients with violent tendencies first."

Harper put down the file he was paging through. "Good thinking." His phone buzzed, and he glanced at the screen. Frowned. "I have to go out on another case."

"I can handle the files here."

Harper was already halfway through the door. "Thanks."

Joe rolled up his sleeves and dove in. He looked for behavioral abnormalities that showed a potential for violence. The work was slow, pages and pages of therapy notes, drug prescriptions, lab work. Each file ate up considerable time. *Depression, phobia, anxiety, depression and more depression, PTSD. Anxiety, anxiety, insomnia, depression, phobia. Depression with suicidal thoughts.*

Captain Bing popped his head in. "Anything?"

"Not yet."

"Let me know what you find." He paused a beat. "About Wendy's accident... Thank you for being there for her. I'm not sure how I feel about that *brake failure*. Is Keith Kline still locked up?"

Just hearing the guy's name was enough to make Joe's muscles tense. "As far as I know."

The tight look on Bing's face said he was looking into all that deeper, but he let the subject drop." Are you coming to Jack's party tonight? If you don't finish with this by then," he nodded toward the files, "Mike can give you a hand tomorrow."

Jack was a hell of a detective. He deserved a good send off, and Joe wanted to be part of it. "I'll read through as much as I can then head over to Finnegan's."

"If anyone jumps out at you, in the meanwhile, call me." The captain pulled back and closed the door behind him.

Joe picked up the next file.

By the time he read through as many as his brain could absorb at one go, wrote up his notes, then headed out, most everyone else was already gone. Only Robin Combs still sat behind her desk, handling incoming calls.

Since she was talking to someone, Joe didn't interrupt, just passed by her with a wave.

"Go for it," she called after him, pausing the phone conversation. "Go with your heart, and you'll never go wrong."

She was the resident town psychic. Her random outbursts were nothing out of the ordinary. As a confirmed skeptic, Joe responded with a smile. And then he didn't give the words another thought. He hopped into his car and drove over to Jack's party.

Finnegan's, Broslin's one and only Irish pub, was bursting with people. The place was comfortable and masculine, its gleaming wood matched with green upholstery. The prospect of good beer and the rich aroma of Irish food made Joe feel instantly welcome and relaxed as he stepped through the door.

"Hey." Rose Finnegan sailed by with a tray. "I was wondering where you were. Party's in the back."

She ran the kitchen like an admiral, while her husband, Sean, manned the bar. What Sean didn't know about beer wasn't worth knowing. They were good, honest people, cheerful, hardworking. They treated their customers like family.

Since they were also the proud parents of Detective Harper Finnegan, they were the unofficial cop bar in town, the obvious place for Jack's good-bye party.

Joe walked over to the conglomeration of pushed-together tables. "What did I miss?"

About two dozen people had shown up. Mike and Chase were drinking soda. They were on duty, might have to go out on a call. The rest of them, including family, friends, and neighbors, were hanging on to their pints.

Chase grinned. "Jack just told us he's going to be an exotic dancer next. Like the ones who go to bachelorette parties in a fake police uniform and rip it off. Offered a free preview, but we talked him out of it."

Jack shouldered him aside, laughing. "I did *not* say that." A devious glint came into his eyes as he nodded toward the door. "Look who just came in."

Chase groaned. Joe turned to look and bit back a comment.

Luanne Wayfair stood inside the entrance—Chase's high school flame. He'd been soooo gone over her, it'd been ridiculous.

And if the expression on Chase's face now was an indication...

Holy shit.

Still?

"Harper said she started a rumor back in the day that you were bad in bed." Jack clearly enjoyed the hell out of the situation. "Should I ask her to give you a second chance? You must feel the need to prove yourself."

Joe stepped between the two men to prevent murder. And acknowledged that Chase very much looked like he would like a second chance. While Luanne spotted her friends in a corner booth at last and headed over to join them, without noticing Chase whatsoever.

Before Jack could comment on that, Harper walked in and headed straight to Joe. "Found anything in the files?"

"Not yet."

"We'll get back to them in the morning. Now, where's that Guinness? We might as well relax while we're taking a break."

He was right. Finnegan's was the kind of place where a man could forget his troubles for a night.

Except, for the first time ever, Joe's beer didn't taste right. Wendy was messing with his brain. He put on a smile anyway, and clapped Jack on the back. "Any chance you'll change your mind and stay?"

"Not likely." Jack's face lit up. "I have a baby coming."

A year ago, Joe would have bet good money that he'd never hear those words out of Jack's mouth. When they'd first met, Jack carried the weight of the world on his shoulders, a lone wolf obsessed with a gruesome serial killer. And now here he was with a goofy grin. He was a cautionary tale about how love could change a man.

"I hate to say this, but we'll miss you." Joe tapped his glass against Jack's. Odd how he could see even Jack Sullivan—former champion in surly and snarly—as a father before he could see himself in that role.

"If you start missing me too much, you can always come out to the house and help me chop wood," Jack offered.

"I don't think I'm going to miss you *that* much." Joe bumped his shoulder.

Harper started into a toast in the middle of the room. And then Chase took over. Then the next guy and the next.

As Joe grabbed a handful of peanuts from the nearest table, he caught a curvy blonde smiling at him from the bar. He nodded to her before turning back to his friends.

Jack was hugging Ashley, the love of his life, close to his side. She wasn't showing yet. Then again, Wendy wasn't either.

Wendy had said she was carrying Joe's baby. Like hell she was. Joe was responsible with women, always had been.

She'd seemed so sane and decent. Why would she lie about this? Did she think he'd do a better job at protecting her if there was a stronger personal connection? Did she think he had some secret pile of football money left?

Across the room, Ashley laughed, then kissed Jack, the kind of kiss that said "love" plain and simple, and a look in her eyes that promised more affection, of the X-rated type, later.

Bing stepped to the middle of the floor and launched into a speech. Sophie was hanging on to his every word. She looked at Bing as if he walked on water. The captain lucked out with her.

Joe had only met Wendy because of Sophie. *Ah hell*, there he went again. He drained his glass. He couldn't keep Wendy from his thoughts for five damn minutes.

While Captain Bing entertained the gathering with tales of every blunder Jack had made during his time with the PD, Joe strode over to the curvaceous blonde at the bar.

Her smile was openly inviting, blatantly suggestive, and almost expectant, as if she would have been offended if he'd ignored her a minute longer. "Hey, handsome."

"Hey, yourself. How are you doing?"

"Better by the minute." She looked him over, not missing an inch. Her gaze hesitated on his scar, then dropped to his lips. This wasn't her first rodeo with a stranger in a bar. She leaned closer, close enough for him to see down her dress. She had a rack that could hold beer mugs. "You could buy me a drink."

"I haven't seen you around here before."

"In town for a friend's wedding." She rolled her eyes. "Small town, huh? Not much excitement. Your party looks interesting. Why don't you invite me over?"

"Why don't I give you the dime tour of Broslin? I'm Joe, by the way."

She slid off her barstool slowly, sinuously, making sure her dress would ride up her long thighs as high as possible. Then she laughed and gave a halfhearted effort to tug the material down, to draw his attention to her legs, in case he'd missed the show. "I'm Candice."

Sean Finnegan behind the bar came over. "What can I get you?"

"Just her tab."

Sean shook his head at Joe, mumbling, "New record," under his breath when Candice turned to grab her purse.

Joe gave the man a good-natured shrug. He'd taken women home from Finnegan's before, but on previous occasions, they'd at least had a conversation first.

He had his Camaro with him, which made Candice laugh with delight. "Oooh, dark and dangerous."

Which, for some reason, annoyed him, so he went around to the driver's side and let her get her door herself.

As soon as she was inside, her gaze dropped to his crotch. "I want to see everything worth seeing."

Normally, he would have laughed at an innuendo like that. This time, he just said, "Buckle in."

He drove to the end of the street then turned right at the light. "Broslin's a mushroom town. Horse and cow country, originally, then someone figured out what to do with all that shit."

Candice giggled, not the least offended by his coarse language.

Joe pointed out a few historical buildings like the First Broslin Bank that had gone out of business during the most recent financial crisis and still stood deserted. He drove by the old county airport and pointed at the nearest hangar. "They have a good flea market here on Sundays, if you're around."

Candice shifted as close as she could without taking off her seat belt. "My plans are flexible."

"Farmer's market's in the other hangar on Fridays and Saturdays."

"Are you a farm boy?" She reached over and put her hand on his thigh, her blood-red fake nails a contrast to his faded jeans. The nail tips were slightly curled, vaguely reminiscent of talons.

"I come from a farming family, but that's not what I do."

The Kesslers had been living in Broslin for generations. He was the first of his family to break tradition, turn his back on working the land, and join the police. His parents had never resented his choice for a second. They'd always supported him.

The job suited Joe. Candice didn't. When her hand began moving up his thigh, he was more irritated than appreciative.

He liked easy, he really did. But he wasn't able to get into the spirit of the evening. He blamed Wendy.

To put her out of his mind, he placed his hand on Candice's and smiled at her. "Over there is the reservoir."

"Not much to look at, is it?"

Joe drove past the turnoff to Broslin Creek, a great place for a walk with the perfect make-out spot a little farther in. He turned at the next intersection instead, heading back to Main Street.

By the time he reached Finnegan's, Candice had her seat belt off, her body plastered against Joe's side, and her flawlessly manicured fingers massaging his crotch.

He stopped the car in the parking lot. "Here we are."

She shot him a confused look. "Why are we back at the bar? I thought we were going to your place."

"Sorry. That's not on the dime tour." He got out and walked around to open the door for her, so she'd know he was serious about dropping her off.

"Are you coming in?" she asked with an uncertain smile.

"I have work in the morning. You have a great evening."

He closed the passenger side door, then strode around the Camaro, dropped behind the steering wheel as Candice called something after him that sounded like "Stupid small-town hick."

He forgot her the second he drove away.

His mind was full of Wendy. *Wendy. Wendy. Wendy.*

Since he was thinking about her, he called Officer Mayfair of the Wilmington PD, the responding officer at Wendy's accident. They'd exchanged phone numbers as a professional courtesy.

"Joe Kessler," Joe identified himself when the man picked up. "We met on Route 202 this afternoon at that Prius that drove off the highway ramp. If you could give me an update on that, I'd appreciate it."

Silence stretched on the other end, then a few choice swear words in a sleepy voice. "At midnight? I have to get up at four thirty for my shift."

Joe glanced at the dashboard. The clock showed 12:23. "Sorry. Time got away from me."

The man grumbled. "You said the Prius?"

"Yeah. I was hoping it would have gone through inspection by now."

"Hang on for a second." Another pause. "Okay. Yeah. We got it. Looks like someone tampered with the brake lines. I'll be going out to talk to Miss Belle about it in the morning."

Tampered. Messed up on purpose. To hurt her. Each thought tightened Joe's muscles another notch, made him want to do things unbecoming an officer. "What time do you think you'll see her? As a friend, I'd like to be there for her."

"Around eight, unless something else comes up. Want to get that out of the way before the day goes crazy."

"I know how that is. Thank you. And sorry for calling so late."

Joe stopped at the stop sign. He would have to turn left to go home and grab some sleep. Or, take a right turn, back to the PD to look through a few more files.

He turned right, then he glanced at the clock again.

Too late to call Wendy, but not too late to call the Wilmington jail. They'd have someone on duty 24/7. Joe dialed, and when the call was picked up, he gave his badge number.

"Could you please tell me if Keith Kline is still in custody?" Technically, the police could hold the man without charging him until tomorrow—*today,* it was after midnight—but maybe his lawyer had pushed hard and gotten him released.

Nails clicked on a keyboard on the other end of the line. "Still here."

"Thank you, Ma'am."

Joe liked the thought of Keith in jail. A lot. With some luck, the fingerprint reports on Wendy's broken furniture and the bloody wig would come back a match for the idiot, and then he would be formally charged and kept locked up a good while longer.

Except...if Keith was still behind bars, who cut the Prius's break lines? Who was trying to hurt Wendy?

CHAPTER SIXTEEN

WENDY WOKE TO HER CELL PHONE RINGING AND GROANED INTO her pillow. She would have given her favorite pair of high heels for another hour of sleep. Her night had been restless, with a bunch of weird dreams. In some of her dreams, Joe was making love to her. In others, he was walking away from her.

She squinted at her phone's screen. *Talk about the devil.*

"It's barely past eight. Did you know it's not a crime to sleep in?"

"I'm here."

Her brain struggled to wake up. "Here where?"

"Outside your door."

"I didn't buzz you in."

"Came in with one of the neighbors. Open the door, Wendy."

He wants to talk about the baby.

"Give me a minute."

She put the phone down and crawled out of bed. Advance warning that he was dropping by would have been nice. She could at least have had a cup of coffee first.

She washed her face in a hurry then brushed her teeth, ran a comb through her hair. She dragged on a simple T-shirt with blue jeans, didn't want him to think that she was dressing up for him.

On her way to the front door, she checked on Justin. He was still sleeping.

"Hey." Joe's dark hair was mussed; his clothes wrinkled as if he'd slept in them. He looked sexier than ever.

Life was damned unfair.

He offered a lazy smile, but his eyes were somber, no glint of mischief. "May I come in?"

She stepped aside, responding to his good manners and rumpled, sexy look. Keith usually just pushed his way in and acted as if he owned the place. "Partied a little too hard last night?"

"Go hard or go home. Right?" He passed by her and looked around. "You cleaned up. I meant to come back and help more."

He had green carpet fibers—the same color as the hallway carpet— on the back of his pants, as if he'd spent some time sitting outside her door.

She headed to the kitchen. "Coffee?"

"Yes, please. Where's Justin? Was he all right last night?"

"Still snoozing." Wendy's heart softened. Joe always asked about Justin, and brought him little gifts half the time. He seemed to genuinely care. So why couldn't he deal with their baby? She'd just have to ask him. *After* she'd had her morning shot of caffein.

She changed the filter in the coffee machine. "I thought he might have nightmares, but he didn't. Thank you for making the accident a game and an adventure for him."

"Kids are pretty resilient." Joe stopped a few feet from her and held her gaze, as if trying to figure out how to say what he wanted to say next.

Wendy steeled herself. Here came the part where he blamed her for getting pregnant and told her that the baby was her problem. She turned on the coffeemaker, then moved away to put a few more inches of distance between them.

"You don't have to do that," he said.

"What?"

"Prepare for the blow. I've never hit a woman in my life, and I'm not going to. Ever."

The truth of his words washed over her. "I know."

"Do you?"

"Yes." Joe wasn't Keith. He was *nothing* like Keith. "I'm sorry. It's a body reflex."

"You don't have to apologize for it either."

"Feeling bossy much this morning? Is there anything else you'd like to tell me to do or not to do?"

An almost-smile twitched at the corner of his lips. "Sorry. I haven't slept much. I've been up most of the night, working on my friend's case and thinking about yours." He held her gaze. "Your brake lines were cut. Your accident wasn't an accident."

The news sucked all the air out of her lungs, stole all the strength from her muscles. She braced against the counter. "Is Keith out?"

"Still in jail. First thing I checked."

That tripped her up for a second. "Then who? It has to be him." She couldn't think of anyone else who'd want to harm her. "He found a way. Maybe he paid someone."

"From behind bars? Sure, it happens, but with people who have extensive criminal connections before they go in. He's in county jail, not federal lockup. How does he connect with an assassin?"

"He made some kind of agreement with someone who was getting out." Her chest hurt. "He can talk anyone into anything."

"Has he tried to contact you since he's been arrested?"

"He had his cell buddy call to let me know he's mad at me." She wrapped her arms around herself. "And that he'd take care of me when he got out."

"When were you going to tell me about this?" Joe's tone was pissed but restrained.

"I don't know. I had other things I had to tell you that I was worried about at the time."

His jaw worked silently for a second. "The baby can't be mine."

His pronouncement felt like a slap in the face, the sense of rejection overwhelming. Of course, he would assume that she slept around. And, of course, he couldn't imagine having a baby with her. She was fluff. Nothing. Keith had told her that often enough.

Well, Keith was wrong. And so was Joe. "I haven't slept with anyone else. Why would I make this up? I have no reason."

"I could think of a few." His dark gaze bore into hers. "You know I'm attracted to you. Maybe you see that as something you can use to your advantage. I'm a cop. That's a bonus. You know I would protect you and your children from Keith." He shook his head. "Here's the thing. I'm going to protect you, no matter what. You have that. Okay?"

"Thank you." She was grateful for the last part of his declaration. The rest.... She turned from him to the cabinets. She didn't want him to catch the stupid look of disappointment on her face.

She grabbed a travel mug and took her time pouring him coffee, then steeled herself as best she could before she turned back to him. She put on her most carefully neutral expression. Life was a runway. You held your head up, never let anyone see behind the mask, pretended that nothing hurt. "Here you go. See you later."

He accepted the mug and glanced at the clock on her microwave. Then he went and sat at the kitchen table. "Wilmington PD will be here in a couple of minutes to talk to you about the crash."

She'd been taking the first big gulp of her own coffee. She burned her tongue. Coughed.

Joe was watching her. "Other than Keith, is there anyone else who might want to hurt you?"

"I'm a small-time model." She rubbed her free hand over her thigh. "I don't know any murderers. It's not like I live a life of crime."

When Wilmington PD arrived five minutes later, she told them the same thing.

Justin woke while she was being interviewed. Joe changed his diaper, dressed him, fed him breakfast in the kitchen while Wendy answered questions in the living room. Both officers were female. They did a terrible job at ignoring the jaw-dropping, sexy-hunk picture Joe presented with Justin on his hip.

Keith had never questioned Justin's paternity but was never there for Justin. Whereas Joe had been there for them so far, every step of the way. Even if they didn't always see eye-to-eye, Wendy was ridiculously grateful for his presence. Until he decided to completely take over the second the police left.

"Pack your suitcases."

"I just unpacked them."

"I can protect you better in Broslin. I have no jurisdiction here. No backup."

"Sophie already promised the house to someone else. As eager as that neighbor was to get her parents in there, they are probably already moved in."

"Then you're coming to my place. I have a guest bedroom. You'll be safe there."

She couldn't think. The morning had hit her with the force of a tidal wave. She had trouble finding her footing. "One minute I'm a liar, making up a baby, the next minute you want me to move in with you? How does that work?"

"I never said you made up the baby, just that I'm not the father," he said quietly. "I know this is a rough time for you. You could have died yesterday. Justin could have been hurt. Give me time to figure out who is behind all this."

"Keith."

"If he is, he's going to be put away for a good long time. I promise you that. Let me help."

"I don't..." *I don't need help*, she'd meant to say, but didn't finish, because it was a lie.

There was being independent, and then there was being stupid. She would have liked to think she didn't fall entirely in the latter category. Even if she might have been willing to brazen the situation out alone, no way would she put Justin in danger.

She tried to picture what it'd be like to spend a few days with Joe. Talk about entering the lion's den.

"I want you safe." He stood in front of her, hands in his pockets. "But it's your decision."

If he'd been impatient, if he'd pushed, it would have gotten her hackles up. The kindness in his eyes disarmed her. Joe was convinced he couldn't be the father of her baby, but he stepped up to the plate anyway and would do whatever it took to keep her and her children safe.

Wendy's heart softened another notch toward him.

"Thank you." She walked over to the couch, to the two large travel bags she'd just emptied. "I'll have to repack everything."

"No rush. I cleared my morning for this. You pack, I'll keep Justin entertained." He turned to her son. "Hey, buddy. Want to come over to my house to play?"

Justin's eyes lit up. He was always game for a playdate. "Do you have a doggy?"

"I don't have a dog, but the neighbor's cat visits all the time. I give him treats. You could do that."

"Kitty!" Justin clapped, bouncing and beaming as if he'd won the pet lottery.

"He's a pirate cat," Joe warned. "He's missing an eye and half of his tail."

Justin's eyes snapped wide.

Joe gave an exaggerated nod. "His name is Prince, but I call him Pirate Prince."

Wendy bit back a smile. He definitely knew how to talk to kids.

Just like that, Justin was sold on going. "I want to see the Pirate Prince!"

Wendy walked to the bathroom cabinet and grabbed what she would need for a couple of days.

"I'll have to pick up diapers," she said on her way back to the living room. "And a car seat. The police haven't released my car yet, and Justin's car seat is in the back."

"I have one." Joe wiped off the juice Justin spilled on the table. "For my nephew. We hang out sometimes to give my sister a break." He crossed to the couch for her bags. "Let me take these down. I'll come back to help you with Justin. We can stop by the store to pick up diapers on the way over to my place."

Then he was walking out with her luggage, leaving her to stare after him.

He helped without being asked. He saw what needed to be done and did it. He didn't think dealing with Justin was "the woman's job." When Joe was around, it was like having a real partner—like in books and movies.

A sharp sense of longing exactly for that, a real partner, cut through Wendy. A useless longing. He wasn't exactly offering, beyond the current, *temporary*, situation.

She picked up her son. "Hey, how about we get dressed?"

Joe was not her partner, and he never would be. He'd made it more than clear that he couldn't even accept that the baby was his. No sense in losing herself to some girlish fantasy.

He returned a few minutes later and carried Justin down to his car while Wendy made sure that all the lights were turned off, the heat turned down, and that there were no dirty dishes left in the sink. She filled her last bag with Justin's baby accessories—sippy cups and toys—then locked up the apartment.

They were leaving. Because staying wasn't safe. The thought hit her with renewed force as she walked away from her home, for the second time in a week.

Somebody wanted to kill her, and they wanted it badly enough not to care if they hurt Justin.

Would Keith really do that? Would a father endanger his own son?

She didn't want to believe that about him. She couldn't. But if not Keith, then who?

She hurried after Joe, more rattled than she cared to admit.

She had a deadly, unseen enemy, hiding in the shadows. And she had no way of knowing when he might strike again.

CHAPTER SEVENTEEN

WHILE JOE TRAILED AFTER WENDY AND JUSTIN IN THE GROCERY store, he called the captain with an update.

"They'll be safest at my house. Whoever is after Wendy might know about her friendship with Sophie, that she stayed at Sophie's place recently. I don't want them to go back there."

"Are you sure that's why you're taking her home? That's a little more *personal* protection than we normally provide."

"She is a friend. Any development on Phil Brogevich? I could come in. Other than you, nobody knows I have Wendy. I feel comfortable with leaving her at my place alone. I have a security system."

"Glad to hear that, because Chief Gleason wants you back in the city. He wants to make sure Ramos isn't going to move on the Twentyniners without him knowing. He wants to prevent another bloodbath."

"Ramos is waiting for the guns I promised." And the gun shipment wasn't going to happen. It'd just been bait.

"Chief Gleason issued a warrant for Officer Tropper's arrest yesterday, but Tropper didn't show up for work. He isn't at home either. The chief wants you to drop in on Ramos. Maybe Tropper figured out that the chief was on to him and he decided to hang out with his gang buddies."

Wendy breezed through the self-checkout, and Joe followed her out to the car.

"I'll go see Ramos," he told the captain, "as soon as I settle in Wendy and Justin. Let me know if there's any progress on the Brogevich case. I promised Marie I'd keep an eye on it."

"Harper is going to the hospital in West Chester this afternoon to check on people the victim worked with there, before he opened his private practice in Broslin. If you're back from Philly by then, you can go with him."

"I'll make sure to get back in time."

"Another thing," the captain said. "Doris called in, Phil's reception-ist. She just remembered that the doc had weekly anger management group sessions at the hospital. He kept that even after he switched to private practice."

"Sounds promising." Someone with anger-control issues might deliver the kind of deathblow that had bashed in Phil's skull.

Joe slipped behind the wheel, thanked the captain for the update, then hung up. As he pulled out of the parking lot, he checked for suspicious vehicles behind him. Nothing.

"Does Pirate Prince bite?" Justin asked.

"No. He's pretty sweet," Joe answered, and for the rest of the ride, they talked about the cat.

"I have to go in to work," Joe told Wendy as he pulled into his driveway.

Her eyes softened with sympathy. "Your friend's case?"

"Something else."

"How many cases do you work at the same time?"

"Depends. We split up whatever we have coming in."

"Wouldn't it be easier to do one thing at a time?"

"That's pretty much prime-time TV show stuff, when all the detec-tives go off after the killer and push until the bad guy's caught. In real life, police work is nothing but interruption after interruption." He shrugged. "You prioritize. What's on top can shift from day to day or even hour to hour. You try to get everything done while doing your best not to drown in the paperwork."

"That doesn't sound as glamorous as on TV." She got Justin out of the car.

Joe grabbed her bags from the trunk. "It has its moments."

"Do you miss football?"

He opened the front door for her. "A little. But I'm what I'm supposed to be. This is it for me. I'm part of the town. I work to make things better here. As sappy as that sounds, it makes me happy."

She walked inside. "It's not a crime to like your job. Nice house."

"Thanks." He set her bags down in the hallway. "Do you like modeling?"

Justin ran past them, to the living room, already busy discovering.

Wendy smiled after him, then looked at Joe. "What I thought was the most amazing thing and the best life ever at sixteen is not the same when I look at it at twenty-six. Not that I'm complaining," she added quickly. "I have a job. It pays the bills."

"But you want more."

"I want different. Something that requires more from me than holding a pose or putting one foot in front of the other. I'm aging out anyway."

"At twenty-six?"

She offered a flat smile. "That's like a grandmother in modeling."

"Sure. Come on, Grandma." He grinned at her. "Let me show you to your rocker."

"Why don't you show us around first?"

So Joe did that, surprisingly self-conscious. He cared more than he thought he would about whether Wendy liked his place.

After the grand tour, he showered and changed, then drove into the city. On his way, he called Keith Kline's arresting officer and told him about Wendy's cut brake lines.

"I'd like to have a list of people Kline had contact with since he's been in jail, the ones who were released before yesterday."

"You think he hired someone? Doesn't seem the type."

"Yeah. Maybe not." Abusers were hands-on. Violence allowed them to let off steam. They fed off the fear of their victims. Battery was hot,

uncontrolled anger, while hiring a hit man was cold and calculated. But
... "Kline's the only one who makes sense right now." Joe thought of
the fear in Wendy's eyes every time she said the bastard's name. "I'm
not going to rule out anything at this stage, just to be on the safe side."

The officer promised to look into it and get back to him.

Joe called his sister, Amber, next. "How is my favorite nephew?"

"He just finished locking all his *bad* toys in jail."

Joe grinned. "Good boy."

"He used the toilet as a holding cell. His stuffed animals are in the
washer right now. On the *sanitize* cycle. Don't you dare laugh. Max
pretends to be a police officer because he thinks you hung the moon
and the stars."

"I'm not ashamed to admit that I am *the* best."

"You think you're funny. I think it's time for a nephew-uncle weekend. See what Max can do at your house."

"He's welcome anytime." And that brought Joe to the reason why
he was calling. "I wanted to let you know that I'll have someone
staying with me for a couple of days."

"Which one of your friends got kicked out by his wife this time?"

"It's not like that. Not a guy. You don't know her."

Shocked pause. Then Amber sputtered on the other end. "You're
living with a *woman?*"

"Her name is Wendy Belle. Single mom with a son Max's age.
Justin."

"You moved a single mom with a kid into your house? Your bachelor sanctuary?" Incredulity tilted Amber's voice up and up. "Who are
you, and what have you done with my brother?"

"I'm going to ignore that undeserved jab. Anyway, I thought you
might want to stop by if you have some time. Maybe the boys could
play."

"Oh my God. You want me to meet her." Stunned silence. "How
long has this been going on? How serious are you about her?"

"It's not like that."

"What is it like?"

"We're friends." All right, so that wasn't the full truth. Joe cleared
his throat. "She says she's pregnant with my baby."

"Oh, wow." More joy and worry echoed in the reaction than two short words should be able to hold. "How do you feel about that?"

"It can't be mine."

"I hope you didn't tell her that. I mean, unless you think she's a total liar like Erika. If this woman is in your house, you must like her and trust her at least a little."

"Hm."

"Joseph Peter Kessler." Amber sounded like their mother, to an uncanny degree. "Did you make a complete mess of things?"

"I might have."

She sighed loudly enough to make sure he would hear it. "Are you in love with her?"

He didn't do love. He did fun. Short. Hot. Then a consensual good-bye. "Definitely not."

"You don't normally mess up with women. I think she got to you. This is something serious."

"It's not."

"She's expecting your baby and living in your house."

Not expecting *my* baby, the words were on his tongue.

He didn't say them. Because the truth was, he didn't know Wendy for a liar.

Shit.

Joe had always been in control of his relationships. *Always.* How in hell had he dropped the ball here?

"Can you see yourself with her long term?" Amber asked.

Joe navigated traffic, tapping his fingers on the steering wheel. Truth was, he *could* see himself with Wendy. All too easily. Not only could he see them together, but he liked the picture. "I hate when you ask me questions and I don't like the answers."

"That's what sisters are for." Amber laughed, way too cheerful. *Nothing* made sisters so happy as seeing their brother in misery. "I'll stop by to check her out," she said. "Can't do it tomorrow, but the day after, for sure. And then you and I are going to have a talk." Then she hung up, before Joe could tell her that he didn't need a relationship lecture.

He took Route 95 to South Philly, through Tinicum Park then past the Navy Yard. He refocused on what he needed to accomplish in the next couple of days: find a way to keep Keith away from Wendy permanently, figure out who cut her brakes, catch Phil's killer, stop a gang war, and find a dirty cop. Think more—*a lot* more—about the baby.

He turned down Brant Street, saw Paco in Ramos's driveway, half under the hood of his car. Paco worked at a local garage, mostly so he could use the tools and get discounts on parts for his lowrider. His electric-blue 1984 Buick Regal didn't have much more than six inches of ground clearance. *Touch it and die* was calligraphed on the back bumper.

Rusty Red was blaring from the radio. His rapping could be heard halfway down the street, a song about taking out enemies.

Joe got out of his car and rolled his neck. He had a rough game ahead of him, but he was ready to tackle the first quarter.

CHAPTER EIGHTEEN

"Yo!" Joe strode up the driveway. "What's up, bro?"

Paco shot a surly look his way. "What the hell does it look like?"

All right. Bad mood. Maybe he ran out of weed. Or had a fight with his girlfriend again about money for the kids. He was the father of two little girls.

Joe paused by him. "Any word when we'll be stoppin' by to say hello to J.T.?"

Paco shrugged and leaned back under the hood.

Trigger was more welcoming. The dog ran to greet Joe and escorted him to the front door, his entire body wagging.

"You're a good boy." Joe scratched behind the dog's ear.

Inside, Rashard was lounging in the living room. He didn't stop playing his video game, just nodded at Joe. "Yo. S'up, man."

Rodrigo was in the kitchen in the back, sitting on the linoleum floor with his back to the wall, a couple of empty beer cans scattered around him. He was twenty, with an alcohol and crack addiction. No education, no job, no prospects—a damn sad state of affairs. He wasn't stupid, just lacked opportunity. "S'up, bro?"

"Qué pasa, amigo?" Joe glanced around. "Where's Ramos?"

"Went out to pick up some guns. He got tired of waiting for you to bring the goods."

"I'll get the guns. No problem." Joe wished he'd come sooner. He could have gone with them, figured out who their connections were. "Let's hope they don't get caught. I want J.T., man. Gomez..." He shook his head. "I loved that kid. I'm not part of the crew, but you guys took me in when I needed help. You offered protection. I appreciate that. Your family is my family."

"Yo, bro." Rodrigo offered him a beer and Joe took it. "They'll be back. Ain't nothing gonna happen to them. We'll get J.T."

"Yeah. Ramos has the devil's luck."

"El Diablo." Rodrigo grinned.

"Maybe he's got someone on the inside. Ever thought about that?" Joe sat on the floor across from Rodrigo. "That'd be nice. Having a friend in the PD. That's what I need in Trenton, man. Should have invested more in protection."

He waited, but instead of giving up any information about Tropper and his whereabouts, Rodrigo finished his booze, his head flopping over as the can dropped from his limp fingers. He was too far gone to answer.

Joe pushed to his feet, leaving his unopened can behind. "Gotta take a piss."

He headed toward the bathroom but stopped in front of the basement door, out of Rodrigo's sight. He turned the knob, then without making a sound, he padded down the stairs.

If Officer Tropper was hiding in the house, he could be anywhere.

An ancient washer and dryer sat against the wall, dusty old boxes taking up the rest of the space. No dirty officer. Joe checked a few of the boxes. Doilies and old clothes, picture albums, stuff that must have belonged to Ramos's aunt.

Joe hurried back upstairs, stepped into the bathroom, flushed the toilet, then backed out fast. The place stank to high heaven. Every once in a while, one of the guys would bring a girlfriend around who might do the dishes, but nobody cleaned much of anything else.

He headed back through the kitchen. "Things to do, people to see. I'll stop by later to catch up with Ramos."

Rodrigo gave no indication that he heard him.

Rashard was still immersed in his game in the living room, his full attention on the big-screen plasma TV. Joe paused by the front door, glanced up the stairs to the second floor where Ramos's aunt lived. As far as Joe knew, nobody but Ramos and Gomez went up there. Upstairs was off-limits to the crew.

The perfect place to stash a dirty cop.

Rashard was lost in a shooting spree. Trigger appeared at the top of the stairs, tail wagging. Joe put his foot on the first step just as the front door banged open and Ramos strode in.

Joe patted his thigh, as if he was only there to call Trigger downstairs.

"Hey," he greeted Ramos. "Stopped by to see what's up. If I can help with anything. When are we moving on J.T., bro? I'm ready."

Ramos watched him, that odd look in his eyes again.

Joe kept his right arm loose by his side, ready to grab for the gun tucked into his waistband at the back.

"Tomorrow night." Ramos walked inside. "Be here by eight. You'll be with me. We'll take your car. J.T.'s crew doesn't know the Camaro. They know my ride."

At last, specific details Joe could give Chief Gleason. "We're splitting into teams?"

"Three cars, three houses to hit."

"What houses?"

"You'll see when we get there." Ramos dropped down next to Rashard in the living room and joined the game, finished with the conversation.

Joe left, drove a couple of blocks, looped around, and made sure he wasn't followed. He got lunch from a fast-food drive-through then drove back to Broslin, straight to the station to report to Chief Gleason through Captain Bing. Nobody on Gleason's team knew Joe was working undercover, and the chief wanted to keep it that way.

Leila was working behind the reception desk. Nobody in the bullpen.

Joe glanced at the bulletin board that looked like a rainbow, every notice printed on a different color paper. Best not to bring that up. Had to be Robin's work.

Leila caught him looking, and her eyes narrowed dangerously. "She thinks we need more color around here."

A high school kid swaggered in, saving Joe from having to pick sides.

"Hi." The kid scanned Leila and adjusted his letterman jacket, flashed a smile that brought out twin dimples. "Hey, beautiful. Are you the angel who's going to help me talk my way out of a parking ticket?"

Joe bit back a grin. The kid had moves, but he seriously had to learn how to read his target better.

Leila raised a strict eyebrow. "Watch it, Romeo. I'm old enough to be your mother."

The kid grinned. "Can I call you Mrs. Robinson?"

"You can call me, Mrs. Please-don't-throw-the-stapler-at-my-head. How is that?"

The cocky grin only widened. "God, I love me a feisty older woman."

Leila pulled her spine straight, her eyes narrowing to slits as she leaned forward to give the kid a good look. "Aren't you Brian Taylor? You know I go to church with your mother? She raised you to talk to your elders like that?"

The kid shrank two inches, the cocky attitude sliding right off him. "No, ma'am."

"Where's that ticket?"

The kid dug through his pocket and handed over a crumpled piece of paper.

"You can pay right here. Anything else?"

Joe watched the transaction silently, holding back laughter.

"Kids these days," he offered in support after the boy left.

Leila scoffed. "What are you talking about? He reminds me of you at that age. You propositioned the vice-principal's wife at the senior prom. Remember that?"

Memories best left forgotten. "In my defense, she was a pretty young woman. Completely wrong for an old bald guy." Joe cleared his throat. "You wouldn't know by any chance when the captain is coming back, would you?"

"Didn't say. He's out at a fatal motorcycle accident. Might be a while."

"Who?" A couple of faces flashed into Joe's mind, buddies who rode bikes. Half the time the bodies he had to scrape off the pavement were friends. That was the most difficult part of being a cop in a small town where he knew everybody.

"Not from Broslin." Harper lumbered from the back with a cup of coffee. He nodded at Joe. "I'm about to go back to the hospital to interview a few more of Brogevich's ex-coworkers. While I'm there, I'm going to look into those anger management classes. Want to ride along?"

"I'll follow you over." That way, Joe could call the captain on the way and report in. Call Wendy too, and check on her. He hoped she was settling in all right with Justin.

"All right." Harper headed to his desk. "Just give me a minute to check my email."

Leila's cell phone rang. She picked up the call and listened for a few seconds, her eyebrows drawing tighter and tighter together. "You tell him he better not leave the house. He's grounded."

When she used that tone, it usually had to do with one of her teenage sons.

"Anything I can help with?" Joe offered after she hung up.

"Put my kids in lockup till they grow a brain?" Her growl would have done a she wolf proud. She wasn't the type to sigh. "Zak has his first girlfriend. Tad decided it's a good idea to sneak smokes behind my back. Bobby wants to drop out of sports."

That last one seemed like the worst problem to Joe. "He's good at football. I saw him play. He shouldn't quit."

"I keep telling him that."

"I could take them to a game in Philly."

"They'd love that. Thanks. With all your pictures and trophies in the glass cabinets at the high school, they think you're *da man*."

"I try not to brag," he said modestly.

She laughed. "For some reason, they think you're not lame like the rest of us adults. Apparently, I don't know anything anymore. I'm out of touch." Dreamy nostalgia filled her eyes. "They were such sweet little boys. Used to pick me flowers. What happened?" Then she answered her own questions. "Testosterone tornado. And I'm in my own hormone hurricane."

Before she could move on to the vagaries of menopause, Joe quickly said, "It's tough to be a single mother."

"Being a mother is a full-time job. Being the mother of more than one is like juggling chain saws."

"If anyone could actually juggle chain saws, it's you." Joe thought of Wendy, because he wasn't able to go five minutes these days without thinking of her. Wendy would soon be a mother of two. With a violent ex, who was possibly out to have her killed.

The second he had his list from the jail in Wilmington, the names of the men Keith Kline had interacted with after his arrest, Joe was going to set everything else aside and jump on that.

"I'll get tickets for the next game," he told Leila. "You let the boys know." He liked her sons. They always came for the Broslin PD fund-raiser cookouts. A few times, Joe had tossed a football around with them out back. They were good kids.

Harper strode up to the counter, shrugging into his coat. "Ready?"

"Let's go."

They were in the parking lot when Joe's phone rang.

"This is a courtesy call. Cop to cop," Officer Conti said on the other end. He was one of the officers who'd processed Wendy's apartment after the break-in. "I just heard that Keith Kline was released on bail."

"I appreciate the heads-up." Joe caught up to Harper. "I have to run off on another case. I won't be able to go over to the hospital." He wanted to, he owed that to Phil and Marie, but he needed to tell Wendy about Keith in person.

"Might all turn out to be a giant waste of time anyway." Harper slipped behind the wheel of his cruiser. "Running down a thousand bad leads before we get the one that takes us somewhere. I'll let you know if I find any useful information."

"Thanks."

As soon as Joe was in his Camaro, he called the captain and filled him in on the planned gang hit.

"I'll let Chief Gleason know. Are you going back to Philly tomorrow?"

"Yes, sir. I want to see the job to the end. All we know right now is that Ramos is going to hit J.T.'s crew at three locations. I don't know where. If I can get that and pass it on, the chief can have SWAT teams waiting. Catch everyone with the guns. Intent to commit murder, gang activity, illegal weapons charges, probably some drug charges."

"I'm sure Chief Gleason would appreciate that. You be careful."

"Yes, sir. But I need a favor."

"What is it?"

"Keith Kline is out on bail... If I'm in Philly, I can't keep an eye on Wendy. I'd like someone to watch my house while I'm gone."

CHAPTER NINETEEN

WENDY KISSED THE SILKY HAIR ON HER SON'S LITTLE HEAD. "ARE you finished, sweet pea?"

"Done!" Justin shoved his empty bowl toward her. He was nestled into the throw pillows on Joe's couch, watching cartoons.

"Good job." Wendy brushed a handful of runaway Oat Loops from the couch into the bowl. "We have to keep Joe's house clean, okay?"

"Okay." Justin's eyes stayed riveted on the screen.

Joe's TV. In Joe's living room. Because they were now living with Joe.

After about five seconds of independence.

Nobody realized how hard she'd had to work to escape Keith's lair. She couldn't just ask to move out. She'd had to make him want them to leave. She'd *let* Justin cry at night. Let him spill juice on the carpet and throw toys around. Then she had to put the thought into Keith's head that everything was calmer and nicer when they weren't there. She'd stayed away, beginning with a weekend with Sophie. Then a week. And every time she'd returned to the penthouse, she'd let Justin run amok, for contrast. It'd taken her a massive amount of maneuvering to escape, but she had.

Or so she'd thought. Now she knew better. There was no escaping

Keith. And coming to live under Joe's roof certainly wasn't the path to making it on her own, which was her goal.

"Jump, jump, jump!" Justin clapped on the couch. "Weeee!" He shouted at cartoon sheep who were making their escape from their corral.

At least, he's happy.

She liked Joe's gleaming black granite countertops and cherry cabinets. His eighties colonial had been converted to an open floor plan, the original kitchen and dining room combined into a large eat-in kitchen. The family room and living room had been opened together to create one large space, with a floor-to-ceiling fireplace, a large-screen TV, and comfortable, masculine furniture.

The upstairs bedrooms had been updated too. Two of the three original, small bedrooms had been merged into one spacious master suite. The bathroom had an oversize shower that had more shower-heads than she would know what to do with, but she'd developed an instant crush on the large whirlpool tub.

The remaining bedroom was Joe's office, thoughtfully including a pull-out couch. More than enough room for her and Justin.

Everything was low-key, homey, and welcoming. Joe had put plenty of thought into the design. He'd renovated the house for himself, not for show, and not for a flip. His house showed a different side of him from what Wendy had seen before. She'd expected a frat house party vibe. Instead, Joe lived in the kind of home that she as a single mom could only daydream about living in someday.

She washed Justin's bowl, looking out the window over the sink. A fancy cedar swing set, complete with a playhouse, sat in the middle of the backyard. A black cat ran around the sandbox, straight to the patio doors.

"I think Pirate Prince is here," she called to Justin. "Do you want to let him in? Joe said it was okay."

Before the last word was out, Justin was already halfway across the room, the TV all but forgotten. No cartoon sheep could measure up to a live, one-eyed cat. "Kitty!"

"Hold on." Wendy ran behind him.

She opened the door, pet the cat first, holding Justin back until she was sure the animal was friendly. He was sweet, rubbing against her shin first, then Justin's. When the cat purred, making instant friends with both of them, she left her son to their visitor and went back to the kitchen to put on some coffee.

She checked out the fancy coffee maker. Trouble was, she didn't just like the kitchen and the rest of the house. She liked the house's owner.

The physical attraction was too strong to deny. So, fine, she could admit it, at least to herself. She just couldn't give in to it.

Resist, resist, resist.

She glanced back at Justin.

"Be very nice to the kitty, okay? They like petting, but you can't pull his ears or his tail. You have to be gentle."

"Like a good little boy?" Justin echoed what she always told him.

She smiled at her son. "Exactly."

He *was* kind and gentle. She was proud of him. He hadn't inherited his father's temper, a fear that used to keep Wendy awake at night.

The coffee machine just finished brewing when Joe walked in.

Wendy hadn't realized how tense her shoulder muscles had been all day, until they suddenly relaxed. Having Joe home made her feel better, an unexpected reaction she set aside to analyze later.

Justin looked up, but only for a second, lost in cat-petting bliss. "Hi, Joe."

"Hey, buddy. I see you've met Pirate Prince. Want to feed him some treats?"

"Yes!"

Joe strode to the kitchen, shot a devastating smile at Wendy, then pulled a handful of treats from the corner cabinet. "There you go. You can lay them down in a line, and he'll follow them. Sometimes that's how I get him to go home for the night when I'm ready to go to bed. I just lead him right out the door."

Justin ran over, grabbed the treats, and he managed to carry them without dropping any. He lined them up, one by one, a foot apart, to the living room couch. When the cat followed, Justin laughed with an unselfconscious, abandoned glee that was the very essence of childhood.

"Thank you." Wendy, unsure what to do with the sudden swell of gratitude toward Joe, grabbed milk from the fridge. "Coffee?"

"Yes, please."

She handed Joe the already finished cup and filled the machine again, for herself. "Pirate Prince is good with kids. And so are you."

"We're both used to playing with my nephew, Max. By the way, Amber said she'd stop in the day after tomorrow."

Wendy wasn't sure if she was ready for meeting Joe's family, but she couldn't very well ask Joe to tell them not to come. She had more pressing issues, in any case.

She lowered her voice to ask, "Did you find out who messed with my brakes?"

"Not yet." Joe stepped closer. Concern reflected in his eyes as he watched her. "Keith is out on bail."

Anxiety wound around her and squeezed, like a giant cold snake. Fear pushed her to grab her son and run. But where? *No, no...*this was Joe's place. Keith didn't know about this house. They were safe. "He won't find us here."

"I'll have to go out on a job tomorrow, but other than that, I'm going to stick around as much as I can. While I'm gone, there'll be someone else here from the station. I'm going to make sure you're protected." His determined expression said he meant every word. "You can stay here for as long as you want. You can sleep in the master bedroom with Justin. I'll sleep on the pullout couch in my office. You write a list of things you both need, and I'll make sure to get everything."

Wendy stepped back from him. "When I told you the baby was yours, I did not mean I was expecting financial support from you."

"You have every right to expect financial support from me. And every other kind of support too. I'm not going to be a deadbeat dad." Annoyance threaded through his voice. He shoved his hands into his pockets. "Not that I have any idea how this happened. Considering the precautions we took."

"If you think I'm faking it, you're welcome to come to my twelve-week checkup tomorrow. There'll be an ultrasound."

"I do believe that you're pregnant." His tone switched to exasperation. "I'm sorry I was a jerk about all this before. I had a bad experience with an ex. I have this hang-up, which is stupid, because you're nothing like her. I'm going to work through it, because this is not fair to you. I know you're not a liar."

"Thank you." She'd needed to hear that. "I wouldn't blame you if you didn't believe me, but I appreciate that you do."

"I'm having a hard time dealing with the baby." He cleared his throat. "Because I haven't dealt with the other stuff yet."

"What other stuff?"

He looked at her as if she should know. As if the answer to her question was obvious.

"I want you." Heat filled his eyes. "I want you all the time. I lost all interest in other women." He took her hands and pulled her to him slowly. And then, even slower, he brushed his lips over hers. "Wendy?"

Electricity zinged through her, followed by longing and desire. Her brain short-circuited, and she sank into the kiss. *So much for resisting.*

He was incredibly gentle, didn't rush, didn't pressure her. He was just showing her what could be, and the brief glimpse stole her breath.

She was falling, as softly as a feather.

Joe Kessler made her *feel.*

So incredibly unfair. She wasn't ready for any of this. Terrible, horrible timing.

She pulled back, even if every cell in her body protested. "We can't."

"Why?"

"Because we're having a baby. I don't want to complicate things."

"We have six more months to figure out the baby thing." He let her hands go but didn't step back. "Why don't we figure out all this other stuff in the meantime?"

Because the other stuff is scary.

With his local celebrity status, and charisma, and, fine, all those muscles, Joe was larger than life. Wendy didn't want to lose herself to him. She'd lost herself to Keith, and she hadn't recovered from that yet.

"I want to kiss you again," Joe said in a brusque whisper. "I want to keep kissing you. I want you upstairs, in my bed, naked, with your mysterious gray eyes rolled back in your head with pleasure. That part I'm pretty clear about. Except, I'm also supposed to protect you, which complicates things. Although probably not enough to hold me back, if you give the green light."

Heat flooded her. Her nerve endings paired up and whirled into a waltz, scattering tingles across her skin in their wake.

"But if you don't want me, tell me," Joe added. So close. Too close. Too hot. Too sweet. "Your choice. Obviously."

CHAPTER TWENTY

A STRAINED, OVERHEATED SECOND PASSED BEFORE WENDY FOUND her voice. "Can I think about this?"

"Take all the time you need." His slow smile teased her. "But just so you remember what we're talking about..." He pressed his lips against hers again, and let them linger.

If he was a comic-book hero, his name would have been Wonder Lips. He could disarm her just by dragging his mouth across hers. Wendy couldn't help herself. She yielded. And when he swept inside to taste her, her brain malfunctioned then put out a sign that it was closed for repairs.

She had to stop letting him kiss her like this.

She was supposed to gain control of her life. But *control* was a fantasy word around Joe.

She had no idea when and how, or *if* she would have been able to stop the kiss.

Thankfully, Justin yelled, "I'm hungry!"

And Joe let her go.

"You just had your afternoon snack," she told her son.

"I'm hungry!"

"I'm down for an early dinner." Joe's gaze lingered on her mouth for another second before he gathered himself and pulled out his cell phone. "What would you and Justin like? Pizza or Chinese?"

"Justin likes pizza." A miracle that she could talk. "Me too. Pizza would be great."

He ordered, then put his phone away. "I need to wash up."

"I'll set the table."

Ten minutes later, he was coming down the stairs again. "Out of curiosity, do you know if Keith owns a weapon?"

"Yes." She set her empty coffee mug in the sink. "I've been thinking about getting one, too, actually."

"Discharging a firearm is not to be taken lightly." He was all cop in a blink. "Most officers never discharge their service weapons during their entire careers, other than for target practice. You do everything you can to avoid having to reach that point." He was dead serious when he asked her, "If you had no other choice, could you pull the trigger?"

She hesitated, but ended up nodding. "I think so."

"All right. Think about it some more, then we'll discuss it again. If you decide it's the right thing for you, I'll help."

He surprised her. She'd expected a long lecture, expected him to tell her she'd be too jittery, too indecisive, not the right type of person. But Joe was not Keith. He kept proving that over and over. She hoped one of these days she would be able to believe it, accept it on a visceral level, on the level where her fears currently lived.

The doorbell rang.

Joe passed by Justin on his way to answer. "Ready for pizza?"

"Pizza, pizza!"

While Joe handed over a generous tip, Pirate Prince slipped out past his feet.

"Come back soon!" Justin yelled after the cat.

Joe put the box on the table and opened it. The mouthwatering aroma of tomato sauce and cheese immediately filled the air. "How many slices, big boy?"

"Three!"

One Wendy mouthed and helped Justin wash his hands.

While Joe pulled plates from the dishwasher, she put Justin down then grabbed glasses from the corner cabinet. "What would everybody like to drink?"

"Juice!"

"Ice tea is fine," Joe said.

He served the pizza, giving Justin the largest slice, the two laughing easily together. Their quick connection, the warmth and the joy of the scene scared Wendy.

Here was everything she never dared to admit that she wanted. At the worst possible time, when her life had never been a bigger mess. She was living with Joe and having his baby. Keith was out of jail. Somebody—possibly other than Keith, which boggled the mind—wanted her dead.

And all Wendy could think about was kissing Joe again.

No. She didn't need another man in her life right now. *Absolutely not.* She and Justin needed calm, peace, and security. And she swore that they *would* have those things. She would never give Keith control again. *Never.*

But Joe.... She took a bite of cheesy goodness and looked at the man across the table from her, meeting his eyes and not missing the heat in them as he watched her.

What was she willing to give him?

———

Joe slept poorly.

He kept thinking about Wendy down the hall. He'd offered her the master bedroom with Justin, but she'd insisted on the guest bedroom with the pullout couch. And because he knew making her own decisions was important to her, he hadn't pushed.

He woke early, shaved, went downstairs, checked his email, then caught up with a couple of friends on the internet. Wendy started moving around upstairs around eight, running water in the bathroom.

He was looking forward to seeing her at breakfast, but he needed to do one more thing first.

"Find out anything useful at the hospital yesterday?"

"The hospital only provided the room for the anger management group. It was Brogevich's brainchild, a free support group, people coming and leaving as they felt the need. He didn't have patient records on anyone, because they weren't really patients."

"How about a log-in sheet for the group sessions? Wouldn't attendees have to sign in with security, at least?"

"Technically. Except all the sign-in sheets for all the health classes are dumped into giant file boxes that are discarded after a couple of months. And the signatures are little more than scribbles. I had a quick look. Couldn't make out half of them."

"Does the warrant you have extend to the sign-up sheets?"

"It does now," Harper said with satisfaction. "I had it amended. I'm taking the boxes home tonight. I'll get a magnifying glass and scrutinize each name. Can't do work that needs that much focus at the office. There's a call coming in every five minutes. I was in and out all day yesterday."

"Anything serious?"

"Had a runaway teen we found hiding in the garage. The worst was mediating between neighbors who like to set dog shit on fire on each other's porches. Maybe it's the full moon."

"Either that or spring fever. Hey, I'm on protection detail for the next couple of days. If you drop some boxes off at my place, I'll go through them when I'm free. Split the workload."

"That'd be great."

By the time Joe finished talking with Harper, Wendy was padding barefoot down the stairs. She wore yoga pants and a T-shirt, her hair pulled back into a simple ponytail, no makeup. She was perfectly put together, yet still had that fresh-out-of-bed look about her. She looked like she was modeling in an ad campaign for a high-priced, artisanal coffee brand.

Joe couldn't look away. *Damn.*

He needed to think about something other than how much he wanted to take her straight back to bed. "Justin?"

"Still sleeping."

"Breakfast?"

"I'll wait for him, if you don't mind. We have our little routine."

"That's fine. I'm not hungry yet either." Not for food, anyway.

"Coffee?"

"Oh God, yes, please."

The breathless way she said the words, *the tone*, melted Joe's self-restraint.

"Still making your decision about us?" He hadn't planned on asking, not as soon as she came downstairs, but there he was.

"I don't make decisions before caffeine."

"Smart rule. And, like I said, no pressure."

She stepped up to him and kissed him on the cheek. Lingered.

Hope rose. Among other things.

She was completely relaxed with him. She'd initiated contact. She was beginning to trust him. That could be the start of something.

Joe inhaled the scent of her citrusy face cream, mixed with the scent of minty toothpaste. He touched his lips to hers, briefly, not pushing for anything, just enjoying the contact, enjoying that he had her in his morning.

The soft sound she made cut to the core of him.

The visceral response was new, the sheer strength of it, the feeling that things were slipping out of his control.

He gathered her closer. She didn't pull away. In fact, she put her arms around him.

He was hard, obviously so, but he didn't let that hurry him. He simply enjoyed the fact that she didn't flinch away.

He nibbled her lips, kissed the corners of her mouth, nudged her into opening up for him. Slow exploration was the name of the game. He tasted her, drank her in, kept that slow, easy mood, even if part of him wanted her then and there, on the kitchen counter.

Worth waiting for.

He drank his fill of her, for the moment, before he pulled away.

"That was no pressure?" she asked weakly, still hanging on to him, smiling, a little dazed.

He'd never seen anything more beautiful. "Think of it as a sample of coming attractions."

"You don't play fair." She skirted him, heading for the coffee machine.

He looked after her, a little stunned himself. *Not playing.*

CHAPTER TWENTY-ONE

THE MORNING FLEW BY.

Wendy glanced up from her laptop and smiled at Joe who was coming down the stairs. Hopefully, for lunch. Her stomach was growling.

He'd spent the first half of the day with a stack of file boxes Officer Mike McMorris had dropped off for him.

"Hey!" Justin chased Pirate Prince around the couch because the cat stole one of his plastic dinosaurs. "Give it back!"

"With that long tail, it does look like a mouse." Joe walked over to Wendy at the kitchen table. "How about I take you two out to lunch? Finished?"

"I still have a ton to do. Computers are not my strength. But food sounds great."

He checked out her screen, standing too close, making her too self-aware, making her recall his kisses. While he seemed oblivious to the fact that her skin was tingling. "I wouldn't think you need a huge website."

"That's what Sophie said. She thinks I'll get most of my bookings from social media." They'd spent half the morning on the phone, Sophie guiding her step by step to set up a photography business online. "Until I find a place I can afford to rent as a studio, I can do on-location work. I just need to give customers a way to find me."

"You could put an ad in the local weekly. And I could talk to the mayor about you being the official photographer at the Easter egg hunt. If people like the pictures you take of their kids there, they'll be back to ask you for birthday party shoots."

"That would be great. Thank you. I have to find income beyond the royalties my stock photos generate."

"I meant what I said about helping with the baby. I want you to have everything you need. And I'd like you to tell me what I should have here. I can borrow Max's crib from my sister, but I'm sure there's more to it than that."

Wendy's heart filled with warmth. It might even have melted a little.

"We could shop together. I should have more of Justin's things, but I don't." Keith hated clutter at the penthouse, so as soon as something was no longer necessary, he got rid of it. "I was planning on buying stuff from Craigslist."

"Recycle and reuse?"

"That too. But also, once I start showing, the modeling gigs will come to an end, so I can't blow my budget."

"Couldn't you model maternity wear?"

"You'd think so, but no. Maternity wear isn't advertised with real pregnant models. Size zero models wear padding for it. Nobody wants to see swollen ankles."

To Joe's credit, he looked honestly indignant on her behalf. "That's bullshit."

"Bullshit! Bullshit!" Justin chanted.

Joe cleared his throat. "Sorry."

Wendy waved off the apology. "That's one of the first things you learn about kids. Don't say anything in front of them you don't want them to repeat."

"I'd better distract him." Joe strode over and swung Justin into the air. "How about we go out to eat?"

Justin's face lit up. "Can we take Pirate Prince?"

Wendy closed her laptop. "Pirate Prince can play with his cat friends in the neighborhood while we're gone. If we keep him inside too much, his friends will miss him."

"They might think Pirate Prince ran away." Joe backed her up, fetching Justin's shoes from the front door. "All those poor kittens, crying into their mittens." He shook his head with a tragic expression, as if his heart was breaking.

Wendy bit the inside of her cheek.

After a torn second, Justin nodded, way too sweet to intentionally cause the neighborhood felines emotional stress. The corners of his mouth dropped, but in a blink, he cheered up again. "Can I have cupcakes for lunch?"

"You can have a cupcake *after* lunch." Wendy grabbed Justin's coat, hat, and scarf.

It was such a small thing, the two of them helping Justin's clothes on. And, at the same time, it felt like such a big thing. The way Joe did it without having to be asked. As if the two of them working together was natural.

Almost as if she had an actual partner.

Don't be stupid.

"Thanks. You can set him down." She put on her son's coat last, didn't zip it up. They were only going to the car.

The Broslin Diner was packed, people lined up two-deep at the counter to pick up their takeout orders.

"There you are." Eileen greeted them as if they were family. "I was about to call Joe to ask him how I can reach you." She seated them in the only free booth and handed Justin a box of crayons from her half apron, then dramatically swept her hand toward the display case behind her. "Sales of take-home baked goods have been up over fifty percent since you rearranged the display. I've been meticulously keeping the pattern." Her smile widened. "Hardly anyone walks past without stopping. And then they buy. I have no idea how you did that, but you're a genius."

"I wish."

"Cecilia at Cecilia's Broslin Boutique a couple of doors down wants your phone number." Eileen plowed ahead. "The girl who used to do the window display quit. Cecilia could use your help. And she'd be happy to pay. Me too, of course. For starters, today's lunch is on me. I owe you that much, at least. And if you think you could come in maybe once a week and rearrange the display to keep things interesting, I'd love that. Let me know your fee."

Wendy's head spun with the sudden possibilities. "Sure. I'd love to do that."

Eileen slapped a blank sheet from her order pad on the table then held out her pen. "If you give me your number, I'll pass it on."

"Thank you." Wendy scribbled down her contact info so fast, she was surprised the paper wasn't smoking. *New opportunities? Yes, please!*

After they ordered and Eileen left, Joe checked out the display. "I didn't know you did window dressing."

"Me neither." Wendy laughed. "But I think it would be fun. I've been surrounded by fashion most of my life, listening to designers and photographers discuss color and composition and harmony and contrast. And sales," she added. "It stuck with me. Do you think I could run a business on my own successfully?"

"That's an unconditional *yes* from me. But the important thing is, what do *you* think?"

"Yes?"

He waited.

"Yes, I can!" She embraced his brand of self-confidence and enthusiasm.

He smiled at her. "That's the spirit."

"It's scary to do something new all alone. With the modeling, there's a whole team around me. I'm not responsible for everything. I'm already stressed about how I'm going to get photography gigs. Can I take on another thing?" She flinched. There she went, slipping back into doubt again.

"You're not alone."

Wasn't she?

The waitress bringing their food over forced a pause in the conversation and gave Wendy a chance to think.

"I felt alone this past year," she said once the woman left. "I was having issues with Keith that I couldn't tell anyone about. Secrets are like walls. They box you in."

"You're out of the box now. Your friends have your back. I'm not going to walk away. I'll help with the baby. And if there's anything I can do to help with any of your gigs, all you have to do is let me know. I'm not always at work, believe it or not. It just looks like that right now, because I'm on a special case."

He sounded too good to be true.

"Eileen does it, right?" Wendy looked over at the woman who was back behind the counter, handing a box of takeout to a young couple with a motherly smile. "She runs this diner. I envy how strong she is. And Sophie, too. She overcame all that life threw at her this past year. Maybe there's something in the water here in Broslin."

"You should move here permanently. Just in case."

She didn't respond. She had no intention of leaving her apartment long-term. She'd fought for that freedom.

Justin pushed away his empty bowl of macaroni and cheese. "Cupcake!"

"I'll take him." Joe scooted out of the booth. "Would you like anything?"

He definitely wasn't counting her calories for her. Keith would have never offered dessert.

"I'm good. I need to keep my waistline acceptable for work for as long as possible. But thank you."

She watched them walk to the display. There was a lull in customers, nobody up there for the moment but the two of them. The men in her life. Joe said something to Eileen then crouched to Justin's level to consider their choices.

While they discussed the pros and cons of various trays, Eileen came over to Wendy and slipped into the booth across from her.

"Joe asked me to share a little of my story with you. He didn't tell me why. I didn't ask. You take pictures. Maybe you work for a newspaper and you're doing research for a story on abused women." She paused a beat. "I was one."

Wendy dropped her hands to her lap, her stomach instantly in a knot. *Okay.* She had no idea what to say. She was far from being comfortable with the topic. She'd just admitted her problems to

Sophie, her best friend, for the first time. She so wasn't ready to discuss it with strangers.

She opened her mouth to deny that abuse was an issue for her, personally, but then she stopped herself. *No more clinging to secrets.* No more boxing herself in and away from everybody. She wasn't ready to share yet, but she wasn't going to lie about it either.

"I'm really sorry," she said simply.

Eileen nodded. "There are people who'll say *It made me stronger. It made me who I am today.* But I won't tell you that. I made me stronger. I made me who I am today. I overcame the asshole."

She reached to her mouth, and popped out her teeth. She held her dentures hidden in her hands under the table. Her lips collapsed without the support, making her look ten years older.

Wendy nearly fell out of her seat. *Oh.*

This time when Eileen smiled, she kept her lips together. "My ex-husband used to beat me daily. When I moved out, he found me and knocked my teeth out. He choked me so hard, I lost consciousness. A good thing, actually. He thought I was dead, so he left."

She smiled a toothless smile that broke Wendy's heart, then popped her teeth back in. "Sorry for the ick factor. Anyway, that's my story. If you want to work with abused women, great. If your story is like my story, I want you to know that you're not alone. One out of four women have violence committed against them by a man. That's the statistics. I know three, in addition to me, right here in the diner, right now." She smiled again, back to her usual self. "It's a small town. People know each other."

Wendy glanced around, scanned the other women at the tables. Everybody looked so normal and happy. Including Eileen.

"You're so self-assured," Wendy told her. "So independent."

"Like I said. I'm this way because that's how I built myself back. It's possible." Eileen stood. "And now I'm off to wash my hands before I go back to handling food. If you ever have any questions or want to talk, I'm here."

Wendy looked after her. *Eileen.* And at least three other women. Right in the room with her. Even if she didn't know who they were, she felt connected to them, linked by an invisible thread. Emotions choked her, lodged themselves in her throat.

She'd been feeling all alone for so long now. Alone and stupid.

One reason why she hadn't reached out for help had been that she'd been scared of Keith finding out. But another big reason was that she'd been so ashamed. Who would even understand her?

Eileen. And others like her.

The terrible loneliness inside Wendy began to dissipate as she sat there, her hands folded on her lap. By the time Joe and Justin returned, she could sincerely smile at them.

"We picked shoofly pie to share." Joe put a mini pie in the middle of the table then helped Justin up. "Feel free to join in."

He said nothing about sending Eileen over. He went on goofing around with Justin, playing Freeze & Wiggle, in between bites of pie.

Their interaction was so lovely and normal. Anyone looking at them would think they were just a regular family. Wendy let herself enjoy the moment. She pushed her troubles out of her mind. She needed a break.

When they were leaving, Eileen gave Justin a sheet of animal stickers. "For being a good boy."

Justin puffed out his chest and showed off the gift. "See, Mommy?"

Eileen was already talking to Joe. "Can I put you down for the Mushroom Festival *Darts and Tarts* booth again this year?"

"Can I wear Kevlar underpants? Last year, Mrs. Harris pinched my ass." But he nodded.

"What's darts and tarts?" Wendy held back her curiosity until they were in the car.

"You buy a ticket, get a dart, and if you hit the bullseye, you win a free tart or pie. Volunteers donate the baked goods. The proceeds go to the Historical Townhall Renovation Fund. You'll have to come and try next year. The board is shaped like a giant mushroom."

"This town is seriously mushroom crazy."

"We prefer to think of it as fungi fabulous. We like our mushrooms and we're not ashamed of it."

She rolled her eyes at him, grinning. *Happy.* The thought caught her off guard, but it was true. It'd been a long time since she'd felt this light.

"Eileen told me about...her life. Thank you."

"I wasn't sure if you'd be mad. I should have asked you first."

"I would have said no. But I'm glad we talked."

At home, Joe went back to work on his boxes of paperwork while Wendy put Justin down for his nap. Then Wendy wrote up a handful of ads and posted them on local online bulletin boards, advertising her on-location photography services. She also called Cecilia about the window display for her boutique and set up an appointment for the following week.

Justin woke from his nap just in time for Wendy's ultrasound appointment. She was putting cheesy crackers in a little bag for him for the road, when Joe came downstairs.

He leaned against the counter, all tall, sexy male. Wendy did her best to pretend that she wasn't affected.

He watched her put a small coloring book into her purse for Justin. "Are you ready to go?"

"Almost." Then, as a terrible possibility occurred to her, she stopped in her tracks. "What if Keith shows up?"

Joe pushed away from the counter. "Does he know you have an appointment?"

"He knows I'm pregnant, and he knows who my doctor is. He knows I'll show up there sooner or later. He might have called to confirm when my appointment was, pretending to be my husband. I don't think he's that obsessed, but also, I can't really rule it out a hundred percent."

"If he shows, I'll take care of him."

"Thank you, but I would really prefer *not* to have a fight at the doctor's office." She hurried to grab Justin's coat from the hallway, but her phone rang. She picked up. Joe took over the dressing.

"Hi. This is Officer Perkins from Wilmington PD," the caller said. "I wanted to let you know that your car has been released. You'll need to pick it up within the next day or two." He rattled off the address of the police holding lot.

Wendy glanced around desperately. "I don't have pen and paper handy right now. Could you please text over that address?"

"No problem."

"Thank you. Also, could I ask if you were able to obtain any finger-prints from the brake lines?"

"Nothing. Sorry."

She thanked the officer then hung up, a heavy sense of hopelessness weighing on her. She would just have to muscle through it. She couldn't curl up in a corner. She was a mother. She went to help Joe with Justin's shoes.

"I have to pick my car up from the police." She tied Justin's shoelaces double so he wouldn't take them off in the car. "Except that parking at my apartment building is provisional. The cars have to be operational. They don't want busted-up junkers surrounding the build-ing." She kissed the top of Justin's head and stood. "I have no idea where to park my car, or how to get it there."

"Artie can pick your car up. Local tow truck guy." Joe magically produced a tiny plastic dinosaur from behind Justin's ear, and Justin giggled. "He can tow it straight to his garage. He has the best rates in town."

"Thank you. Please tell him I only want a quote. I don't want him to start any work until I know what repairs will cost."

"If money is an issue, I'm good for a loan. You look stressed out."

She unclenched her aching jaw. "It's not just the car."

"What else?"

"Ultrasounds make me nervous. I was this way with Justin too. I just desperately want to hear that everything is all right and the baby is healthy."

He froze. "I didn't even think about that. *Not healthy* being an option."

He looked so stricken, the urge to hug him was nearly irresistible.

She ended up patting his shoulder. "We'll find out in a few minutes."

"The baby will be fine."

He had no way of predicting that, but the tension in her neck eased. Somehow, not having to worry alone made it a little better.

CHAPTER TWENTY-TWO

THE ALIEN-LOOKING BLOB ON THE MONITOR COMPLETELY mesmerized Joe. He was going to be a father. The thought hit him harder than when that tree had smacked him in the face in the river. He was stunned and disoriented.

Dr. Pederick slid her white wand through the blue jelly that covered Wendy's barely noticeable bump. "Here we go. That's a better angle."

Wendy squeezed Joe's hand. "Surreal, isn't it?"

"Yeah." He was going to have a child. For real this time.

He didn't know at what point he'd decided to let himself believe it. But the more time he spent with Wendy, the more he knew that she was neither a liar nor a drama queen. She had a quiet strength that she wasn't even aware of. She faced hardship head-on and fought her way through it.

Wendy was nothing like Erika, Joe's ex. Wendy would never set a trap. And Joe was no longer the young idiot he had been back then either. He'd better not be. He was going to be a father. He grinned at Wendy, then at Justin, picturing another little boy like him.

Justin was busy coloring on the floor. The blob on the monitor didn't interest him nearly as much as an entire coloring book of dinosaurs driving trucks.

The doctor finished the ultrasound and handed Wendy a wash-cloth. "Everything looks perfect. You can have a printout, or for a fee, 3D pictures or the video."

She let Joe's hand go to wipe off the goo. "We don't—"

"We want it all." Joe stepped away from the examining table and scooped up Justin. "Hey, buddy. Let's go play with those trucks in the waiting room." There might be things Wendy would want to discuss with her doctor in private.

He walked out with the kid on his shoulder, happier than if he'd just scored the winning touchdown at the Superbowl. The future stretched before him, an endless vista of possibilities.

"I want the dump truck!" Justin squirmed to get down, then, as soon as he was free, he ran for the toy.

"I like the firetruck better anyway."

Only two women were out there, one sitting in the back, one by the door. They didn't even look up from their phones when Justin shouted, "Race!"

Dump truck versus firetruck it was, around and around the toy chest in the corner, until Wendy finally appeared.

"Everything okay?"

"Perfect." She glowed.

The relief he felt was staggering. He helped her with her coat, pulled her in close, snug against his chest, brushed a kiss against her lips. "Kid definitely looked like a football player."

She laughed. "We don't even know if it's a girl or a boy."

"I don't care either way. As long as he grows up to be a wide receiver."

All the way home, Joe sang along with Justin.

They ordered Chinese food for dinner. He taught Justin to eat with chopsticks. Almost. Justin preferred using them as drumsticks on the table. Actually, the kid wasn't bad with a beat.

After their shared meal, Wendy and Justin tossed out the empty containers. They looked comfortable in his house, as if they were at home.

Joe wiped off the table. "I'm going to have to go into work tonight."

"Your special case? Stay safe."

He changed upstairs in his room, then called the captain. "I'm heading over to Philly. I'd appreciate if you could send someone out to watch the house."

"Mike is on his way."

"Thank you, sir."

Downstairs, he found Justin watching cartoons with Wendy and Pirate Prince.

"When did the cat get here?"

Wendy turned. "Just let him in. Hope that's all right."

"Fine. He'll ask to go home when he's ready."

Justin piped up. "Can I give him treats?"

"Sure. You know where they are."

The kid ran to the kitchen, Pirate Prince on his heels. The cat knew all about the snack cabinet.

Once again, a sense of *this is right* hit Joe, strong enough so that for the first time, he didn't want to go to work. He wanted to stay home.

This was going to be his last high-risk assignment in the city. He wasn't going to volunteer for another one. He was going to be a family man.

He was grinning as he strode to the front door. "I might not be back until morning." Taking down two gangs the same night was not going to be easy, then processing everyone, then all the debriefings and paperwork. "Officer Mike McMorris will be outside. If you need anything, you let him know."

"Okay." Wendy's gaze dropped to the weapon tucked into his waistband. "How much danger are you walking into?"

"Some." He didn't want to lie to her. "Part of the job." He smiled so she wouldn't worry, but she didn't look convinced. He shrugged into his coat then walked over to her and leaned in. "Good luck kiss?"

The corners of her mouth turned up. "Do you ever pass up a chance to hit on a woman?"

He pulled back, affronted. "What kind of a chump do you take me for? Losers pass up opportunities. Winners grab the ball."

"Is that some football wisdom?"

"Would it turn you on if it was?" He wiggled his eyebrows. "I think you're secretly into jocks. You had me marked from the beginning. Admit it."

Her wide smile relaxed the tension in his chest. He leaned in again, slowly, and kissed her, waited until she kissed him back. The feel of her soft mouth buzzed along his nerve endings.

The kiss made him feel invincible, activating some primal male part of him: the warrior going off to battle, kissing his woman good-bye.

He pulled her off the couch, into his arms, his entire body hardening. This was why, millennia after millennia, women kissed their men before battle. To remind the befuddled bastards what would be waiting for them at home when they returned triumphant.

Egyptian pharaohs and Napoleon, all the generals of all the armies —they conquered for this.

His hands slipped lower. "Mind if I cop a feel?"

A burst of a laugh escaped her. Then her hands went around him, mirroring his movements. The breath caught in his throat. He deepened the kiss.

She tasted sweet and hot. He wanted her now, her long legs wrapped around his waist...

Justin laughed at something the cat did in the kitchen.

Right. Kids. Joe was going to have to get used to a new paradigm.

A car horn beeped outside.

He hated to pull away. "That's probably Mike."

Wendy's eyes were glazed with passion, her face flushed, her hair disheveled.

Oh hell. How was he supposed to walk away from her?

"Stay safe," she whispered.

"I'm coming home. Count on it."

He brushed one last kiss over her lips, then he walked over to Justin and ruffled his head. "Have fun while I'm gone. Hey, did I tell you I have a secret stash of cookies too? It's in the drawer of the kitchen island. You can have some if it's okay with your mom."

"Cookies!" Justin ran to find them.

Joe smiled at Wendy one more time, then he walked out, leaving a *home* behind when he went off to work, instead of an empty house as usual.

Unfamiliar emotions churned in his chest, twisting into a tangled mess. He needed to make sense of them, but it would have to wait. He strode up to Mike. "Thanks for coming."

"Sure thing. Hey, have you heard the one about two seventy-year-olds getting married?"

"If I said yes, would it stop you from telling me?"

Mike's eyes glinted. "So, old Liam and Moira are finally tying the knot. Moira, having been an independent woman for some time, says, *I have conditions. I want to keep me own house.* Liam says, *Fine with me.* Then Moira tells him, *And I want to keep me own car.* Liam says, *Yer welcome to it.* Finally, Moira announces, *And I want to have sex every day.* Liam thinks about it, nods. *"Alright. Put me down for Tuesdays."*

Joe shook his head and tried hard not to laugh. God knew, Mike and his questionable sense of humor needed no encouragement. He failed and snorted, a weird sound like an offended hippo popping out of the water, which made Mike laugh in turn.

Joe left him with a wave.

All right, so the moment of lightness was appreciated. Especially, since Joe was on his way to Ramos and crew to do some damage. He prepared himself mentally, but Wendy, Justin, and the ultrasound popped into his head every five seconds.

Ramos was waiting for him out front in the waning light, standing next to Paco's tricked-out Buick. Music blared out the windows, Rusty Red again. Tension sat on the driveway like a heavy fog. Nobody was joking around, nobody was even talking. Joe went over, bumped fists.

"All right." Paco finished off his coffee, in a green travel mug with a pink piggy sticker on it. He spit on the ground. "Let's go."

Three guys got into his car without a word. They drove away.

Ramos frowned at Joe. "Nothing for me?"

"Sorry, man. I can't get those guns out here until tomorrow. They're in my cousin's garage, and the cops have eyes on him. They know he's connected." He looked around. "Where is Rashard?"

"Gone with Chuck, Andre, and Will. He's taking the long way to make sure nobody sees us all together and tip off the enemy." Ramos grabbed a semiautomatic from the porch, then strode to Joe's Camaro. "We're taking your car. I'm driving."

"Where are we going?" Once he knew the location, he could excuse himself to go to the bathroom and text it to Chief Gleason.

"Don't worry about it. Get in."

Joe slipped in on the passenger side without argument. Now was not the time to show hesitation or challenge the guy's alpha status. He couldn't stay back at this stage without arousing suspicion. He had to go along. He might get a chance at minimizing damage.

Ramos patted the semiautomatic on his lap. "Good thing someone else came through this morning."

"You'll have my crates too. Tomorrow, the latest. I swear, man."

Ramos pulled away from the curb. He drove with his shoulders relaxed, a man without a care in the world.

The Camaro's engine purred.

"Got a fine sound," Ramos acknowledged, sounding nothing but friendly.

Yet there was a bad vibe in the car that had Joe's cop instincts prickling. "So, just the two of us, huh?"

The other vehicles had gone out with a full crew each.

Something nagged in the back of his mind.

Something wasn't right.

Something didn't fit.

And then it hit him.

The green travel mug with the white infinity logo.

Wendy had one of those in her car. Keith had left it there, she'd said. And Justin had put a pink piggy sticker on it.

Paco could have taken his kids to the diner. They could have gotten the same sheet of animal stickers from Eileen as Justin had. But Paco wouldn't—in a million years—have bought a hundred-dollar yuppie-brand travel mug that was a status symbol for rich white boys.

Shit.

Joe slid his hand closer to his gun.

If Paco had the mug, that meant he'd been in Wendy's car, which meant he'd been the one who cut her brakes. *Why?*

The only thing that made sense was that Paco had followed Joe at one point, saw him with Wendy, and thought she belonged to him. But why hurt her? The only reason the crew would have to hurt Wendy was to hurt Joe.

He glanced over to Ramos, but Ramos was looking straight ahead, his jaw set at a determined angle, a hard gleam in his eyes.

Nobody in the gang did anything without Ramos's approval. Ramos had to have sent Paco. Even as Joe figured that out, another puzzle piece fell into place.

When he'd been shouting, "*I'm an undercover officer*," in the back of the sinking police cruiser, Officer Tropper *had* heard him. He'd just acted as if he hadn't. Tropper had left him to drown so Joe couldn't finger him as the dirty cop. Gomez had been collateral damage. Then Tropper reported back to Ramos.

Ramos had put a payback plan together. A plan to hurt Joe any way they could. A plan that no doubt would culminate with his death.

Joe reached over with his left hand to slap some music on while, at the same time, he took the safety off his gun with his right. Ramos had his hand right on his semiautomatic. Joe watched from the corner of his eye, for the smallest movement.

Ramos didn't aim the weapon. He drove on without a word. But just when Joe was beginning to think he was being paranoid, they reached the boulevard, and Ramos didn't turn left, toward J.T.'s neighborhood.

Joe did his best not to tense up. "Did you set up a meet with J.T. somewhere neutral?"

Maybe he could send a text from his pocket, blindly, without Ramos noticing.

"Rashard and the others will take care of that." Ramos kept looking straight forward. "You and me are on a special op today. Got a little surprise up my sleeve."

He drove a quarter of a mile then turned onto a side street of graffiti-tagged row houses, and then down another side street that led them to an industrial area with rusty fences and abandoned factories. Everything dark out there, no streetlights.

Ramos bobbed his head to the music, a cold smile on his lips. "Rashard and Paco are hitting J.T.'s house. You and me are gonna take out the motherfucker's business." Ramos reached to the dashboard and pumped up the volume until the car was rocking. "This is where J.T.'s crew cuts their cocaine," he shouted over the music.

Joe reached into his pocket for his phone, just to make sure it was still there. Wilmington PD was tracking his cell phone signal tonight, so at least they would know where he was at all times.

Among the abandoned buildings, a beat-up shoe warehouse sat maybe three hundred feet ahead, lights on inside, a familiar yellow Hummer sitting in front.

This is it.

Survival mode.

Joe rolled down his window all the way. He pulled his gun, then leaned back in his seat so Ramos could shoot by him.

And then they were lined up with the warehouse, with its open, corrugated metal door. Three guys were working on a gleaming black GTO inside, another three watching. They all looked up at the music that blared from the Camaro.

Ramos stepped on the brake and opened fire, knocked one guy to the ground immediately. Bullets ricocheted off the pavement.

Joe was firing too, aiming at hands and weapons. He was hoping the enemy would run. But, of course, they didn't. They dove for cover, then shot back.

Ramos was squeezing the trigger nonstop.

"Go, go, go!" Joe shouted at him as more guys rushed from the back, shooting at the Camaro.

He didn't have time to worry about his car. The fifteen bullets left in his magazine weren't going to get him far. Ramos was squeezing them off by the dozen.

"For fuck's sake, get out of here!" Joe shot back for real, aiming at central mass. He took out one guy then went for the next. "Go!"

Ramos had his foot on the brake, open hate on his face as he switched his gaze to Joe for a second.

He wants me dead, right now, right here.

Of course, he did. If one of J.T.'s guys shot Joe, Ramos would be off scot-free; he wouldn't be the cop killer going to federal prison.

A bullet flew by Joe's face so close he felt the wind of it. He opened the door and threw himself to the pavement while squeezing off one shot after the other at the warehouse. He rolled behind his car, but didn't dare stay there. Ramos might run him over.

Nearest shelter? Nothing close enough. Joe dashed toward the side of the enemy warehouse, bullets whizzing by in every direction around him.

He didn't look back to see if Ramos was shooting at him too. He ran like hell for cover.

He got maybe thirty feet away when a bullet knocked him face-first into the pavement.

His dazed mind cut to Wendy, Justin, and the baby. He wanted, desperately, to go home to them. He shook off the pain in the middle of his back and rolled into the cover of a jumble of rusty dumpsters. The bulletproof vest concealed under his jacket might have just saved him.

Tires squealed.

Ramos was driving away. Hopefully with a couple of bullets in his ass. Joe struggled to catch his breath as he pushed to his feet. *Move, move, move.* Some of J.T.'s boys would go after Ramos. The rest would come after him.

He staggered into the narrow alley between the shoe warehouse and the next derelict building. The alleyway stretched two hundred feet, less than ideal. If anyone came after him before he cleared the other end, he'd have nowhere to hide, nothing but brick wall on either side. The gap was maybe three feet wide, filled with dead weeds and garbage—a freaking deathtrap.

Somewhere in the distance, police sirens sounded. *Too damn far.*

Engines roared to life behind the warehouse. J.T.'s crew was mobilizing. If Joe darted out of the alleyway in front of them, they'd either run him down or shoot him dead, probably both. He couldn't go forward, and he couldn't go back.

He spotted two basement windows near the ground behind the weeds. One had its glass broken out. He stuck his head in. The dim, cavernous place seemed uninhabited, no sound or movement.

Jeezus, it stunk in there. He gagged as he dove in.

Concrete floor, concrete block walls, a mess of broken industrial equipment thrown around. He held back a coughing fit, but he wasn't sure how long he could keep from throwing up.

Voices reached him from outside, coming closer.

He waited another second or two, until his eyes adjusted to the lack of light, then he moved forward. An odd-shaped pile sat in the corner. He took half a dozen steps in that direction before he realized he was looking at three decomposing bodies. The one on top was Officer Tropper.

Joe cupped his left hand over his nose, pulled his cell with his right hand, and dialed Chief Gleason's direct number. Didn't get anywhere. The basement had no reception.

He snapped a picture of the bodies, then moved toward the door, ready to get the hell out of there. The police were on their way. Maybe J.T.'s guys had run off.

No. No such luck.

Two men lurked at the top of the stairs. They spotted him the same time as he spotted them. And they opened fire. "Down there!"

Joe had to retreat into the unbearable stench.

If he could get back out the window—

No, not that either. Someone was climbing in. The men who'd come into the narrow alleyway after him had figured out where he'd disappeared.

"Right there!"

Joe pulled into the nearest empty corner, put his back to the wall, and squeezed off a rapid volley of shots. He hit his targets, and the men dropped, one after the other. Unfortunately, the second one had enough life left in him to fire back. Then his buddies reached the bottom of the staircase and opened fire on Joe from the other side.

"Gonna put you on the top of the pile!" one of them shouted.

Joe shot at him. Missed. He had two bullets left.

CHAPTER TWENTY-THREE

A CAR PULLED UP OUTSIDE THE HOUSE. JOE WAS BACK, THANK GOD. Wendy had spent half the night worrying about him. She stirred the pancake batter she'd just mixed up for breakfast. *Perfect timing.* She turned to the window, giddy with relief that quickly disappeared. *Oh. Not Joe.* A tow truck parked up front, her Prius on the back.

Wendy swallowed her worries about Joe's "special assignment" and put a smile on her face for her son. "Hey, tow truck is here. Want to see?"

"Yay!" Justin, nuts for cars and trucks, beamed as if he'd swallowed a sunlamp.

They were outside just as fast as they could get dressed.

Officer Mike McMorris was sitting in an unmarked car a few houses down the street. He didn't get out. Probably didn't want to draw attention to himself. Which meant she shouldn't go over to him either, to ask if he had any news on Joe.

"Miss Belle?" The tow truck driver climbed out of the cab slowly. He was an older guy. Looked like his knees weren't bending properly.

"Hi." Wendy hurried forward to help, but he thumped onto the ground before she was halfway to him. "You must be Artie. I'm Wendy. Thank you so much for doing this."

"I figured I'd swing by to see if you want anything from your car before I take it to the shop."

"Tow truck!" Justin ran up and hugged the oversized front tire.

Watch your clothes! Wendy bit back the words. Little boys needed to be little boys sometimes and get dirty. She would clean him up later.

"You stay right there, okay?" she told Justin, then climbed in the back. She exercised plenty to keep her model figure. Those muscles and having good balance came in handy at moments like this. "I'm just going to grab the car seat."

"I could have lowered the back end." Artie was looking at her as worried as she'd been looking at him a minute earlier.

"It's all right. Got it." She jumped back down with the car seat in hand. "How much do I owe you?"

Artie batted away the suggestion. "Tow is free. Call it a favor to Joe. He's done me plenty. I'll call you with an estimate once I take a closer look at the damage, but unless you have a special attachment to this car... It's pretty much totaled. Let the insurance deal with it."

Totaled. The word hit Wendy hard. "I didn't think it was that bad."

"You should get enough money to buy another one."

When? In a week? Two? A month? How was she going to get to her shoots in the meanwhile?

"Insurance usually pays for a rental until you get a new car," Artie added. Clearly, she wasn't the first person he'd seen in this situation. "Check your policy before you call them." He climbed back into the cab. "Don't let them give you the runaround either."

"Thank you." Wendy picked up Justin so he wouldn't dart under the large tires. Then, as Artie pulled away, she called another thank-you after the man.

The free tow was a huge help. "And we owe this to Joe, too. He is a good friend. Maybe this is why everyone in town likes him."

She set Justin down and followed him in, leaving the car seat just inside the door.

"You're such a big boy." She took Justin's coat that he'd tugged off all by himself. He even kicked off his shoes. "I'll make us some pancakes. Then, after breakfast, we'll check out the back yard. Okay?"

The doorbell rang.

She wiped her hands on a dishcloth and went to see who came for a visit.

A woman about Wendy's age stood on the front stoop, short brown hair cut after the latest fashion. Pretty. She held a toddler boy who had her eyes and mouth.

"I'm Amber," she said with a warm smile. "Joe's sister. He said he had guests staying over. Max and I wanted to stop by to say hi."

"I'm Wendy." Wendy opened the door wider and stepped aside. "Come in. We were about to have some pancakes. Why don't you join us?"

"Where's Joe? I thought he had the night shift."

"He hasn't come home yet. I'm trying not to freak out. I don't know what's normal for him."

"Work can drag on. If something happens right at the end of shift, they have to stay to do the million pages of paperwork."

Justin stared curiously at the visitors, holding on to Wendy's pants. She nudged him forward. "This is Justin. Max, would you like some pancakes?"

Max looked at his mother.

"Go ahead." Amber nodded. "What do you say?"

"Thank you!" Max ran for the kitchen table, Justin right behind him.

Amber watched with an indulgent smile as her son climbed a chair. "He's not one to turn down maple syrup. Unfortunately, my metabolism doesn't allow a second breakfast."

While Wendy made the pancakes, Amber chatted about how much better the kitchen was now than when Joe had bought the house. But the whole time, Wendy had a feeling she was being assessed, which made her twitchy.

The boys too measured each other up during the meal, but once they were outside, they found a collection of plastic cars in the sandbox and played demolition derby as if they'd been best friends forever.

Amber leaned against the picnic table next to Wendy. "Mind if I ask how long have you known my brother?"

"A couple of months."

"He said you two were having a baby. That's...unexpected."

"At least as much for me as for you. Believe me."

Amber smiled, a genuine smile, no anger, no resentment. "Honestly, I can't wait to be an aunt. Why aren't you *together* together? He's a great guy. I'm not biased. I swear. Okay, probably a little. Are you two fighting? How can you be fighting with him? He's so not the type. I could barely eke a good fight out of him when we were kids. He's too easygoing. I had to do my sibling fighting with my best friend's brother. I'm not kidding."

"We're not fighting."

"Good." Amber's smile brightened another notch. "You're living in his house. I keep telling myself that means something. It never happened before."

"I'm here only temporarily."

Amber's expression telegraphed *we'll see.*

"Do you live in Broslin too?" Wendy asked to regain control over the conversation.

"All my life. I'm a realtor. Where do you live? Are you looking to move here?"

"I have a place in Wilmington, but thank you."

"Daryl was from Wilmington before his family moved to Broslin. My husband. That best friend's brother I was talking about that I used to fight with like crazy when we were kids." Her mouth tightened. "He died two years ago from cancer." She blinked. "Sorry. Didn't mean to dump my gloom and doom on you. My point is, when you love somebody, you can't put things off. You can't know how much time you've been given together."

"You don't have to apologize. I'm sorry for your loss." Wendy glanced at the boys. "Must have been difficult for Max to lose his father."

"You're a single mom too." Amber attempted a smile, but couldn't quite pull it off this time.

"Did Joe tell you?"

"I assumed. My big brother might have done a lot of stupid things in his life, but he's never gone after a married woman."

That tidbit of information didn't surprise Wendy. Joe had a good, honest core. One more thing that pulled her to him.

Amber tilted her head. "If you're not here because you're *together* together, are you living with Joe because of some police business? I mean, like witness protection. That would explain why Mike is sitting in an undercover car two houses down the street. I'm totally not going to ask you about that, by the way. You know what? Never mind. Forget it."

Wendy relaxed. For a second. Then Amber was off to the races again with her questions.

"Where do you work?"

"I've done modeling mostly, but I'm transitioning to something new. I'm starting my own photography business."

"Women need to take charge of their careers. Hey..." Amber's eyes lit up. "For my realty work, I take adequate pictures for the internet listings, but the finer homes get their own flyers. That means staging and a professional photographer. Would you be interested in something like that?"

"Absolutely."

"If you give me your phone number, I'll call you the next time I need help."

They exchanged numbers, then Amber switched topics again. "Tell me what you like most about my brother."

Wendy was getting whiplash. "He's kind. Honest. Dependable."

"You didn't say hot."

"Not the most important thing." Although, it didn't hurt.

"What do you like least about him?"

"That I'm attracted to him." A heavy sigh escaped her.

"You don't have to sound so miserable about it." Amber laughed. "I like you."

"I have no idea what to think about you," Wendy told her the truth. "You're a whirlwind."

"I get that sometimes."

"You and Joe both have that larger-than-life personality. I'm just an ordinary mortal."

"I have no doubt that you're special to him. I couldn't believe when he called to talk to me about you. Especially, when he told me to come over to meet you and Justin. And now that I've seen you... I think he's finally met his match." Amber's tone was thick with satisfaction. "My brother and women.... Here is the thing. We have twelve cousins, all boys. Joe was grandson number thirteen. The grandchild novelty had worn off by then. And then I came along. Everybody spoiled me rotten. I think Joe looked to girls at school for that extra attention he wasn't receiving at home. And, of course, he got validation there in spades. That's where he got spoiled. He needs a good, strong woman to set him straight."

"I'm so far from strong, it's not even funny."

"Don't believe it." A conspiratorial glint lit up Amber's eyes. "Do you want to hear something creepy about my brother?"

"Mr. Perfection has a dark side?" Wendy leaned forward. "I'm all ears."

"His exes don't hate him. They're all friends. What woman doesn't hate her ex? I can't stand my high school ex. I hope my college ex has chicken pox right now. On his balls."

Wendy laughed. She liked Joe's sister.

Amber plowed on. "When are you due? I'm going to throw you a baby shower. Don't say no, and don't ask me anything about it. I want it to be a surprise. I just need your due date so I don't run out of time."

More whiplash. Wendy gathered herself. "In the fall. Around Labor Day."

"Going into labor on Labor Day?" Amber grinned. "How appropriate is that? Do you have a big family?"

"My parents live in Florida." They didn't even know about the pregnancy yet. Wendy had wanted to tell Joe first.

"What do you think about..." The questions kept coming.

Joe's sister was the definition of nosy but so sweet about it as to be irresistible. And the conversation wasn't one-sided, not an interrogation. She volunteered information about herself too. An hour flew by. Wendy felt as if they'd known each other for years.

When the boys tired of racing their trucks, Max showed Justin where some of his other toys were buried in the sand. They kept burying them, then excavating them, until their little ears turned red.

"Time to get out of the cold and go inside," Wendy told them, some of her loneliness gone. She'd made a new friend. Justin did too. "All right, guys." She held the door open. "Who wants hot chocolate?"

"Have to put the top on the sandbox." Max grabbed the sheet of plastic they'd cast aside when they'd come out.

Justin went to help. "How come?"

"If you don't cover up the sand, Pirate Prince poos in it."

Justin's eyes snapped wide. Wendy could tell he thought that was a very *piratey* thing, and he liked it quite a bit.

The kids played another hour inside before Amber and Max left. Wendy locked the door behind them, then she picked up the scattered toys. Since Justin was all tuckered out, she set him on the sofa and put on the cartoon channel. Glanced at the clock. *Almost noon.*

She thought about calling Joe, but if he was doing undercover work —which she suspected—she didn't want to interrupt something important, or get him in trouble. He was probably fine. Like Amber had said, probably filling out a mountain of paperwork.

Wendy kept telling herself that, but it didn't keep her stomach from tightening into a knot as another hour passed.

Justin was asleep on the couch.

Wendy set aside her laptop and went to grab a drink, looked out the window above the sink while her glass filled. Max's red scarf waved from the swing set. She drank her water, then ran out to get it. She would text Amber to let her know they'd left it behind, save her from having to look all over. God knew, she spent half her life looking for Justin's stuff.

She unwrapped the scarf from the swing and was turning around when Keith stepped out of the holly bushes that separated Joe's property from his neighbor's.

"Hey, babe."

Nonono.

Her heart banged painfully fast. "What are you doing here?"

"Where's my warm welcome?" He spread his arms. He wore his black wool coat, the one he liked for work. Fresh out of jail, dressed every inch the successful businessman. Did he think that was going to impress her?

She edged toward the house. "I'm glad they let you go," she lied. The key was not to get him angry.

"That's odd, considering you called the cops on me."

"I didn't. I swear. Somebody broke into my apartment. I told the police it wasn't you." She would have said anything to reach the back door safely. Mike was up front in his car. She could signal him from the living room window.

"Damn right." Keith advanced. "All they have is fingerprints. Can't put anything on me with that. I'm over there all the time. Of course, my prints are on everything. You're my girlfriend."

She wasn't, hadn't been in a long time, but Wendy didn't correct him. She had maybe twenty feet to the door. "I think Justin is crying."

She might not make it all the way to the living room in front, but her cell phone was on the kitchen counter. She lurched forward.

Keith caught her halfway to the door. "What the hell are you doing here?"

"Visiting."

"Screwing cops now?" His fingers dug into her arms. "Who the hell is Joe Kessler?"

"He's Sophie's friend."

"The kind of friend that knocks you up? That's right. I found the test. And I know this one isn't mine. You keep your legs crossed when I come over." He shook her hard. "You're a cop's whore?"

"Please let me go. You're hurting me."

"You were lucky I ever looked at you twice. You thought you could hide from me with your new lover? I saw him with you at Sophie's place. You thought I wouldn't find you? Too bad Lover Boy paid me a visit in jail. Took me a second to realize he wasn't a local cop. Wrong uniform." Keith flashed a superior smile. "Had his name on it. Turns out, plenty of people in Broslin know where Officer Kessler lives. They were happy to point an old college friend in the direction of his house."

Blood rushed so loudly in Wendy's ears the swooshing nearly drowned out the last few words. How was it possible that she kept underestimating him? Maybe he was right and she was plain stupid.

"Joe's a friend. I swear. I was scared of staying at the apartment after the break-in. And I couldn't call you over. You were locked up."

He shook her so hard her teeth chattered. "Are you lying to me? I'll know if you're lying, you cheating whore."

He threw her against the picnic table.

Oomph. The pain in her ribs stole her breath. She surged up to run, but he caught her by her hair and yanked her back, slapped her so hard she fell to the ground.

"Please don't." She gasped. "It doesn't have to be like this. I'm sorry." She had to get to the phone. "Let's go inside and talk about it."

"With me, you want to talk. But this asshole you fuck?"

"I'm sorry, Keith. I'm sorry." She scrambled back, pushing to her feet. "It wasn't like that. It was a mistake. I'm sorry."

Her begging seemed to calm him. He extended a hand to help her up.

She took it because she didn't dare anger him any further. "Thank you. Hey, you want a beer?"

He backhanded her so hard she fell again. "You think I want your new boyfriend's beer?"

And then he kicked her in the back. The pain that sliced through her, robbed her of breath. She saw stars. Anger flooded through her, hot and fluid. If Keith touched her one more time, so help her God—

She reached for the nearest stone.

"Hey!" Someone was shouting from the front of the house. "Wendy?"

Amber's voice.

Stay quiet. He'll hurt Amber.

Wendy pressed her lips tightly closed. And she meant to keep them closed, but then she looked up at him, and his cocky expression, his sure knowledge that he had her under control, made something snap inside her.

"Back here!" Wendy screamed.

She threw the stone.

Missed.

Oh God.

Keith swung his foot to kick her in the face. When she rolled out of reach, he spit at her. "This isn't over."

Then he jogged back to the bushes he'd come from and disappeared through them again.

Wendy lay on her side, trying to catch her breath. *Gone. He's gone. It's over.*

"What happened?" Amber rushed toward her with her son in her arms. "Did you slip? Where's Justin?" She set Max down and helped Wendy up. "What did you hurt?"

"My back." Wendy shuffled to the picnic table and sat down, forced herself to breathe evenly. *Stay calm.* "I think I need to get checked out. Justin's sleeping inside."

"Yes, of course you do. I'll drive you to the emergency room. Thank God, we came back for Max's scarf."

"Thank God. I'll get Justin ready." But Wendy didn't get up just yet. "Could you please go and tell Mike that Keith was here?"

"Who is Keith?" Amber tensed, looked around. "Did somebody hurt you?"

"Just tell Mike, please."

"Okay." She picked up her son and hurried away.

In the end, after some discussion, she stayed at the house with the boys. Mike drove Wendy to the hospital.

She called Sophie from the car on their way to West Chester. "Joe had the night shift yesterday, but he hasn't come home yet. I don't suppose you know anything about the special assignment he's working on?"

"I'm not supposed to say." Sophie's voice was strained.

Wendy closed her eyes, breathed in and out slowly. "I had another *accident*. I'm on my way to the ER."

"Are you all right? I'll come and meet you there." The words rushed from Sophie.

"If you don't mind, would you go to the house instead? I left Justin with Joe's sister. She seems nice, but Justin doesn't really know her."

"Of course. Leaving right now."

"Thank you. Could you tell me what's going on with Joe? Please?"

A brief pause. Then a ragged sigh. "He was in a shootout last night."

Wendy's heart lurched. She gripped her phone so hard, the plastic edge cut into her palm. "Is he okay?"

"I don't know. I'm so sorry, Wendy. They can't find him."

CHAPTER TWENTY-FOUR

BY THE TIME JOE FINISHED WITH ALL THE BRIEFINGS AT THE Philadelphia Police Department, had a private meeting with Chief Gleason, then got sewn up at the hospital, his dashboard clock read twenty minutes past noon.

Ramos and his crew had been arrested. So had most of J.T.'s gang. J.T. was dead. Rashard had gotten him before he'd been killed himself. Ramos had been shot in the arm. Twenty pounds of cocaine had been confiscated at J.T.'s warehouse, more drugs at Ramos's place, and about two dozen illegal weapons.

Out of the major players, only Paco slipped through the dragnet, but Philadelphia PD was looking for him.

Joe's new cell phone was in pieces, took the brunt of the bullet that had ripped into his thigh. His torn pants were hanging off him, but he couldn't care less. He was ready for a shower, lunch with Wendy and Justin, then some sleep.

The only good part of his morning was that he'd gotten his car back. The Camaro had taken an insane number of bullets, but it was still running. He'd worry about the damage to the body later.

He was tired to the bone, beaten up, bruised all over, and starving.

The first thing he noticed when he turned down his street was that Mike wasn't there. Amber's car sat in the driveway, along with Sophie's.

Maybe Mike had to go out on a call and the captain sent Sophie over so Wendy wouldn't be alone. Joe had asked Amber to check in on Wendy, so her car in the driveway didn't surprise him.

Looked like Wendy was having a girls' get-together. She deserved a break. Joe had news for her that he would have preferred to give her when they were alone, but he could wait until her visitors left.

He pulled over by the curb in front of his house so he wouldn't block in anyone, crossed the lawn, then walked inside where an enthusiastic Peaches greeted him.

Wendy was lying on the couch, pale. *And bruised*, he noticed the next second, his muscles tensing, his body ready for the next battle. "What happened?"

Sophie came from the kitchen with a bag of frozen peas.

Behind her, Amber was entertaining the boys at the kitchen table. "Thank God, you're back."

Joe kneeled next to Wendy and took her hand. "Are you all right? What's going on?"

She wouldn't meet his eyes. "Keith stopped by."

Cold, murderous anger filled him. He had to work to keep it in check, to not let it show on his face. "How bad is it?"

"I'm just a little bruised."

His gaze snapped to her son. "Justin?"

"He was inside. Keith caught me out back." Her eyes filled with guilt.

"This is not your fault." She had nothing to feel guilty about. "The baby?"

"The baby's fine. They did an ultrasound at the ER. I'm just supposed to take it easy for the rest of the day."

Sophie handed over the peas then returned to the kitchen to help Amber with the kids. Peaches followed her.

"Where do you want this?" Joe offered Wendy the bag.

She took it and covered the purple on her cheekbone. "He came through the neighbor's yard. We argued and he knocked me down."

Joe wanted to pound the bastard into the ground. See what he thought of having to face someone his own size. "Did you file a police report?"

"Yes. But it's my word against his. Mike was up front, didn't see anything." Her gaze sharpened. "And don't you blame him."

"I won't. *I* should have been here with you. Where is Mike now?"

"Bing has the whole department looking for Keith. I told him I'd be safe here with Amber and Sophie and Peaches." She made a good show of being brave, but her voice held a slight tremble. "What happened to you? Bing said you were in a gunfight and then disappeared."

Had she been worried? He should have found a way to call her. He wasn't used to anyone waiting at home for him.

"Long night." He took her hand again. "You have to fill out a stack of paperwork for discharging your firearm. Then another stack for getting injured in the line of duty. I also spent an hour at the hospital. Sorry I didn't call. My phone took a bullet."

"You were shot?" She bolted upright. "Where?"

"The phone in my pocket deflected the bullet. My hip was grazed. I just had to get it disinfected." He pulled her into his arms. "It's barely a nick."

She buried her face into his neck and hugged him.

The bag of peas was freezing his collarbone, but he didn't care. He held her as tightly as he could without hurting her. "How did Keith find you?"

"He saw us together at Sophie's. He figured out that I was with you. Everyone in Broslin knows where you live."

He should have thought of that. Joe cursed his carelessness. "Is the whole PD really out looking for him? Everyone?"

"They are," Sophie called from the kitchen.

"Could you let them handle it and stay home?" Wendy whispered. "Just today. Please?"

He could feel her baby bump between them. That and the way she burrowed into his arms decided it for him.

"I'm right here. I'm not going anywhere."

Sophie's phone rang. She picked it up, listened for a second, then brought it over for Joe.

"I just caught up with Chief Gleason," the captain said on the other end. "I'm glad you're home in one piece."

"Anything on Keith Kline?"

"Not yet. But I have a warrant for his arrest. We'll find him. You stay with Wendy today. I'll send someone to take over in the morning. I want to see you at the station. We need to talk."

"All right. I'll see you tomorrow." He clicked off the phone, then turned back to Wendy. "I want to hear the whole story from the beginning."

She started with Keith stepping from behind the holly bushes. Then she recounted the attack, her face pale, her voice brittle with emotion.

By the time she finished, Joe was rigid with fury. "I'm not going to let him hurt you again. Ever. And you don't have to worry about him getting custody of Justin. He's going to prison."

"Thank you."

Her round abdomen drew his gaze. "Do you think I could..."

A ghost of a smile flickered across her face. "Of course." She took his hand and placed it over her belly. "No kicking yet, but soon."

He registered a flicker of disappointment. He wanted to feel the baby. He wanted a connection, to know for sure their child was all right after the ordeal.

They stayed like that for several seconds, until his stomach growled and he let her go. "Have you eaten?"

"Your sister made me lunch. She and Sophie are trying to outdo each other spoiling me. They can be scary bossy together."

Her faint smile loosened some of the tightness inside Joe.

The kids were laughing in the kitchen, the dog barking. Happy sounds filled his house. It would have been idyllic if not for Wendy being hurt.

"I swear," he told her under his breath so the women in the kitchen wouldn't hear. "Whatever I have to do to stop him. *Whatever.* If I lost my badge in the process, so be it."

Amber walked over, cutting him off. "Max is getting cranky. I think it's time for a nap for this little bandit. Are you two going to be okay here?"

"I'm fine," Wendy said, shifting back. Her smile tightened. "Thank you so much for your help. Thank you for everything."

"Are you in pain?" Amber never missed anything.

"The acetaminophen I got at the hospital should kick in soon."

"I'll stop by tomorrow to check on you. And then we're going to have a long discussion about me becoming an aunt. I so love you for that."

Sophie piped up from the kitchen. "I can stay and take care of Justin if you'd like."

"Thank you." Wendy let Justin climb onto her lap, and snuggled him. "But I can handle it. Honestly. I already took up everybody's morning. Justin needs a nap too, anyway. He's tuckered out from all the excitement. As soon as I put him down, he'll be out like a light."

"I'll be home for the rest of the day," Joe put in.

"Good." Sophie came for a kiss on Wendy's cheek. "Then I'll get out of your way. Call me if you need anything."

"Me too." Amber went for a hug.

Justin, not liking to be crowded, climbed over into Joe's lap.

He scooped him up and walked the women out, thanked them for their help again and locked up behind them. Then he carried a wiggling and jiggling Justin back into the living room, holding the kid under his arm like a football. He faced Wendy as he set the kid down. They were finally alone. *Here we go.*

"I have some new information about your car." He hated what he was about to say, but she had a right to know. "I know who cut your brake lines. A gangbanger I was dealing with at work figured out I was undercover, followed me, and saw your car, thought you were maybe my wife. He hurt you to hurt me. I'm so sorry. I feel guilty as hell." The thought of what could have happened if they'd been a hair less lucky twisted his guts into a pretzel. "You should never be in danger because of me."

She stared at him. "Are you sure it wasn't someone Keith hired?"

"We can't blame this one on him. But I'm blaming him for every-thing else. And I *will* hold him responsible."

"Is the guy who cut my brake lines in jail?"

"Not yet, but there's a city-wide dragnet to catch him. They'll have him. The rest of his gang was rolled up today. He has nobody to watch his back."

Wendy shifted again, leaning more into the pillows, winced, pressed a hand to her lower back.

It killed Joe to have to watch her in pain. "Why don't you lay back completely?" He caught Justin who was running circles around the sofa, and scooped him up again. "I'll put him down for his nap."

"Are you sure?"

"I watch Max for Amber all the time. I'm an experienced babysitter. Top-notch Yelp ratings." Joe grinned and swung Justin up to his shoulders. "Ready, buddy?"

"Readyreadyready!" Justin drummed on his head.

All the way up the stairs.

Other than that, the kid didn't give him any trouble. His last burst of energy ran out pretty fast. As Joe settled him in and picked a book to read, Justin was yawning. He fell asleep, missing the end of his naptime story.

By the time Joe went back downstairs, Wendy was yawning too. He picked his work laptop off the bookshelf, moved it to the side table, then sat on the end of the couch and put Wendy's feet on his lap.

She flinched when he touched her. "Sorry."

"You don't ever have to apologize. I should have asked. Is this okay?"

"Yes. I'm not falling apart. I swear."

He could tell she was working on relaxing, and she did, eventually, as he massaged her soles. She relaxed enough to fall asleep.

He turned to his laptop and signed in, then he brought up everything the PD had on Keith Kline so far. He read through every detail, highlighted everything that might be a clue to where to find the bastard. Then, keeping his voice down, he called in his suggestions to the captain.

He opened the Brogevich case file next and scrolled through the crime-scene photos again, then read the transcript from Doris's official interview. With most murder cases, the killer ended up being someone who knew the victim, often their domestic partner, but Joe ruled out Marie. Marie adored Phil just as much as he adored her.

As far as business rivals went, Phil had his own practice and no longer worked at the hospital. He hadn't been competing with anyone for the next staff promotion.

Joe typed *Broslin psychologist psychiatrist therapy* into the search engine. One other name came up: Gerta Fischer. He knew Gerta, a sixty-five-year-old woman who was about to close shop and retire. She had crippling arthritis. It would have been nearly impossible for her to swing the phone as hard as the killer had. She had no motive either.

But if not a rival, then who?

According to Doris, Phil spent his time either at work or at home with his wife and new baby. What time he didn't spend with his family, he spent with his patients. Joe's every instinct said that the killer was someone Phil was seeing in a professional capacity.

He pushed the laptop aside and lifted Wendy's feet gently so she wouldn't wake. He stood up and covered her with a blanket. Then he went upstairs for the boxes that held the hospital sign-in sheets. Since Wendy and Justin had moved into his office, he'd stashed the boxes in his bedroom for the time being, but he didn't want to work up there now. He wanted to stay near Wendy.

He'd already separated out the sign-up sheets for Tuesdays, the days when Phil had his anger management group. Now he began to read through them.

He squeezed in about two hours' worth of work before Wendy and Justin woke up.

Joe was bushwhacked but didn't want to sleep, in case Wendy needed him. Not that she would stay put. She wouldn't even let Joe cook dinner. But when bedtime for Justin rolled around, she did let Joe take the little boy up to bed.

He stopped halfway up, Justin squirming on his shoulder. "Bath?"

"I don't think I can bend over the tub. It won't kill him if we skip one day." She smiled at Justin. "Just wash your hands and face, and brush your teeth, okay?"

Joe cleaned the kid up, following instructions, then wrestled a tiny pair of pajamas on him. "Story time!"

Justin picked up the book next to the bed. "Dancing sheep!" He bounced on the mattress. "Dancing sheep!"

When Joe finished, the kid "read" the book back to him, nearly word for word. Had the whole thing memorized.

"You're one smart peanut, you know that?" Joe tucked the boy in.

Then he walked over to the master bathroom and turned on the water in the tub, before heading back down the stairs. "Okay, the dancing sheep are so wrong on so many levels."

"It's a very wholesome series." Wendy cranked her neck from the couch. "Teaches creativity."

"They're boy sheep and they spend all their time dancing, painting, and cooking?"

She raised an eyebrow. "Do you have a problem with that?"

"How about sports? And they could fix a car now and then. Maybe take some girl sheep out?"

"You think men need women to feel complete?"

"Are you mocking me?"

"Is that a trick question?" She smiled.

He liked seeing her joke around. "Dancing sheep is a book a mother would buy." He walked over to her. "I'm going to set Justin up with some studly books."

"Hey, maybe America's Most Wanted has a bedtime storybook edition."

"I'm going to check on that. Or something like *Tool Time for Bedtime*. If that picture book doesn't exist, somebody needs to start writing it."

"Good night, hammer, good night, saw?" She shook her head, still smiling.

Joe walked over. "I'm drawing you a nice warm bath." Warm, not hot. Pregnant women weren't supposed to sit in a hot bath. He'd learned that when Amber had been pregnant with Max. Amber wasn't the type who was shy about sharing. Joe knew about mucus plugs and water breaking and the whole nine yards.

"A bath sounds really, really great."

"Hold on." He bent, and, before she could protest, he gathered her into his arms.

Her cheeks flushed. "My legs are fine. You were shot today."

"Barely a scratch." He carried her up the stairs, enjoying every minute. She was with him, safe. "I feel guilty because I wasn't here to protect you, all right? You have to let me do something."

He set her on her feet in front of the tub then stepped to the linen closet for towels. He lay them on the towel bar. "Do you need anything else?"

"I can handle it from here. Thank you."

He wished he could do more. He checked the hallway closet, in case Amber left some goodies in there the last time Max had spent the night. *Bingo.* Joe grabbed a yellow bottle and carried it back to Wendy.

He knocked.

"Come in." She was still fully dressed.

He held up his find. "Bubble bath?"

"That'd be lovely."

He dumped some into the water, and it frothed up in a blink, layers of bubbles. "Don't get lost in there."

She was lifting her arms to tug off her sweater. Instead of smiling at his lame joke, she was wincing.

"Do you need help?"

"Could you please?" She turned her back to him.

He reached for the hem, lifted it slowly, waited until she worked her hands up above her head. From the way she moved, he knew she was hurting. Then he saw the bruises on her bare back and forgot about everything else.

The bastard kicked her.

She'd said Keith had knocked her down, but seeing all that purple marring her skin hit Joe a lot harder than just hearing the words had.

He was a calm kind of guy, which was helpful for police work. He wasn't used to hot violence surging through his veins, pushing him to find Keith and—

"Joe?"

He'd stopped moving. He began again, slowly, and swore that he was going to bring Keith Kline in and see to it that the asshole spent his prime years in prison.

"Let me finish."

Joe gently tugged the sweater over Wendy's head and off her arms, then tossed it on the small stool next to the tub. He reached up and unclasped her pink lace bra. "You shouldn't turn and twist."

She didn't protest, so he pulled the lacy material away from her body and laid it on top of her sweater. As she folded her arms over her breasts, he reached to her waist and tugged her pants down, helped her step out of them. Then he reached for her panties.

"Joe?"

Steam filled the room.

"I'm not looking. And even if I was, I've seen you naked before. This is not a romantic thing. You're a purple blob."

"Don't overwhelm me with all the compliments all at once."

"What I mean is, I'm not here to ogle you. Think of me as an officer of the law assisting you in a professional capacity."

"Do cops strip women naked a lot in the course of the average workday?"

He could hear the tentative smile in her voice. He liked it. "Not as much as we wish."

He felt none of the calm he was projecting, his heart rate kicking up as he tugged her pink lace panties down inch by inch, over the smooth curve of her incredibly fine behind. He helped her step out of the soft material. Bruises or not, she was perfect. She was the woman he had X-rated dreams about. And she was standing in his bathroom naked.

He was as hard as the cast iron tub next to them.

He scooped her up and lowered her into the water, grateful that he'd had the foresight to add bubbles. At least, they covered her. *Mostly.*

He turned off the tap. Cleared his throat. "I'll be right outside if you need anything."

"I don't think I've been fussed over like this since I was a kid."

"Pregnant women should be pampered."

She looked away.

He doubted she'd gotten any pampering from Keith when she'd been pregnant with Justin. Not that Joe was some knight in shining armor. He'd been pretty much a jackass, in fact. When she'd told him about the baby, he'd run away. And then he'd denied that the baby could be his.

"Listen." He ducked his head. "About before. I'm sorry. The idea of having a kid... I needed a moment to absorb that."

"It's okay. I did kind of spring it on you. I'd been trying to figure out for a while how to tell you." She smiled toward her belly under the bubbles. "The pregnancy was a pretty big surprise to me too."

He nodded, stepped away, but didn't leave. "I'm not sorry about the baby."

"We're not going to ruin your bachelor lifestyle. I promise."

"I'm not worried about that." He frowned. "I don't know why I'm not scared. I should be." The truth was, he hadn't really taken advantage of being a bachelor in a while. "Maybe I'm maturing."

She laughed out loud, the best sound he'd heard in a long time. "Let me know if it hurts. I have some painkillers the hospital sent home with me."

"So funny." He fought a grin. And because he wanted to step back to the tub and kiss her senseless, he walked out, leaving the door open a crack behind him. "Holler if you need anything."

Of course, what he was really hoping for was that she needed *him*.

CHAPTER TWENTY-FIVE

WENDY BRACED HER ARMS ON THE SIDE OF THE TUB TO PUSH herself to standing. Groaned. Every time she moved, it hurt. For a second, she hesitated.

Joe had said to call him for help.

He *had* seen her naked before. He'd helped her into the tub. But she wasn't ready for him again. Not just yet. Not naked. Too vulnerable.

She heaved and pushed, and stood at last.

Drying herself was a pain, but her nightgown was loose enough to slip into without much trouble. She even managed to comb her hair.

The hallway was empty, the TV on downstairs. She walked straight to her room. Justin slept peacefully on his side of the bed. Wendy eased her tired body onto the mattress.

"Goodnight, peanut," she whispered, then kissed her son's forehead.

She didn't like Keith, but she could never hate him, because without Keith there wouldn't be Justin, and she loved her son above everything else in the world. Justin was *not* a mistake.

Keith had impressed her at the beginning, with all his success and smooth manners, but the more she'd gotten to know him, the less she thought of him. Joe was the opposite. When she'd first met Joe, she'd put him down as a superficial, womanizing jock. But the more time she spent with him, the more she had to admit that she'd been wrong.

Joe Kessler was kind, caring, and brave. He stuck around. He took care of what needed to be taken care of. He seemed like a man a woman could depend on to be there but not take over. If she could ever trust a man, he'd have to be a lot like Joe.

His footsteps fell softly on the stairs as he came upstairs. Wendy lay still in bed and listened to him take a shower, tried not to picture him naked, failed. Then he went back downstairs, and she could hear him moving around for a while before everything went silent. Was he sleeping on the couch?

Maybe he wanted to be downstairs in case Keith came back and tried to get in.

He wouldn't. Keith wouldn't come unless he thought Wendy was alone. He was a coward at heart. He was only tough enough to beat up a defenseless woman.

Wendy stared at the ceiling. Every time she closed her eyes, she saw Keith grabbing her, the vicious hate on his face. She tossed and turned.

She'd better stop that, or she was going to wake up Justin.

In the end, after another twenty frustrating minutes, she went downstairs. "Hi."

Joe was lying on his back on the couch, snug under a blanket, the TV turned down low. "Everything okay?"

"Can't fall asleep. I thought I'd grab a glass of milk."

"Are you hurting? You know, taking another one of those pills they gave you doesn't mean you're weak."

She nodded and walked into the kitchen without turning on any lights. Plenty of moonlight came in the windows and the sliding glass door. She poured her milk, drank it, then left her rinsed glass in the sink.

Instead of walking back to the stairs, she plodded over to Joe.

"Thank you for having us here. If we were at the apartment when Keith came...." She dug her bare toes into the carpet. *If Amber hadn't come back....*

He turned off the news then shifted his muscular body to the back of the wide couch and held his blanket open. "Why don't you lie down here for a while?"

He wore nothing but sweatpants, moonlight glinting off his impressive pecs.

"All I want," he said, "is to provide comfort. Women need comfort from men, not just sex."

She tilted her head, amused. "Maybe you *are* maturing."

He flashed a sheepish smile. Definitely a new look for him. "Actually, Amber texted that to me before she went to bed. She wanted to make sure I was taking good care of you." Hand in the air, he waited, exercising admirable patience. "Maybe we both need comfort. I wasn't here today when you needed me. If you're right next to me, at least I'll know that you're safe."

His words fluttered inside her chest then divebombed straight into her heart.

He was right. They'd both had a rough day. What would be the point of denying that they both needed comfort? The couch was wide enough for two, so she lay down next to him, her back to his impressive front. He settled the blanket over them and left his arm around her.

She relaxed against him.

Three months ago, they'd had sex, but they'd never done this. Turned out, she loved lying in his arms. This was what she'd missed the night she'd kicked him out of her bed. She'd kicked him out because of the power of their attraction. How she'd felt around him had scared her.

And here they were now, nicely snuggled together. Expecting a baby.

A despondent sigh escaped her. "Everything is all messed up."

"What is?" he asked quietly.

"Us."

"We're doing okay."

"I didn't set out to trap you. I swear." Keith had accused her of that a hundred times.

"I don't feel trapped."

"Why?" She didn't understand him, how he could be so different.

"I'm a simple guy. I have a beautiful woman in my arms. What's there to complain about?"

"I look like an eggplant."

"Purple is my favorite color."

She smiled into the darkness. "There's a really annoying dinosaur you might want to watch with Justin over breakfast."

They lay next to each other in silence. She didn't feel any sleepier than she had upstairs. She couldn't shut off her brain. "I turned your life upside down. We're intruding here."

"You're not intruding. I get to invite whoever I want to my home, and I'm entitled to enjoy their company." He snuggled her in closer.

And then she could feel just how much he was really enjoying her proximity. "That better be the remote."

"You can think whatever makes you sleep easier."

She couldn't help a small laugh. "I'm not going to have sex with you..." She winced. Joe wasn't Keith. Joe didn't push. He didn't deserve all her crap baggage dumped on him. "Sorry. I have all these reflex defense mechanisms that have nothing to do with you. It's not fair."

"Sex is never far from your mind, is it? Shocking from the mother of two, really." He gave a dramatic sigh. "Still, I can't say I don't like it. Relax. This is nice. It doesn't have to be more."

And, of course, as soon as he said that, as soon as he set her at ease, she *wanted* more. And how stupid was that, today of all days—with her aching all over? Or maybe it wasn't so strange. She'd been beaten up this morning. And she knew what Joe's touch would be like. She could sink into his gentleness.

Actually, she was already doing that, more relaxed than she'd been all day. She pondered that for a moment. "So the town Casanova is a snuggler?"

"Don't tell anyone. I have a reputation to protect."

"Mum's the word."

"Oh, I'm still hoping the word is *hot sex*. I'm just saying I'm willing to wait for it."

"Technically, those are two words." Again, she smiled into the night.

She could get used to this, him, his easy, laid-back ways, his arms around her, the promise of passion in the future.

"I don't want to fall in love," she blurted, then caught herself. *Oh God.* She needed to shut up.

"Okay." He didn't sound concerned. "Mind if I ask why?"

"When Keith gets caught...." She tried to pull her thoughts together. "I need time between that, dealing with that part of my life finally being over, and whatever I do next. I want to figure out what I'm doing. I want to grow into a person who will make good relationship decisions. I don't ever want to be the way I've been with Keith. I want a balance of power."

He didn't respond immediately. He thought for a while before he said, "How about this? Whatever happens between us, you're in control."

She so wanted to believe that. But he was the Wonder Boy of Broslin. "What about all your other girlfriends?"

"I'm not a total dog. I don't chase after every skirt."

"Just the short ones?"

"I used to like short skirts." He grumbled. "But since I met you, I haven't been able to think of anyone else but you."

Her heart lurched. "You should see if there's a pill for that."

"People rely on pharmaceuticals too much these days. Most problems can be solved with natural remedies." He hinted heavily. "But you're in charge. I mean it."

He did, she could tell, and it stunned her. He didn't exactly have a Type B personality. Why would he ever give up control like that?

She had a difficult time accepting the only answer that came to her —that Joe Kessler, small-town hero, Officer Cop Casanova, actually cared about her.

CHAPTER TWENTY-SIX

THE NEXT MORNING, READY TO LEAVE FOR WORK, JOE CARRIED Wendy up to her bed and lay her down next to Justin who was still snoozing. She might catch another hour of sleep. Might as well be comfortable. He covered her up, then brushed a kiss over her lips. And when she sleepily murmured something unintelligible, he lingered.

Wendy and Justin were in his life. In his house. Snuggled under his blanket.

And he didn't want them to leave. He wanted them to stay with him.

For the first time, he could almost understand Keith Kline. Not the violence, never that. But the concept that if a man was lucky enough to have a woman like Wendy in his life, he would fight like hell to keep her. Although, he knew that wasn't Keith's motivation. What Keith had done was about control, not love.

Joe paused by the bed for another second to watch Wendy and Justin sleeping peacefully. They would always be part of his life on one level. Wendy was going to be the mother of his child. Justin was going to be the big brother. They'd see each other. Regularly. Except, Joe wanted more than a visitation schedule regulated by shared custody.

He could see them as a family.

Could *she?*

How many times had she told him that she wanted nothing to do with him?

The thought needled him as he went downstairs.

Outside, Mike was pulling up in his cruiser. When he spotted Joe, he got out of the car and hurried across the street. They met in the middle of the walkway.

"Don't let her out of your sight."

"I won't." Mike's face was haggard. He couldn't have slept much the night before. "I'm sorry about yesterday, sitting out here like an idiot." He sounded as miserable as he looked. "I had no idea that bastard was sneaking around the back."

"Nobody expected him to actually show up. If I thought he would, I wouldn't have gone to Philly. I don't think he'll come back, but keep an eye out for him. And keep an eye out for a short, skinny guy called Paco."

"What for?"

"He cut Wendy's brake lines. I got tangled up with him in an unrelated case. He wants to hit back."

"Nobody's getting through me." Mike puffed out his chest. "I'll be patrolling on foot and checking in with Wendy regularly."

"They're still sleeping. Give them another hour or two before you knock on the door."

Mike nodded. "I'll walk around the house."

He must have really felt bad about the day before, because he never even cracked a joke.

Joe hopped into his shot-up Camaro. A call to Artie was on his to-do list for the day. Not only because it hurt him to look at his poor car all banged up, but also because the bullet holes would draw too much attention.

He glanced toward his house, acknowledging that he wanted, very much, to go back inside. He didn't want to leave Wendy and her son. He wanted her, their baby, wanted to be there for Justin, raising the kids together as a family. He wanted it all, wanted everything.

He pulled away from the curb shaking his head.

In the past, the very idea of something permanent with anyone had always made him feel trapped, but the possibility of a future with Wendy filled him with happiness.

When he walked into the station ten minutes later, the captain greeted him with, "First things first, you need to fill out another injury report." Followed up by, "How bad is it? No bullshit."

"It's nothing. My cell phone took the brunt of the hit. I was stuck in a basement, had to shoot my way out. I shot down the first two guys, clipped the third, ran out of bullets so the fourth one got me before I rushed him. I ended up escaping through the roof. There was a bloody war going on the ground."

"Gleason said you were missing. We were worried about you."

"Had to sit down next to a chimney to catch my breath. Might have blacked out up there for a spell."

"How much blood did you lose?"

"Probably more than advisable, but it's been all replaced. A pushy nurse dripped a couple of bags of IV fluid into me in the ER."

"Doesn't mean you're fit for duty. How is Wendy?"

"Banged up. I'm going to put that bastard away."

"Alleged assailant. You want to be a detective, you better start using correct terminology. But, yes, we're tossing Keith Kline's bastard ass into jail."

They spent ten minutes arguing over whether Joe should go back on sick leave. Joe won on that, so after he was done at the station, he drove into Wilmington.

The day before, Wilmington PD had searched the city for Keith Kline while the captain and the rest of Broslin PD had combed Broslin, but Joe wanted to take a shot at it himself. He was more determined than anyone else to find the guy. For Joe, the case was personal.

He planned out his morning as he drove, where he wanted to go first, but then his thoughts returned to Wendy once again. He needed to figure out how to convince her to stay with him.

Sadly, he reached the insurance company where Keith Kline worked, without having come up with a brilliant plan.

"We had police here already," the department director told him, an older guy wearing an impeccable three-piece suit, Italian leather loafers, and an old-fashioned gold signet ring. Clearly, the insurance business was going well. "Keith didn't come in yesterday, and he hasn't shown up yet today either."

"Does he have a personal relationship with anyone at the company?"

"Sure. He's a great guy. He goes out golfing with the other brokers all the time. Some people grab a beer after work now and then. He's fun to be around. Outgoing. Good at sales."

"Any female friends? Maybe something that goes beyond friendship?"

The director shook his head. "I don't think so. If people have intraoffice relationships, they don't flaunt them. We have a company policy against fraternizing with coworkers. I've never noticed Keith spending extra time with anyone."

"Any history of violence?"

"Look, he's a great guy." The man's tone changed to wary.

Joe waited him out.

"It wouldn't be fair to harm his reputation because of one mistake," the director said finally.

"This is a police investigation."

"He had an argument over a project with a coworker six months ago. Keith threw a chair in the heat of the moment. A laptop got knocked off a desk and broke. He paid for damages, made apologies. He worked it out with HR."

Joe asked a few more questions, but none of the responses proved helpful toward figuring out where Keith might be, so he ended with, "Could you show me his office?"

"I'll have to call security to let you in. I'm not sure if you'll find anything useful. The other officers already looked through it yesterday."

He made a call, and then they walked over together. They only had to wait a couple of minutes before a uniformed guard showed up with a master key and let them in.

The director stayed. "If you want to take anything, I'll need a warrant. He has client files in here. Those are confidential."

"No problem. I'm not interested in his files. Just want to get a better feel for the man, for the way he thinks, to figure out where he would go to hide."

Keith had to know that he'd gone too far, that Wendy would have to go to the hospital, that there'd be police involved. So where would he run to regroup? Not far. He had too much: good job, nice apartment, Wendy and Justin. He would consider them as *his*. He wouldn't leave everything behind and take off permanently.

Nobody had seen him attack Wendy, no witnesses. He might think that the case against him was too weak to go to court. He could afford a lawyer who was good enough to have the charges dismissed.

Joe looked around carefully.

Several awards and certificates bragged on the wall about how successful Keith was at work. He had pictures up too, taken at golf courses, with people Joe assumed were key clients—but nothing personal, no pictures of Justin.

Joe hesitated over the photo of a boat. "His?"

Maybe he had a boat Wendy didn't know about. *The perfect hiding place.*

The director stepped closer. "That? I rented it for a team-building event last year. It was a big hit. Might do it again."

"Where does he like to vacation?" When people ran, they usually went to someplace familiar.

"He takes golf trips to Myrtle Beach, but not this time of the year."

Joe thanked the director. He was done with the office.

Keith's penthouse apartment was next, although Keith probably wasn't dumb enough to be sitting on his couch, waiting for the police. Also, Wilmington PD would have checked there already. Still, Joe liked dotting his I's and crossing his T's.

On his way down in the elevator, he thought of something else. He got off on the next floor and asked the first person he saw, a young woman in her late teens, probably an intern. "Could you tell me where I might find the HR department, please?"

"Third floor."

"Thanks." Joe hopped back on the elevator and rode to the floor below.

The HR department had its own reception desk. Joe flashed his badge and asked to see the person in charge.

The middle-aged woman who came to meet him introduced herself as Lashanda Jefferson, director. She was nearly as tall as Joe, wore her hair in a tight bun, dove-gray suit well-cut and crisp high-heel shoes, no jewelry, no frills. She had a let's-get-it-done air about her, reminding Joe of Leila. If she kept her department as shipshape as Leila kept the station, they were in good hands.

Joe introduced himself and showed her his badge. "I understand that one of your employees, Keith Kline, had some issues six months ago and worked out a deal. I need to find out more about that."

The incident had to have an HR report written up about it. That would prove that Keith had a history of violence, which would improve the chances of the assault and battery case going to trial. As it was, the attack on Wendy would come down to Keith's word against hers. Her injuries had been documented at the hospital, but she had no way to prove that Keith had been the attacker.

"I'm sorry, Officer, but I can't discuss employees." The HR manager flashed a tight smile. "If you want to look at Mr. Kline's file, you're going to need a warrant."

"But there's a file?"

"All incidents requiring disciplinary action are fully documented," she said smoothly.

"You should probably find the file and get it ready. Wilmington PD will be here with a warrant to pick it up. Thank you for your help."

Joe called the captain on his way to his car and relayed the information he'd found. The captain promised to call Wilmington PD. He had a higher rank and more pull.

Asking for help didn't bother Joe. He'd learned team-playing on the football field. It didn't matter who scored any one point; everyone worked together to make the team win.

Back behind the Camaro's wheel, he gave Keith Kline's address to the GPS.

Time to check out the villain's lair. And, hey, with a little luck, he might, just might, even catch the villain there.

CHAPTER TWENTY-SEVEN

KEITH KLINE LIVED IN A FANCY-ASS APARTMENT BUILDING. THE doorman's uniform looked like a theater costume for the toy soldiers in the Nutcracker: red wool with golden braids. First time Joe ever met a doorman, come to think of it. He'd only seen them in Christmas movies set around Central Park, NYC.

The old guy was as stiff as an English butler. "Mr. Kline is not in."

"Do you expect him back?"

"He did not leave word of his schedule."

"When did he leave?"

Imperious silence. Chin tilted up. A slightly offended air, but not so offended that it would rule out a discreetly slipped twenty-dollar bill.

Joe flashed his badge.

The man made a poor attempt at stifling a sigh. "Yesterday morning."

"I'd like to go up."

"May I enquire why?"

"I'd like to talk to his neighbors."

The doorman hesitated, but then nodded at last. "As you wish, Officer."

Marble foyer. Mailroom to the left. Gleaming brass elevator straight ahead. Joe rode it all the way.

Four apartments occupied the top floor. Joe knocked on Keith's door first, just in case. "Police, open up."

No response.

Joe knocked again, louder. Waited. Tried the knob.

The round brass handle didn't budge.

A neighbor stuck her head out with a tiny white dog in her arm. They wore matching pink tops. At least the dog didn't have on sequined gold pants with it. The woman dripped jewelry, and Joe could swear the dog's collar had gemstones embedded in the leather.

"Ma'am." Since Joe wasn't in uniform, he held up his badge as he strode over. "Officer Joe Kessler, Broslin PD. I'm looking for your neighbor, Mr. Kline."

"I haven't seen him in a couple of days. What's this about? The officers yesterday wouldn't tell me anything."

"I'm afraid, I can't divulge details either." Joe shot her an apologetic smile. "Official police business."

She scowled, probably not used to being denied.

"Any idea where Mr. Kline might be?"

"Certainly not. We up here on the twenty-second floor like to respect each other's privacy."

Joe could see that. *Living in their own towers and looking down on the rest of the world.* Their neighborly relationship probably consisted of polite nods in the elevator.

Joe handed her his card. "If you happen to hear him come in, would you mind giving me a call?"

The dog nipped at his wrist. The woman said nothing.

"You have a good day, Ma'am."

Joe moved on and knocked on the other two doors, but nobody else was home, so he rode the elevator back down. He handed a card to the doorman, asking for his help as well, then he drove to Keith's country club.

"Keith was in this morning," the gym manager said, a young woman with an ardent love for Spandex and painted-on eyebrows. "Must have changed his mind, because he was in and out. I don't think he spent more than ten minutes here."

Joe perked up at the news. Keith was still in town. But where?

Not at a hotel. Wilmington PD would have already checked those. Guests had to show ID to check in. They were registered in the system. Maybe Keith was living out of his car. Maybe he'd come into his gym for a quick shower.

"Thank you, Ma'am."

Joe drove to the next address on his list, the home of Brett Astor, ex-coworker, workout buddy, best friend, according to Wendy.

Brett hobbled to the door with a salesman's overly bright smile and apologies for being slow. Apparently, he was on sick leave with a busted knee. He was on some soccer team.

"Yeah, Keith slept here. There was a gas leak in his apartment building. He went back this morning."

Incorrect. Keith had gone to the gym. But probably not for a shower. He could have cleaned up at his friend's place. Maybe he'd gone to the gym to stash something in a locker. Incriminating evidence? Joe would have to drive back there and check.

"I've just come from his apartment," he told Brett. "He's not there. Any other idea where he might be?"

Brett leaned against the doorway, squinting. "What do you want from him?"

Joe could have protected the suspect's reputation for the time being. He usually did. Not this time. "He's wanted for assault and battery."

The guy drew back, squinted harder. "Who's accusing him?" His tone dripped with skepticism. "His girlfriend?"

"Ex-girlfriend. Did Keith say anything to you about Wendy Belle?"

"Just cursing her out. I figured they had an argument. She's a lying, cheating bitch, if you excuse my French. Does whatever she can to keep Keith's son away from him. I wouldn't believe anything she says."

Joe set aside his indignation and didn't correct the guy. Brett only knew the story from Keith's point of view. And Brett's opinion of Wendy hardly mattered.

"You can see why it would be important for us to hear Mr. Kline's side of the issue." Joe handed over his card. "If he comes here again, I'd appreciate it if you could call me." He put steel in his gaze. "If you cover for him, you will be charged with harboring a fugitive, obstruction of justice...."

"That's not right." Brett shoved the card into his pocket, then reached for the doorknob, ready to close the door in Joe's face. "Way to blame the victim."

Joe thanked him for his help, although he couldn't manage more than cold politeness. And then he left, hoping the guy was smart enough not to want to get sucked into Keith's troubles with the law.

He called Wendy on his way back to the country club. "How are you feeling today?"

"Better than yesterday. How did I end up upstairs?"

"I went up to brush my teeth, and you followed me like a puppy. You tried to seduce me."

"Oh, did I?"

"I resisted."

"In your dreams."

He could hear the smile in her voice.

"Frequently," he admitted. "I hope you're taking it easy today. Stay off your feet."

"Yes, sir, Officer Kessler," she mocked him.

"Now, that's what I like to hear."

"Don't get used to it."

"Private citizens must obey officers of the law. That's a fact." He would have gladly bantered with her for a while, but his phone pinged. He glanced at the screen. *Captain Bing.* "I'm sorry. I have to go. Got another call. Work."

"Okay. Don't do anything dangerous."

"I don't run from danger. Danger runs from me." He let himself enjoy her laughter for a second, then he switched to the other line. "Captain."

"We have a situation here at Sophie's place." Bing's words snapped through the line. "That old couple who are renting? Some guy called Paco took them hostage, demanding to talk to you. You know what this is about?"

Shit.

"Brant Street Gang. I'm on my way." Joe burned rubber on a U-turn then stepped on the gas.

Paco clearly wasn't as smart as Keith. He hadn't been able to figure out where Joe lived, had fixated on the house that Joe had driven to the night Paco had followed him, the night the bastard had cut Wendy's brakes.

"Idiot."

Not only was Paco too stupid to lay low when he knew every cop in Wilmington was looking for him, he couldn't even get Joe's house right.

"Out of my way!" Joe slammed the car horn and cut through traffic.

He was thirty minutes away.

He made it in fifteen.

The entire Broslin PD was in front of the house, plus an ambulance idling a hundred feet away. Joe pulled up behind the cruisers and rushed forward in the cover of the other cars, noting everyone's positions.

He dove behind the vehicle closest to the house. "Captain."

"Stay down, dammit." Bing sounded pissed. His girlfriend's house had been invaded. He was taking it as a personal affront.

"I want to—" Joe began to say, but then they ran out of time to strategize.

The front door opened a crack. Paco must have seen Joe from a window. "Motherfucking cop!"

"Hey," Joe shouted back. "Let's talk about this."

"You come in."

The captain shook his head with a dark look that promised disciplinary action if Joe disobeyed.

"Put down your gun first," Joe called back to Paco.

"You come in, or I'll pop Grandma and Grandpa," Paco sounded like he was feeling his strength or, more likely, the false strength some drug was giving him.

Fury hit Joe, burned right through him. All he could see was the Prius with Wendy and Justin as they'd dangled over the abyss. Paco had done that.

Paco was going behind bars. *Today*.

The captain was furiously gesturing *stay put*.

Joe had another plan. There was a time to play as a team, and then there was a time to hold on to the ball and run with it. He held his gun high up in the air and stepped out of cover. Bing swore behind him.

Joe stepped forward before the captain could grab his coat and yank him back.

"I'm coming in." He tossed his weapon to the ground. It hit the pavement with a metallic clang and slid a few inches, visibly out of his reach. "Let those people go, Paco. You don't need them. You got me now." He strode slowly, steadily toward the door, stopping a dozen feet away. "You let them out, I'll come in."

No response. A second ticked by, two, ten.

"I'll come in as soon as you let them out," Joe called to Paco. "No tricks. I swear, man."

Seconds crawled by in tense silence.

Sophie's house was a veritable fairytale cottage, tulips blooming in the grass. The place looked like the set of a Hallmark movie, rather than the scene of a hostage situation.

They waited.

Then an older woman appeared in the doorway, eyes red, thin lips trembling. She stepped outside, pale as the white siding, her husband behind her, walking with a cane.

Joe waited until they scrambled down the stairs.

"Stop!" Paco shouted after them. "You stay right there until he's inside."

Joe moved forward. "Once I'm at the top of the stairs," he told the hostages as he passed them, "you go behind the cruisers. You'll be all right."

Paco stood a few steps inside the door, his eyes bloodshot, anger tightening every muscle in his face. "Fucking cop." Gun in hand, he motioned Joe in, then eased another couple of feet back.

"I'm sorry, man." Joe stopped inside the threshold. "I was just doing my job."

"Close the door."

Joe did. "Anyone else in here?"

"I don't need backup to kick your ass."

The living room looked all right, everything in its place. Didn't seem like Paco had knocked the renters around. Probably didn't have to. Joe doubted they'd resisted.

Paco swore in Spanish, sweat beading above his lips. He looked strung out, beat, and more than a little disoriented. "Rashard's dead."

Joe held his jumpy gaze. "That's a chance you take when you go on a drive-by."

"Shut up." Paco aimed the gun at his chest.

"Hey, I got a kid on the way," Joe told him, hands up. "Just found out."

"Shut up."

"How are your girls?"

"Shut the fuck up!"

Joe kept his shoulders relaxed. "There are a lot of cops out there. Let's work this out so you don't get hurt."

"You lied to me! You're a fucking liar."

"Those girls love you, man, you know they do. The police have nothing on you. They don't even know for sure if you were involved in the shootout. This here—" He shrugged to indicate the situation they were in. "A year. You get out. But if you shoot a cop, it's over. Those girls go to your funeral. That's how you want them to see you next?"

Paco's finger twitched on the trigger. "Motherfucker!"

Joe stood his ground, calm, keeping things level, his fury at the guy carefully locked away. "Drop the gun. We walk out together. I came in because I don't want you to have to walk out on your own. I've met your girls, man."

Behind Paco, Mike appeared outside the sliding glass door. Joe gave a faint shake of his head. *Not now. Not yet.*

Paco lifted his left hand to brace the gun's butt. His gaze hardened. "You've been lying to me all this time."

"Just doing my job."

"Fucking cop."

They were going around in circles.

Joe lunged forward, went low, just as Paco discharged his weapon.

The shot was deafening from that close. If Paco screamed as he was slammed into the floor, Joe couldn't hear. He could barely hear when, three seconds later, half the Broslin PD burst in the house, shouting, "Drop your weapon! Drop your weapon!"

Then Mike and Harper were on top of Paco, like an old-fashioned football pileup, crushing Joe.

One of them kneed his injury from the day before. *Damn.* That hurt. Joe untangled himself and let them have their target. Shook his head. His hearing got a little better. Good enough so he could hear Mike starting to read Paco his rights.

"You have the right to remain silent..." Mike cuffed Paco, both of them breathing hard.

Harper kept the man facedown, with a knee at his back.

Paco swore and promised to murder all of them.

When Mike was done Mirandizing him in English, Harper yanked Paco to his feet and repeated everything in Spanish. They took the guy out together.

The captain stayed back until only he and Joe remained inside.

"Officer Kessler." Bing's face was redder than Joe had ever seen it, a decidedly unhealthy shade, his entire body tightly wound, his lips thin as razor blades. He paused, allowing himself a few seconds to calm down. Didn't quite succeed. "If you ever pull a stunt like that again," he said through clenched teeth, "you're off my force. Are we clear on that?"

"Yes, sir."

"You could have gotten shot."

"Yes, sir."

"You have a death wish, Officer?"

"No, sir."

"What the hell were you thinking?"

Joe hung his head. "Paco was the one who cut Wendy's break line."

"I know that. You know how I know? You told me. Did I lose my head, and put lives at risk?"

"No, sir."

"Do you want to give me a stroke?"

"No, sir. I'd have to answer to Sophie."

The corner of the captain's mouth twitched. But when he turned on his heel and strode out, he still looked ready to punch something. Joe gave him space, not following immediately behind. Truth was, he'd been damn reckless. Truth was, when it came to Wendy, he was no longer his cool-headed, reasonable self. He was grateful the captain had let his rash actions go as easily as he had.

Outside, the ambulance had pulled up, and the paramedics were checking out the old couple. Harper and Mike were wrestling Paco into the back of one of the cruisers.

Paco wasn't ever going to hurt Wendy again.

That's one thing that went right today.

Joe stopped and took a second to appreciate it.

He wouldn't have minded being the one who booked Paco, but he wanted to go home just as much. More, in fact.

He shrugged the tension out of his shoulders and shook it out of his arms. He wasn't going to carry any of this stress with him. All was well.

He was going home to Wendy.

Joe smiled as he crossed Sophie's small yard.

He pulled his phone to call her, just as it rang. Wendy was calling him.

"Are you busy?" she began. "I'm sorry to bother you at work. It's not a big deal, but I wanted to let you know. It's nothing serious—" Her tone was uncertain, halting.

Trouble.

Joe's attention snapped into sharp focus. He was already running for his car as he asked, "What is it?"

"It's just...I'm bleeding."

CHAPTER TWENTY-EIGHT

THE BLEEDING WAS MINIMAL, BUT WENDY CALLED HER OB-GYN anyway, to be safe. The doctor said to go in. Sophie jumped at the chance to watch Justin for an hour. She offered her car too, since Wendy hadn't gotten a loaner yet from the insurance company. But then Joe surprised her by dropping everything and offering to take her. She hadn't expected that.

"I want to be part of our baby's life," he told her as they walked to the medical building from the parking lot. "Every day, all the way. I know you don't believe me yet, but you will. I'll keep showing you that I mean it." He took her hand in his, his warm fingers enfolding her cold fingertips.

"Some spotting is normal. I'm probably overreacting."

They went inside together, hand in hand. They only let each other go when she had to sign in at the reception desk.

They barely sat down in the waiting room when her name was called.

She stood, looked back at Joe.

His eyes were filled with naked worry. "I'll be right here."

"You can come back with me, if you'd like."

He was next to her in a blink, taking her hand again.

"It's probably nothing," she told him as they walked back together. "All kinds of weird stuff happens to the body during pregnancy. And then everything turns out well at the end." With Justin she'd had swollen ankles, and cramps, and brown splotches appearing on her skin.

In the examining room, he helped her undress and put on the green gown. Then helped her onto the table. And then he waited with her until Dr. Pederick entered.

"So how much bleeding are we talking about?" the doctor asked after greeting them.

"Not too bad." Wendy shot Joe a reassuring look. "I wasn't even sure if I should call."

"You should always call." The woman reached into the top drawer under the counter and pulled out a baby heart-rate monitor. "Have you felt movement yet?"

"Not yet. But I hadn't felt any with my first either at this stage."

The doctor pressed the heart-rate monitor to Wendy's belly, moved it around, adjusted it. Staticky noises filled the room. Wendy waited for the unmistakable sound of the baby's rapid heartbeat, similar to galloping horses. She held her breath, but no matter how Dr. Pederick adjusted the monitor, they could hear none of those rapid little baby heartbeats.

———

Joe knew something was wrong. He could see it in Wendy's bloodless face. He moved closer to the table and took her hand again.

"Hold on." The doctor adjusted her instrument. "Sometimes it's hard to get this right. Let's bring the ultrasound cart in here, all right?"

She stepped to the door and called out to the nurse. The three minutes they waited for the ultrasound machine were the longest three minutes of Joe's life.

Out came the blue jelly again, then the wand, things he was familiar with from their previous appointment. Wendy's fingers tightened on his hand as the outline of their little baby came up on the fuzzy screen.

"Let's poke him a bit." The doctor's tone remained upbeat.

She pushed on Wendy's belly. The baby didn't move in response. She tried a few more times. Stopped. And then her smile was gone, replaced by dread and sympathy.

"I'm so sorry."

Joe could hear the words, heard Wendy catch her breath, but then for a moment it was as if he'd gone deaf and blind. The world stopped. The room seemed to drop, drop, drop with him, like an elevator crashing. *Falling to hell.*

On the bed, Wendy was blinking rapidly, staring at the monitor, as if unable to look away, as if desperately needing to see the sweet little shape there.

"Are you sure? Just poke me again." But then she couldn't wait, and she poked herself. And then again. Hard. Until Joe pulled her hand back.

The doctor switched off the monitor. The screen turned black. Their baby disappeared.

"Let me check for dilation." She moved to the end of the table.

The gown slid off Wendy's shoulder, and Joe let her go to fix it.

She grabbed after him. "Please don't leave."

Her small voice shattered his heart into a million pieces. "I'm not going anywhere."

"Dilated to one centimeter," the doctor said. "I'm sending you over to the hospital."

And then came the hardest, darkest hours of Joe's life.

He stood by Wendy as their baby went to heaven, then he drove Wendy home, carried her upstairs. She climbed into bed, curling her body around Justin who was down for a nap.

"What can I do?" Sophie whispered from the doorway with tears washing down her face.

Joe couldn't answer. He couldn't comprehend what had just happened. He felt as if a battle axe was embedded in his chest.

"I just need sleep," Wendy whispered in a broken voice from the bed.

He wanted to lie down next to her and fold her into his arms, but he didn't deserve comfort from her. This was his fault—he'd let Keith get to her. So he followed Sophie downstairs where Mike waited with Peaches.

Sophie gave Joe a big, long hug. "I'm so sorry."

"Me too." Words couldn't express how sorry he was.

"Do you want me to stay?"

He shook his head. "Thank you for taking care of Justin. I think Wendy will sleep now. They gave her drugs at the hospital. Maybe you could come by tomorrow?" He made a helpless gesture with his hands. "I'm not sure what to do."

Sophie gave him a sad smile, an even sadder look in her red-rimmed eyes. "You're giving her exactly what she needs. Protection and support."

"I didn't protect her yesterday."

"Nobody could have known that Keith would come here. And you had Mike watching the house."

It didn't matter. Wendy had been hurt. The baby was lost. Joe couldn't forgive himself for that.

After another hug, Sophie left.

"Want me to stay?" Mike offered. "I'm sorry, man. I should have..."

"Not your fault." Sophie was right. Keith had done this. He was the only one responsible. "You should go. I'll be here. I'm not going anywhere."

Wendy didn't rise from her bed until the following morning. She'd missed supper the night before—Joe had fed Justin. She didn't want to miss breakfast, couldn't give in to her grief. Justin needed his mother. Staying in bed for another day wasn't going to help. Not a day, not a week, not a month. She was never going to get over losing her baby. *Never.* She couldn't imagine a time when the loss would hurt less. She would just have to wade through the thick swamp of pain, day after day. Might as well start.

Joe waited for her downstairs, with his own dark circles under his eyes. "How are you this morning?"

"I'm okay." The three syllables came out halting. "I'm fine." She needed to get better at lying and fast. She didn't want to dump her bottomless grief on anyone. "When do you have to leave for work?"

"I'm staying home today." He stepped toward her.

She stepped around him. "You shouldn't skip work because of me." She couldn't possibly hold herself together all day. "Honestly, I think I'd prefer to be alone today."

"All right. I'm sorry. I understand if you don't want to—"

He sounded bewildered, maybe desperate, and definitely hurt, but she didn't have the bandwidth to figure out what to do with any of that. "I just want to be alone."

"I'm sorry," he said again before he left.

Chase replaced him on guard duty that first day, Harper on the second, then Mike again, then Jack, Broslin PD rotating through the house while Joe was off working. He worked a lot. At one point, even in her grief haze, Wendy figured out that he was hunting Keith. He only came home to sleep.

His sister, Amber, stopped by every day. So did Sophie. Short visits. They intuited that Wendy needed time alone. They gave her that, but they wouldn't give in on everything. They wouldn't let her do housework, and she wished they did. She needed to keep busy.

She played more with Justin instead, took care of him, hugged him more—every time he'd let her, until he squirmed away. When Justin napped, time passed slower, or didn't pass at all. It came to a standstill. Finally, she dragged out her laptop, and worked on editing her stock images to prepare them for uploading.

On the fifth day, Cecilia called from Cecilia's Broslin Boutique. "I was hoping you could help me with my window display design. Eileen keeps telling me how amazing you are. Any chance you have an available spot in your schedule?"

Wendy looked around and realized she was desperate to get out of the house. She'd tried to keep her grief to herself, but it was as if her sorrow had poured out into the rooms, and stuck to the carpet and couch cushions like cat hair. While she'd done a lot of staring off into space, doing her best not to think, not to feel, Justin was bouncing off the walls, displaying definite signs of cabin fever.

"How about today?"

"Are you serious? Today would be fantastic."

"I'll be there in about an hour." She needed to shower first.

"Thank you so much, Wendy."

Mike watched Justin while Wendy got ready, then he drove them over.

Wendy created a vibrant display to Cecilia's delight and praise, and received a nice check.

"Is it okay if I pass your number around?" the boutique owner asked.

"Yes. Thank you."

Life had to go on.

Wendy had to be strong, even if her heart ached with an unending pain for the baby she would never hold in her arms.

She missed her unborn child, and she missed the tenuous connection that had been built between her and Joe. He'd begun to avoid her —another layer of hurt.

"He probably blames me," Wendy told Sophie when Sophie had dropped by for a visit. "Why wouldn't he?"

"Why would he?" Sophie handed a stuffed toy to Justin who jumped up and down with the small, fuzzy Rottweiler.

"Doggy!"

"What do you say?"

"Thank you, Aunt Sophie!"

Sophie kissed the top of his head, then took Wendy's hand. "Joe is not like that. He's suffering too. Have you seen how haggard he is lately?"

"He's working overtime all the time so he doesn't have to stay home and look at me. What happened was my fault. I'm the one who let things get out of control with Keith. I could have left him sooner. Stood up to him. Obtained a restraining order. Got him out of our lives for good before the violence ever progressed this far."

Sophie kept protesting, but the roar of guilt in Wendy's head drowned out her words.

"Joe probably hates me, he's just too polite to tell me. He's too nice a guy to say it. His ex-fiancée had pretended to be having his child and then pretended to lose it. Now I have lost his baby for real. I have no idea how to apologize for that."

What words could she possibly say?

The week passed, a long dark slog through dreary days with freezing rain.

"Winter is returning for an encore," Amber complained on Sunday when she brought Max over once again to play with Justin. "I'm definitely giving this spring a one-star review. One more day like this, and I'm going to have to insist on talking to the supervisor."

The following week, Wendy managed a little more work. Sophie had finished her website. The car insurance company called. They'd processed her paperwork. By the end of the week, she received a check in the mail, and Joe drove her to a used car dealership in West Chester to pick out a car. She chose what she had before, a three-year-old Prius. Justin liked the color, toy-car red.

For the most part, her conversations with Joe remained limited to polite inquiries after each other's well-being in the evening when he got home from work.

"Your stitches are out."

"I don't think the scar is going anywhere." He ran a finger down the angry red line on his face. "What have you been doing today?"

"Talked to my parents."

"Did you tell them about the..." Neither of them had been able to say the word.

She shook her head. "I don't see the point in breaking their hearts too. There's nothing they can do to help. There's no undoing what happened. I don't want to make them sad."

"Of course," Joe said.

And that was the longest conversation they had that week. He usually left so early in the morning that she never saw him leave. She would come downstairs, and a different officer would be sitting in the living room, wishing Wendy good morning.

Joe did take time to play with Justin, though, during the evenings. On one hand, Wendy was grateful for that, because Justin worshipped him. On the other hand, she was worried that when they left—Keith would be caught eventually and it would be safe to return home—

Justin's little heart would be crushed, his all-important friendship with Joe abruptly cut off. Joe had said he wanted them forever, but that had been when Wendy had been carrying his child. Those promises no longer applied.

When Wendy's checkup appointment came around the following week, she hesitated whether or not to tell Joe, but in the end, she did.

"Do you want me to take you?" he immediately offered.

"I'm going with Sophie. But thank you."

"Will you tell me what the doctor says?"

He's just being polite. "Of course."

She was pronounced physically recovered.

Dr. Pederick did her best to sound upbeat. "The vast majority of women are able to have another child, or even multiple children, after a miscarriage."

Wendy barely heard the words.

CHAPTER TWENTY-NINE

THEY WERE LIKE TWO GHOSTS HAUNTING THE SAME HOUSE, JOE thought. The only burst of life energy was Justin. The little boy kept them both going. Because of him, they had to pretend to be all right, so they did.

The early spring chills finally gave way to warmer weather, the flowers and trees in full bloom, tulips and daffodils giving their last hurrah on the front lawns. But even the beauty of spring couldn't bridge the gorge that had opened up between Joe and Wendy. If anything, the distance seemed to grow each day. Joe wanted, badly, to reach out, but he didn't know how, if she'd welcome it.

He wasn't used to letting people down.

Yet he was letting Wendy down, day after day.

"What do I do?" he asked Amber over the phone.

"Just be there for her," his sister advised, without any smart-alecky comments for once. "Just be there and love her."

He did love Wendy, Joe realized, too late. He loved Wendy, and she was never going to forgive him.

He threw himself into work. Harper's father had a heart attack and the family spent their days by his side at the hospital. Since Harper was taking leave, the captain officially assigned the Brogevich case to

Joe. He worked on that. He also ran down every new lead on Keith. Then he ran down every shadow of a lead. Nothing. The bastard had disappeared from the face of the earth.

A month after Keith's attack, Joe dragged out everything he had and printed what he could, carried the foot-tall stack into the conference room, and laid it all out on the table. He took a mug and a full pot of coffee in there with him. He wasn't going to leave until he found something.

He read through every page, grouping related items together. The only thing that stuck out was the HR report on the incident when Keith had lost his temper at work.

Keith Kline had been advised to take an anger management workshop. He had accepted the recommendation and completed anger management training, according to the update scribbled on the bottom of the page.

Joe picked up the paper, then he set it down again. More than likely it only jumped out at him because it reminded him that he'd come to a dead end with Phil's case.

Wait...

Joe picked up the paper again. Could Keith have been attending Phil's anger management classes in West Chester?

It didn't seem probable. Wilmington Hospital was in Keith's backyard, then Christiana Care hospital a few miles away. Traveling to West Chester would have been cumbersome and inconvenient, a waste of time.

And yet.

Joe kept turning the idea around and around in his head on the way home. He was so focused on the possibility; he almost didn't pick up his phone when it rang. Then he glanced at the screen. *Chief Gleason.*

"I wanted to let you know I requested that you be awarded a commendation," the chief said. "You've gone above and beyond helping me. I won't forget that."

"Thank you, sir."

"If there's anything I can ever do for you, all you have to do is ask."

Joe didn't have any favors lined up, but he did have a question. "What happens to Ramos's and Gomez's aunt now?"

"She's been referred to a senior living facility by Social Services. She needs more help than what she's been getting. Medical supervision."

"Do you know, by any chance, where she is?"

"I can find out for you."

"Thank you, sir." He thought he might visit the old woman, for Gomez's sake. "I don't suppose you have any information about Trigger, the dog?"

The chief cleared his throat. "Damn mutt ate my recliner. I brought him home, just until somebody can adopt him."

The chief's update put Joe in a better mood as he drove home. He found Wendy in the living room with Justin and Mike. Mike was on his hands and knees, Justin riding him like a pony.

"What do you call a pig that knows karate?" Mike asked.

Justin attacked the air.

"A pork chop," Mike told him.

Justin giggled. "Mom, it's a pork chop!" Then he spotted Joe. "What's the name of the pig who does karate?"

"Karate Pig?"

"Pork chop!" Justin giggled again, even louder.

Wendy stood up and walked toward Joe, the same uncertain look on her face that she'd worn for the past few weeks. "Your dinner is on the table."

"You don't have to take care of me." He didn't want to give her extra work.

She recoiled, as if he'd offended her. Since they'd lost the baby, he never seemed to say the right thing.

"Anything exciting at work?" Mike asked from his undignified pose on the carpet.

"Slow day at the station. Robin gave Leila a charm bracelet to clear up her aura. That almost turned into something, but pretty calm otherwise. Thanks for being here."

Justin ran out to the kitchen, so Mike stood up. "There's going to be a cat fight between those two one of these days, mark my words. Hey, an old woman and a cat walk into a bar—"

"Maybe I should tell Leila and Robin that you're telling old-woman jokes. A common enemy might bring them together."

"Traitor." Mike laughed as he left, calling back a good night to Wendy and Justin.

Wendy had made beef stew. Pretty damn good too. Joe ate, then cleaned up after himself. Wendy read a book about dinosaurs to Justin, until the boy had to go upstairs for his bath.

Joe dragged out the hospital file boxes and began going through them again. He was looking for one specific signature this time: Keith Kline.

People were supposed to print their names, then sign, but only about half of them followed instructions. Out of those, half had handwriting so bad that even the printed name was undecipherable.

While Joe combed through signatures, he called the captain to check in again, but Bing had nothing new on Keith or on the Brogevich case.

"How's Wendy?" he asked.

"I don't know." Guys didn't talk about their feelings, right? But then Joe said something anyway. "I don't know how to reach her. I messed up with her, and I don't know how to fix it."

"I did that with Sophie. Here's the thing. Men can be stupider than dirt about women. With Sophie, I was stupider than dirt under a toad's toenails. She forgave me anyway." He paused. "The most important thing is to talk to her."

"Yeah."

The captain said to talk to her. Amber had told Joe to show Wendy that he loved her. He used to be good at romance, dammit. Joe put his phone down. How had he gotten so bad? Hell of the thing was, Wendy was the only woman who ever truly mattered.

Since he had no solution to their problems, he threw himself into work.

He was still looking through the first box of papers, and getting more frustrated by the minute, when Wendy came back downstairs.

She'd lost weight. She'd always been slim, but now she looked downright thin. He was worried about her.

She stepped over his stacks of paper on her way to the couch. "Mind if I watch a little TV?"

"Go ahead."

She settled in and pulled a blanket over herself as she glanced at his folders. "I thought police work was all chases and excitement."

"That's how we get suckered in. Nobody tells you that most of it is mind-numbing paperwork."

She flipped through the channels, picked a cooking show, and turned the sound way down. "If it bothers you, I can just mute it and turn on closed caption."

"It's fine."

"I'm sorry we've taken over your house. I'm sure you didn't expect us to stay this long."

"I want you here."

She looked at him, a bundle of sadness and desperation. "Why?"

He tried to remember what he would have said back when he'd known how to woo women. His mind drew a blank. Screw it. Strategy was for football. When you loved a woman, you laid your cards on the table. Joe set down the papers in his hand. "Because I'm falling in love with you." He winced, shook his head. "Believe it or not, I used to be known for my impeccable timing. Listen, I know it's going to take time for you to forgive me..."

She stared at him. "I'm the one who lost the baby."

"I'm not looking for a baby-making machine. I wasn't looking for a baby. I wasn't looking for anything. And then you came along." He shook his head. "I can't explain it."

"Does this mean you forgive me?"

"I already told you none of this was your fault. If anyone's, it was mine." He moved closer to her and took her hands.

She looked torn. Then, after a few seconds, she leaned toward him.

He pulled her onto his lap, his arms around her. He wasn't ever going to let her go, he promised himself, and then he brushed a kiss over her lips.

"I missed you," he whispered against her mouth.

"I missed you too."

"I know you want time to yourself to figure out what you want." He nibbled. "I'm not going to push."

"Okay." She kissed him back.

"I'm falling in love with you, and I don't know how to handle it. Never happened to me before. I don't know how to do this."

"That must hurt your ego," she joked.

"Yes, it does. I'm used to being good at things."

"You're doing fine." She pressed her lips against his again.

Yes, that was more than fine. Joe took it from there. Hell, he had the ball. If he knew one thing, it was how to run with it. The knowledge that he could have lost her along with the baby gave a whole new layer of emotion to the kiss.

Some woman on TV rambled on about crème brûlée, but the words never connected into a sentence in his head, his thoughts and feelings lost in Wendy.

Her arms went around his neck as she held on to him.

His right hand snuck up her rib cage, stopped under her breast, hesitated. "I'm not going to rush you."

"It's been over a month. I'm fully recovered." She shifted, and her breast slid into his waiting palm.

He ran his questing fingers over her. Her nipple pebbled under his touch, and he was instantly hard.

He could barely pull away long enough to say, "Hold on." And then he went for the hem of her nightgown and gently eased it up, running his fingers along warm flesh, dragging the material over her head.

He anchored her by holding on to her hip and leaned forward to claim her nipple with his lips.

She is the one. This was what Amber had had with her husband, Daryl, before she'd lost him, the kind of love Joe couldn't even understand back then. And now he had it.

No way was he ever going to lose this. No way.

He laved her nipple, breathing in her scent, wanting her more than he'd ever thought it possible to want a woman. She held him to her, her head falling back, her neck bared for him. He traveled up with a row of kisses, then back again, then eased her down onto the couch and settled himself between her legs.

He kissed one nipple thoroughly, then the other, moved lower, her slim fingers in his hair.

"Joe?"

He kept kissing his way down.

"Wait."

He stopped. *Too fast.* He'd promised not to push. He glanced up.

She wasn't looking at him. She was staring pale-faced at one of the papers that had fallen to the floor from the couch.

"What is it?"

"That's Keith's signature. What are these?"

His brain needed a second to click over from *lust haze* to *work.* "I'm still working on the murder of that friend I told you about. He taught anger management classes. These are the sign-in sheets."

Wendy pointed to a line in the middle of the page. Shuddered. "There. That's Keith."

The heat disappeared from Joe's body. Now that the signature had been pointed out, he could make out the letters in *Kline.* And if he squinted, he could see *Keith* in the too tight scribbling. "Sonofabitch."

"What does this mean?"

"I don't know yet." He kissed her, quick and hard, then pushed to his feet. "I better call the captain."

CHAPTER THIRTY

ALL JOE WANTED TO KNOW WAS WHETHER KEITH HAD COME TO Broslin on the day of Phil's murder.

For once, Broslin PD was blessedly quiet, nothing to distract from the traffic camera footage. Every time a white Mercedes E450 coupe popped up on the screen, Joe paused the video and checked the license plate.

Mike lumbered by with a slice of mushroom pizza from the break-room. "What are you doing?"

"Considering whether my instincts on the Brogevich case are wrong."

"Wait." Mike yanked his phone from his back pocket. "The great Joe Kessler is admitting he might be wrong about something. I need to record this so I have proof for later. Say it again."

Joe threw a handful of crumpled sticky notes at him.

Mike dropped his hand. "What might you be wrong about?"

"Maybe Keith Kline isn't connected to Phil's death. I can't find proof of him in Broslin that morning. No sign of his car."

"He could have driven a rental."

"The murder didn't look premeditated. The killer didn't bring a weapon. He used the phone he picked up in Phil's office. And if the murder wasn't premeditated, the murderer wouldn't have come in a rental."

"Why do you think Keith Kline was involved?"

"Phil and Keith knew each other. Keith was in Phil's anger management class in West Chester. I can't tell whether it's my instincts that keep pushing me in that direction, or some dark hope. I wouldn't mind putting Keith Kline away for life."

Mike nodded toward the screen. "Let me know if you want me to look through the recordings to double check. Fresh pair of eyes."

"Thanks."

"Anytime."

"Hey, you know why no one ever asks Chuck Norris to fill out an online form?"

Joe raised an eyebrow.

"Because he'll never submit." Mike cackled as he walked away.

Joe shook his head.

He went through the video from Baltimore Pike, the most logical route for Keith, then started on video from Routes 100, 52, 81 and Route 41 in case Keith had taken one of the back roads.

Scanning through the footage ate up the entire day, but he considered the time well spent. Because, in the end, just as he was ready to shut down, he did spot the right white Mercedes with the right license plate.

He paused the recording, rewound, played, paused again. He couldn't fully make out the face behind the windshield, but the chin and jawline sure looked like Keith.

Joe printed a still shot and showed it to the captain.

"Keith Kline was in one of Phil's anger management classes. They knew each other. And he was in Broslin on the morning of the murder. Means and opportunity."

The captain scanned the printout. "What about motive?"

"First thing I'm going to ask Keith when I catch him."

————

Wendy was preparing dinner in Joe's kitchen, porkchops with roasted carrots and potatoes, when Eileen called.

"I was wondering if you'd like to go over to the battered women's shelter in West Chester with me next Thursday. I'll be giving a free cooking class while sharing information about the difference between a temporary restraining order and a permanent restraining order. Over seventy percent of domestic-violence murders occur *after* the victim leaves. I want those women to be careful and have the right protection in place." The noise of the diner ebbed and flowed in the background. "I thought maybe we could bring some makeup, and you could take pictures? Self-image is a huge issue. Abused persons see themselves as less than others, unworthy. And if they left everything behind when they ran, they might not have so much as a picture of their children. Maybe you could take a few mom-and-kids shots?"

Wendy didn't have to think about it. "I'd love to."

"Wonderful. How are you doing? Sorry. I should have led with that. I was just thinking about my schedule, and I thought about asking you to come with me to the shelter, and then I got so excited I got carried away."

"I'm glad you asked. And I'm all right. Honestly."

"I'm really glad. How about if I pick you up Thursday, and we drive over together?"

"Sounds like a plan."

"One more thing, before I forget. I have another friend interested in a window display consultation with you, the beauty salon on the corner. Would it be okay if I gave Sharon your phone number?"

"Of course. Thank you."

After Wendy hung up with Eileen, she picked up Justin and swung him around. "Three customers!"

His smile was dimmer than usual. He didn't squeal *"Again. Again!"*

She checked his forehead. He was a little warm, but she didn't think he was running a fever. She plopped him into his highchair. "How about some OJ?"

She filled his sippy cup from the jar in the fridge. A shot of vitamin C couldn't hurt.

He swung his feet as he drank, tapping on the wood. Keith had broken the chair. Joe had fixed it—a gesture of kindness and thought-fulness. The longer Wendy lived with him, the more she appreciated the man.

She managed to peel one more potato before her phone rang again. She didn't recognize the number. It could be Eileen on the diner's land-line, or Joe from the police station, so she picked up the call.

"Hey, babe."

The voice sent a chill down Wendy's spine. She gripped the phone. "I don't want to talk to you. I don't want to ever see you again."

"I'm sorry I lost it the other day," Keith said. "You know how I get. Doesn't mean I don't love you. I feel so bad about what happened. I swear it's not going to happen again. Hey, I signed the custody papers."

Hope wouldn't let her hang up. "Did you really?"

"I should have done it before." Remorse rasped in his voice. "You're a good mother. All I'm asking is that you and Justin have dinner with me at Torrino's. It's our restaurant. Let me apologize in person. Let me give you the paperwork."

Torrino's wasn't really *their* restaurant. They'd gone there a couple of times during the short period when things had been working between them. She didn't want to go back there. Maybe Keith was feeling nostalgic, but she wasn't.

"I'm ready to do this, Wendy," he said. "I understand that you need to move on. You deserve closure. How about Torrino's at eight?"

She would do anything to have full custody of her son, and he knew it.

"Could we meet in Broslin? I think Justin is coming down with something. It's cold and wet outside. And I don't want to keep him out too long past his bedtime."

A moment of silence on the line. "Fine."

"There's a diner on Main Street. We could get a booth in the back and have more privacy there than at Torrino's."

She held her breath and waited for the answer. If he objected, she'd drive to Wilmington. At this stage, she'd be willing to drive cross country. She wanted those papers. She could practically taste her freedom.

"All right." By some divine intervention, Keith seemed to be in an agreeable mood. "See you at the diner at eight."

CHAPTER THIRTY-ONE

KEITH KLINE LET THE RENTED BLACK VAN IDLE IN THE BACK OF THE restaurant's parking lot. He flipped on the windshield wipers every couple of minutes to clean off the drizzle. He wanted to see the cars coming and going.

"Come on, Wendy. You know I hate it when you're late."

She'd be his or nobody's. He certainly wasn't going to allow her to become some cop's whore.

She needed to learn her place. She needed discipline. Keith's jaw tightened when he thought of her calling the cops on him because he'd lost his temper for five seconds at her apartment. He'd been fired because of her, after the police had gone to his place of work and asked questions about him.

Of course, he'd lost his temper again at the asshole cop's house where she'd gone to hide. Wendy had provoked him. What did she think was going to happen if she moved in with another guy?

She should have been moving back with Keith. At the very least, she should have gone back to her own place. *Not* move in with another man. She didn't think. Sometimes she could be incredibly stupid. God knew, he'd been trying to be patient with her, but she kept pushing him—right over the edge. Almost as if she *wanted* him to hit her.

On some level, she liked it. Otherwise, why provoke him? She enjoyed that he felt guilty afterwards. She was pissing him off on purpose to get the emotional upper hand.

He loved her, but their relationship was messed up. They needed time together, away from her friends' interference, to work things out. They needed to talk to each other. She needed to realize that they belonged together.

He was going to find another job. A better job than the one he'd lost. Then she wouldn't have to work. He would take care of her and Justin, but the new pregnancy had to go. He was prepared to forgive her for cheating—women were weak—but he wasn't going to raise some cop's bastard. She didn't even look pregnant. She should have no trouble getting rid of the kid.

They needed a fresh slate.

They needed privacy to talk. Enough time alone for her to come to her senses. Keith had the perfect place in mind. He was going to take her to the beach house in Jersey he used to rent with his college buddies back in the day. The house would be empty this early in May, the beach deserted.

He had plenty of cash on him. The cops weren't going to be able to trace them. Keith would show Wendy how much he loved her. She needed to see just him, without Sophie the bitch whispering into her ear, or that asshole cop trying to get into her pants.

Once Keith made love to her, over and over again, Wendy would know that there could never be another man for her but him. She would never want to leave him.

If she did....

The dark rage took him swiftly, the urge to hit, to pummel the resistance out of her. He started the breathing exercises he'd learned in anger management. Gave up after a few minutes. *Fuck Dr. Brogevich.* The idiot wouldn't stamp the paperwork that Keith had completed classes. He'd missed a few, so what? His fingers clenched on the steering wheel.

He unclenched them. None of that mattered now. He'd gotten his stamp in the end.

Of course, he lost the damn job anyway. Because of Wendy and the idiot police. Keith smacked the console. Why did people insist on antagonizing him?

"Where the hell are you?" He scanned the parking lot. "Come on, Wendy."

He was reaching for the gearshift, ready to track her down, when she pulled into the lot behind a tour bus, driving her new red Prius.

She parked but didn't get out. She wore the pale blue coat he'd picked out for her from a catalogue at the beginning of winter. She'd wanted red. Only whores wore red. He was tired of having to remind her.

She'd wrapped a matching silk scarf over her head to protect her from the drizzle. Keith could barely see her face. Without the car and the coat, he wouldn't have recognized her. She looked wider. Was she gaining weight?

She was going to bungle her career if she didn't watch herself. She was lucky she had him to help. He was going to slim her down if he had to lock her up and starve her. Sometimes, tough love was necessary.

He was going to help her, even if he had to do it against her will. He was going to take her, and Justin, tonight. If she didn't want to go along, Keith was prepared to convince her the hard way.

He pulled his rented van into the parking spot next to her and got out, walked right up and grabbed the Prius's door handle. "I changed my mind," he told her. "I don't want to go in. We're going somewhere else. You're coming with me."

Joe had the handcuffs ready. "Broslin PD. You're under arrest. Turn around and put your hands behind your back."

Zap!

The pain was instant and debilitating.

Call for backup. But reaching for his cell phone was beyond him. He fell to the ground, convulsing.

Jack was sitting in his car on the other side of the building, ready to block the exit if Keith tried to give them the slip. Chase and Harper had just gone into the diner, in case Keith was already in there. Captain Bing was watching the parking lot from the far end. He'd see that something wasn't right.

Or maybe not.

The tour bus that arrived at the same time as Joe had beeped as it backed up, blocking Bing's view of Keith's van. A flock of chattering girls poured out of the bus.

Keith stayed where he was, pretending to be looking at his phone, looming over Joe, waiting for the kids to be gone.

Then one of the girls ran by them on her way to the diner and shouted. "Gun!"

Joe wanted to yell at her to get back, but his jaw felt fused shut, his muscles still contracting from the Taser's electric shock. He could do nothing. Couldn't even roll away when Keith kicked him in the kidney. Then the bastard was gone, around his van, then jumping in and peeling away.

More girls screamed.

"Is he dead?"

"Oh my God!"

Joe struggled to his feet just in time to see Bing's car roaring into view, but Keith's black van veered sharply and went up the grassy divider between properties, crushing several bushes as it crossed over to the parking lot of the next business.

Chase and Harper running from the diner, weapons drawn, were too late. Their target was gone.

Joe shoved his aching body into Wendy's car to follow Keith and Bing, but he had to dodge high school girls who were darting around in their blue/red uniforms and doing the worst job ever at getting out of his way. All Joe could do was swear and beep his horn, and neither made a damn difference.

He called the captain. "Do you see him?"

"No. But he can't be more than half a dozen cars ahead of me. Hang on, I need to let Chase and Harper know what's going on." Then his voice sounded from farther away as he spoke into his radio. "Unmarked black van, heading south on Main Street toward Route 1."

———

Broslin PD searched the town for four hours, everyone out.

The captain put out an APB so the PA State Troopers were looking too, but Keith could easily have headed straight to Delaware or Maryland. Broslin sat right in the corner where the three states met.

Joe finally drove home to Wendy and Justin around midnight, having accomplished nothing, frustrated out of his skin.

He thanked Mike for his help with guard duty and sent him home, then grabbed a bite quietly so he wouldn't wake up anyone. He planned on sleeping on the couch so he would hear if Keith came around, but wanted to check on Wendy and Justin first.

Mike had been sitting in the dark so nobody could see him through the window, and Joe didn't turn on the lights either. He knew his house well enough to navigate. He just had to watch his feet to make sure he wouldn't step on any of Justin's toys.

At the bottom of the stairs, he heard a small noise from above that snapped his attention to the top.

Wendy stood up there, legs apart, holding a table lamp.

"It's me." Joe held his hands up to show he was unarmed. "It's Joe."

The night-light in the upstairs hallway outlined her figure and her long hair that fell softly around her shoulders. She wore pink pajama pants and a matching tank top that was molded to her torso.

Hot liquid desire shot through him. "Sorry I woke you. Just got home."

She set the lamp on the floor. Then she ran down the stairs and flew into his arms without a word.

Her soft warmth pressed against him. He buried his face in her hair, inhaling her scent, and his entire body buzzed alive.

She held on to him. "Are you okay?"

"I'm fine. He got away. I'm sorry." Joe wrapped his arms around her. "How are you?"

"I was worried."

"I'm here now. You should get some sleep." But he didn't move to let her go. He held her and pressed a kiss onto her forehead.

She snuggled even closer.

Her breasts pressed against his chest through his shirt. He was as hard as a police baton. She couldn't not notice. He tried not to move, not to shift.

She looked up.

"Joe..." Her eyes begged, but he wasn't sure for what. "I can't afford to make another big mistake."

He reached up and tucked her hair behind her ear. "This is not a mistake."

Slowly, she nodded.

He rested his forehead against hers. "I don't want to hurt you."

"I know."

The trust in her voice was humbling.

He liked women. If they came to him and offered, he didn't see a point in refusing. He knew desire. He'd seen lust in more pairs of eyes than he cared to count. But what he saw in Wendy's eyes as he pulled back a few inches was different, more, deeper.

What he felt was new—the need to take care of her, to protect her, to be with her, not just in the bedroom, but to be with her in every way. He wanted the trips to the grocery store and helping her feed Justin and reading books to the boy. Maybe even more kids, with time. He wanted forever. He wanted them to be a family.

Sweat broke out on his brow. He had no idea what he was doing. All around him was unfamiliar territory. How do you make love to the woman you are in love with?

He kissed her and tried to put everything he felt into that kiss, because sure as hell, he couldn't put it into words.

How did anyone ever do this? How did a man love a woman and not be scared to death that he might do something wrong and lose her? He'd never worried about losing a woman before, but now the thought damn near paralyzed him. Love was the freaking pits.

His lips fumbled over hers like some teenage boy with his first kiss.

"How are you so incredibly soft and sweet?" *So perfect.* He nibbled her lower lip.

He'd been an idiot. All this time he'd thought he was some hot stud jock, but he'd just been an idiot without her. Everything he'd thought he knew about women was wrong. Nothing from his past could compare with what he was feeling.

He softly tasted her upper lip. *Slow, slow, slow.* Not to show off his football player stamina, but because he didn't want this moment to end, ever.

He kissed the tip of her nose, her eyes, her brows, then meandered back to her lips again.

"Joe." His name floated from her lips on a soft breath.

She tugged his shirt out of his jeans. Her slim hand slipped under the shirt and she splayed her fingers over his skin, sending more heat through his body.

He didn't dare touch her tank top, didn't dare touch her skin to skin, not yet. He kept kissing her, drinking in her sweetness, trying to settle his brain.

Then she opened up for him, and he was lost instantly. He explored her little by little, tongue to tongue, a sweet, slow dance of desire that brought his blood to the boiling point.

Her hands moved to the front then up his chest, her fingertips brushing across his nipples and making his dick jerk. He put his hands over hers and held them in place until she looked up to meet his eyes. "You matter to me."

She searched his gaze. "You matter to me too."

Then a smile that nearly stopped his heart bloomed on her lips for half a second before she raised her mouth back to his.

The kiss changed tone, gathered steam. When a throaty moan escaped her, Joe lost some of his hesitancy and pulled the tank top over her head. She was pushing his shirt off his shoulders. Then they were skin to skin.

Her pebbled nipples dragged against his chest as she moved.

"Full disclosure. I might lose it, before I ever get my pants off," he confessed. "Last time I embarrassed myself like that, I was fourteen."

She laughed.

He picked her up and carried her to the couch, kissed his way down her chin, her neck, licking and sucking each nipple in turn as she let her head fall back, her hair cascading to her waist.

His fingers fumbled with her pajama pants, pushed them down. He kissed his way down her belly while she kicked those pants away. Then he was on his knees in front of her, eye-to-eye with a lacy scrap of fabric that was so pretty he kissed her right through it.

Then that was no longer enough, so he tugged her panties off, needing to have his lips against her heat. His hands moved up to cup her from behind and settle her against his mouth. As he kissed his way up and down her seam, she braced herself on his shoulders.

"Joe." Her single whispered word dripped with urgent desire.

He drew back a couple of inches and blew on her damp curls to further fan the flames.

CHAPTER THIRTY-TWO

WENDY DUG HER FINGERS INTO JOE'S SKIN. HER KNEES TREMBLED. "Please."

Joe was mad at her for her calling him a jock all those times, so he was going to torture her to death. There was no other explanation for why he was going so agonizingly slow.

"Lean back."

She braced herself on the couch cushion behind her, her feet coming off the ground. He was reaching for her ankles already, hooking her legs over his shoulders as he knelt in front of her.

The whole move took maybe three seconds, then his lips were back on her, his hot tongue parting her folds.

"Joe!"

He explored her as thoroughly as if he were conducting a police investigation. He used his left hand to hold her open to him while he tortured her with his tongue. She was ready to explode even before he inserted two long fingers inside her and started to massage her from the inside.

Her body convulsed with pleasure, and she called his name again.

He rose above her. "I'm going to have an aneurism, if I can't have you right now."

He took care of protection before stretching out next to her. They lay side by side, facing each other. He reached down and hooked her leg over his hip, opening her to him. Then, with endless gentleness, he eased inside her a fraction of an inch at a time, kissing and caressing her body.

"Is it possible to die of pleasure?" she gasped out the words.

"Nobody is dying." He shifted her, rose over her, and made love to her with such care and gentleness, it completely disarmed her. Then, when she felt her body reaching toward the peak again, he shifted their position once more, putting her on top. "Ride me."

The urgent whisper, raspy with undisguised need, was her undoing.

"Harder." Dark fires burned in his gaze but he wasn't ordering. He was begging.

He was letting her have control. All control. That couldn't be easy for him. He was used to being in charge. But somehow he knew, that this was what she needed to feel completely safe.

Experimentally, she pulled up until they were barely touching.

He groaned, but he didn't force her back down, he didn't shove up to surge into her. He waited, letting her decide how much she was willing to give.

And Wendy discovered that she was willing to give pretty much everything.

Slowly, slowly she lowered herself, letting him fill her, stretch her, inch by hard inch. When she thought she couldn't take more, she still didn't stop. She ground herself against him.

"Wendy." His back arched. His long fingers tightened on her hips.

She was in control and she liked it.

He responded to her every move, caressed her hips, her butt, reached up to her breasts. His fingers worked miracles, teasing her nipples into aching, throbbing buds.

Then his hands moved back lower, parted her flesh again. He touched her so gently, so reverently, as if afraid to break her. That tenderness reached Wendy as nothing else could have.

His caressing hands never left her for a second. She began moving faster, her head falling back. Her eyelids fluttered closed as she flew into a million little pieces, at the same time as he soared to his own release.

When they could both breathe again, he tugged her down on top of him and embraced her, her head tucked into the crook of his neck. Their hearts beat next to each other, their breathing synchronizing.

Long, sated minutes passed before he stirred. "Shower before bed?"

"Yes, please."

He carried her to the master bathroom, turned on the water in the shower, and didn't set her down until they were under the warm spray.

They soaped and washed each other, each movement filled with intimacy and caring. She could no longer deny the connection between them, or the fact that he'd breached all her defenses.

After they dried and dressed, he took her by the hand. "Sleep with me?"

They settled on his large bed, her head on his shoulder, his arms around her. He pulled a blanket over them, enclosing them in a cocoon of warmth. She felt content and safe with him.

Which he ruined by saying, "Marry me."

Her head snapped up. "What?"

"Marry me."

Don't do this. "I can't."

"Why?"

Because she didn't want to give herself into a man's control. She didn't want a husband making decisions for her, controlling her finances, deciding what she could and couldn't do. She didn't think she could ever trust anyone that much. "I can't."

She braced for anger that never came.

"I'm not going to marry you, Joe," she repeated, to make sure he understood.

"It's your choice, obviously. But I'd like to point out that is what you said about sleeping with me, and look at us now," he said in an oh-so-smug tone before he took her lips in a lazy kiss.

CHAPTER THIRTY-THREE

JOE SPENT THE NEXT MORNING FOLLOWING UP ON LEADS FROM home, working at the far end of the kitchen table on his laptop—staying out of the splash zone.

"The incident in the diner's parking lot is all over the news." Wendy put her phone down on the counter to clean up Justin who was wallowing in the remains of his lunch.

He was a cute kid, but in a previous life, he'd definitely been a warthog. Joe loved him anyway. It was good to see someone attacking life with that kind of gusto.

"They're showing Keith's picture." Wendy wiped Justin's ketchup-covered hands. "And a picture of the van he drove."

"I know. Leila sent an email. Calls are pouring in." Ninety-nine percent of them wouldn't amount to anything, but Joe only needed one good tip.

Wendy picked up Justin. "You know what?" She kissed a sticky cheek. "We're going to hose you down in the shower before your nap."

"I'm not sleepy!"

"We'll just try all right? We'll clean up, lay down, and if you can't fall asleep, we'll come back down. Okay?"

Justin watched her as if suspecting a trap, but then he said, "Okay, Mommy."

She carried him up and wasn't up there for ten minutes before she was coming back down again, with a smile. "Out like a light."

Joe waited for her at the bottom of the stairs and pulled her into his arms. "I've been waiting to do this all morning."

He kissed her until her arms went around his neck, until she clung to him. But not until he had his fill, because that would be never.

When he let her go at last, he was pretty damn pleased with the dreamy smile he'd put on her face.

Except that then she said, "I'm still not going to marry you."

"But you'll move in with me permanently?"

"I'm my own person. I have my own place."

"You could think of this place as your own. We'll put your name on a couple of rooms."

She raised an eyebrow. "Let me guess, the kitchen and the laundry room?"

"If you want to be the boss in the bedroom, just say so." He coughed. "Dominatrix." Coughed again.

That got her laughing. Good. She needed more lightness in her life.

He leaned in to kiss her again, but his laptop pinged with a message. "I should check that."

Another e-mail from Leila, notes and contact info from the last two dozen calls that had come in on the hotline, people who thought they might have seen Keith or the van. Joe settled in and called back every one of them. By the time he finished—one lonely old man had gone on for half an hour and somehow circled around to his grandchildren who'd moved to Seattle and never visited—Justin was awake and Wendy was bringing him back downstairs.

"Any good leads?"

"Not really. Two hours pretty much wasted."

"I have an idea."

Justin wiggled in her arms until she set him down. He ran to the sliding glass doors to check if Pirate Prince was out there.

Joe let his gaze drift over Wendy and whispered, "Does your idea involve us being naked?"

"You're incorrigible."

"You say that like it's a bad thing." He reached for her hand. "I think we should—"

She shook her head, her smile evaporating as she pulled back. "I have an idea for catching Keith."

Joe could guess from her sudden, nervous expression where this was going. "No."

"You don't even know what I want to say."

"We're not using you as bait."

She stood her ground, solemn and determined. "Keith is my problem. This is about my life. My son's life."

"Even if you manage to convince me, because, God knows, I'm the opposite of clear-headed and objective when it comes to you, the captain would never go for a setup that involves you. A, for professional reasons. B, Sophie would skin him."

"Sophie is the last person who'd buy into the women-are-the-weaker sex bullshit. Sophie has always done exactly what she wanted."

"Point taken. But trust me to take care of it."

"I do. All I am asking is for you to trust me to be part of the solution. I can't be looking over my shoulders forever. I want a resolution, before anyone gets hurt. I want more than wait and hide and see. I want to be the one making the decisions that affect my family."

Joe clenched his jaw. Frustration made his teeth ache. "Dammit, Wendy."

"Dammit, Joe."

She wasn't being unreasonable. If their circumstances were switched, Joe would want a say in what happened, he'd be fighting to take the reins. "It'd better be a hell of a plan."

She gave her chin a confident lift. "It is."

While Justin let in the cat, lost in his own little world, Joe pulled Wendy back to him "I'm pretty sure I'm going to hate your plan. But I can't say I hate this strong, sexy-chick vibe you have going."

And then he kissed her to prove it.

Keith sat in the beach house, alone in the cold. The damned place had no heat, and with the wind coming off the ocean, early May still had plenty of chill in it. He'd bought an electric heater at the nearest department store, but it did little to warm up the living room that stood open to the kitchen and the stairs that sucked all the heat up to the second floor. He didn't want to go back for a bigger heater. His name and description were all over the news.

His muscles were rigid with rage.

Wendy had betrayed him.

She'd betrayed him to her bastard cop.

Blew her chance.

Keith had offered to forgive her everything, offered a way for the two of them to be together.

Stupid bitch didn't get it.

He couldn't stand the thought of her with the cop. Picturing another man's hands on her pumped Keith's blood pressure so high, he felt dizzy.

If I can't have her, nobody can.

He knew where the cop lived.

Keith spat on the heater and watched his saliva sizzle. *His* woman and *his* kid inside that cop's house. It wasn't right. They were all over there like a goddamn happy family while he was sitting in some stranger's house, freezing his ass off. They had everything. He had nothing. It wasn't fair.

Joe Kessler needed to be taught not to go after another man's woman. And Wendy needed to be taught not to be a whoring bitch.

Keith popped the battery back into his phone then walked out of the drafty summer house, cursing it to hell.

He had the black van parked in the back. He'd switched plates with a pickup in the department store's parking lot earlier. For a while at least, the van should be safe.

He opened the back to make sure his five-gallon cans of gasoline were still there. He closed the door, then patted his pocket. He had plenty of matches.

His plans were all in order.

———

"I'm sorry," Wendy whispered into Joe's phone, leaning against the kitchen counter, Joe right next to her. "The police made me do it. I didn't trick you, I swear. They came and took my clothes and my car. They knew I was going to meet you at the diner. They must have tapped my phone."

"Are they listening now?" Keith snapped on the other end.

"No. I'm on Joe's cell phone. He's in the shower."

"You need to get away from those people."

"Yes."

"I want you to meet me."

"I can get out after Joe goes to sleep tonight."

"You can't trust anyone but me."

"I know."

"I was about to come and get you. I'm running out of patience with you, Wendy." His tone turned cold. "You don't want me to run out of patience."

"I don't. I'm sorry. I should have never left. I regret that more than I can say. I'm sorry, Keith."

"I'm the only one who cares about you and Justin. We need to be together again."

"I want that."

"All right. Get out, then drive south on Route 1. Take the Oxford exit. Pull over at the end of the off-ramp. I'll be at the gas station. How soon can you come?"

"In another hour?" She wanted to give the police enough time to set up a trap. "Joe will probably head off to sleep once he gets out of the bathroom. He looked pretty beat."

"This time, you'd better be in that damn car instead of a decoy," Keith hissed, and then the line went dead.

Wendy drew a long, deep breath, drained. She'd completed the first step of her plan. Too late to second-guess herself. She passed the phone back to Joe.

He made a call.

"Anything?" He listened, and then he listened some more, anger hardening his eyes. "Okay. Thanks." He clicked off. "The tracking worked on the call. His cell was activated just outside Philadelphia. As soon as the call ended, he went off-line again."

"How does he do that?"

"Takes the battery out. Cell phones can be tracked even when they're powered off, and he seems to know that. They're not really powered off. If they were, the phone would lose track of time and other things. When you power off, the screen is powered off. But the phone still checks in with the nearest tower periodically. That can be tracked."

Wendy watched the bleak anger in his eyes. "What's wrong?"

"Bing had an update on the Brogevich case too. The paint on the murder weapon is a perfect match to the paint in the hallway in your apartment building. Keith must have had it on his hand. He's officially wanted for Phil's murder."

That last sentence was like a punch in Wendy's face, hard as a fist. She'd known Keith wasn't a good guy. He was violent and mean. *But murder...* She staggered back and shoved her hands under her arms, her fingertips icy cold. "What do we do now?"

Joe drew her hands back and warmed them with his. "You relax. I'll set up everything."

He pulled her in and landed a quick kiss on her lips, then he walked away and began making calls.

Wendy had to keep busy. She made dinner: burgers and fries. She didn't have the mental capacity for anything complicated. Talking Captain Bing into agreeing to their plan had taken a while, and so had setting up the call tracing. The afternoon was gone, dark settling on the street outside.

She ate with Justin at the table, while Joe breezed by, picked up a burger and walked off, still on the phone.

She couldn't eat more than two bites. She called Sophie.

"I have to go out. Do you think you could watch Justin for a couple of hours? There'll be police protection here too."

"I'm already on my way. Bing told me what you're doing. I haven't called you, because I think it's more effective to yell at people in person. But... Are you crazy? No. Just no."

"I can't live like this forever, in suspended animation, waiting for Keith to make his next move."

"Dammit."

"That's what Joe said."

"Listen to him for once."

"I can do this."

"Just because you can, doesn't mean you should. Leave this to the professionals."

"I will. All I'm doing is driving the car. As soon as Keith shows up, the police will grab him."

"Didn't the police try that plan already?"

"With Joe behind the wheel. I should never have agreed to that. Keith realized something was wrong before they could take him down. He isn't stupid."

"No. He's a murderer."

Wendy lost her breath for a second. "You know about Phil."

"I overheard the call."

"Putting Keith behind bars is the right thing to do. Trust me."

"I do. That's why I'm on my way. I'm going to yell at you. Then I'm going to watch Justin while I pray like I've never prayed before."

"Thank you."

"Don't thank me until it's over and you're safe back at home."

After they hung up, Wendy borrowed two towels from the downstairs bathroom, rolled them up and wrapped them in Justin's red coat. She tugged Justin's hat over the end of the towel roll. Then she took the Taser Joe had brought in from his trunk, slipped it into the car seat, placed the towel-roll kid on top, and strapped it in.

Her coat, a high-fashion brand Keith had picked for her, had no pockets. And if she switched to something big and bulky now, Keith would become suspicious and pat her down. Everything had to be perfect, including the pretense that she had Justin with her.

The last time, they hadn't bothered. Joe had planned on grabbing Keith in the diner's parking lot long before Keith realized the back seat was empty. The setup hadn't worked out quite that way. This time, they had to up their game.

"Looking good." Joe came up behind her. "Everybody is getting into position. I called Amber. She's coming over with Max. Jack is bringing Ashley and Maddie over, and he'll stick around for protection. Just in case."

"Sophie is coming too."

In fact, she arrived first, with Peaches, which delighted Justin to no end but made Pirate Prince shoot out the back door with an irritated hiss. Then Jack came with Ashley and seven-year-old Maddie. Amber popped in last, Max wide-eyed with excitement at the prospect of a party.

Wendy stood in the middle of the small crowd, her throat tightening. All those people were there for her and her son. When had she made all these friends?

The women moved in for hugs and wished her safe, promising to watch over Justin.

"I decided not to yell at you right now," Sophie told Wendy. "But I'm going to have *a lot* to say about this harebrained idea when you come back."

Amber offered Wendy a fist bump. "Knock him dead."

Wendy kissed Justin good night, hugged him until he squirmed, then hurried to Joe, who was waiting for her by the front door.

He handed her the slim bulletproof vest Jack had brought. "I want you to wear this. There's a small tracking device in it. In case Keith takes your phone. We'll know where you are, every second."

"Thanks." She shrugged into the vest and let him help with her coat.

He left his hands on her shoulders, as if unable to let her go. "I'm having second thoughts. I should go in your place."

"He's not going to fall for that again. He's not going to approach the car unless he clearly sees me behind the wheel."

"I still hate this plan."

"In another hour, it'll be all over, and we'll be coming home."

"All right. You drive down Route 1. I'll drive the back roads. It's a shortcut, so I'll be in position with the others by the time you get there. The second he shows, we'll take him into custody. Do *not* get out of your car. Stay safe."

"You too." She kissed him.

He kissed her back, with enough heat to melt the arctic icecap.

Amber gave a wolf whistle from the living room.

Jack called out, "Get a room."

Wendy smiled then picked up the car seat and the towel kid.

Joe walked out with her. She headed to her new car, and Joe strode to his cruiser. She strapped the car seat into the back. Justin's red coat and hat had to be visible from afar. If Keith couldn't see Justin, he'd become suspicious. He knew Wendy wouldn't go anywhere without her son.

Joe followed her to Route 1. She took the south ramp; he kept going straight.

She barely drove half a mile down the road when something clicked in the back. Then half the backseat folded down and Keith popped up, surging forward from the trunk.

"Oh my God!" She almost drove off the road. "What are you doing here?"

Nobody had thought to monitor her car in the driveway. People were showing up at her door continuously, coming to stay with Justin. Nobody had thought Keith would come there.

He punched the car seat with the fake kid next to him. "Fucking liar. I thought I'd make sure there were no mix-ups this time. How about we skip Oxford tonight? Take the next exit?"

He scrambled to the front passenger seat and pointed his gun at her.

Fight. Knock the weapon from his hand. She knew what she had to do, but fear froze Wendy to her seat. Her hands were fused to the steering wheel.

"Did you think I was stupid enough to fall for another setup?" Keith shouted. "Do you take me for an idiot?"

"No! I swear. The police made me do it."

"Don't fucking lie to me!"

"Sorry. I'm so sorry, Keith." She begged, like she had begged so many times before. But then she thought, *screw it*. She shouldn't be the one apologizing. She shouldn't be in danger because of him once again. She shouldn't have to wonder whether she'd ever see her son again. The abuse and fear had to end.

It *was* going to end. *Tonight.*

Yet when he dug the barrel of the gun even harder between her ribs and said, "Take the next exit and pull in by the produce stand," she obeyed him. Wanting to be brave and actually being brave, especially when threatened with a deadly weapon, were two different things.

A black van waited behind the dark building. Nobody around.

"How did you get to Joe's house?" She stalled.

"Gambled on Uber drivers being too busy to watch the news. Out of the car," he ordered. "We're switching. And you'll be driving."

He held his gun on her the whole time. She had zero opportunity to reach for the Taser tucked into Justin's car seat.

"Move!"

She got out and hurried over to the van, opened the driver's side door with trembling hands. "Please, just give me a chance to apologize."

"Too little, too damn late. I've forgiven a lot of your stupidity over the years. But whoring for some idiot cop, and then setting me up on top of that?"

"Please—"

"Take off your coat."

"Why?"

"I'm patting you down for a listening device."

"I swear—"

"I don't believe shit you say."

He reached out and ripped, buttons flying. Jabbed at her bullet-proof vest. "Exactly. Take it off."

The police tracker was in the vest. "Please, Keith."

He backhanded her so hard, she stumbled.

She tugged the Velcro open without wasting any more words. Then she tossed her coat and vest on the ground, and stood still while Keith patted her down, his fingers rougher than necessary.

"In the van," he snapped. "Time to get out of here."

The dome light was off, so she didn't see much in the cab. But once she was on the road, oncoming vehicles shined enough light into the back of the van. A glance in the rearview mirror revealed a row of red, plastic gasoline cans, along with rope and duct tape.

Fear whispered into her ears, the same mantra it always had. *Don't make him angry, and maybe he won't hurt you so bad.* But this time, Wendy had another voice inside her head, the voice of budding self-confidence, boosted by long-suppressed anger. She was no longer the woman who used to cower before Keith. The heady realization sent strength surging through her veins.

When he pointed at the next exit and said, "Turn here," instead of slowing down, Wendy stepped on the gas.

"Take the next turn!" he shouted.

"No." She braced, then she whipped the steering wheel and spun the van in a U-turn, the cans of gasoline slip-sliding in the back.

"What the hell are you doing?"

She stomped on the gas pedal. Eighty-five miles per hour. Ninety.

"Slow down, you stupid bitch!"

"Roll down your window and throw the gun out."

He raised the barrel. "I'll shoot your fucking head off."

"Then we both die. Between the two of us, you have more to lose. Wherever you want to take me, you're taking me there to kill me. I die either way."

He swore viciously. "You'd never leave Justin behind. If you kill yourself on the road, who will raise him?"

"Joe and Sophie will," she said with certainty.

"You won't kill yourself all knocked up. You'd kill your little bastard."

"I had a miscarriage after you knocked me down and kicked me the last time." She swallowed her pain because she had to focus on the road and the other cars. "You're right. I'd rather go home to Justin. But dying while taking you out is better than dying and letting you live. You took too much from me, Keith. I'm not giving anything else, not without a price."

"Listen to me you fucking whore!" His voice shook with rage.

She had to get that gun away from him before he lost it completely. "I'm going to start counting." She was going a hundred miles an hour, passing cars so fast that a few beeped at her to slow down. "If you don't throw your gun out the window by the time I reach five, I'm going to drive head-on into the nearest tree, and we both take our chances. I predict a fiery explosion, considering all the gasoline in the back."

For once he didn't sneer at her.

"One." Wendy swallowed. "Two." If a deer jumped in front of them, if she hit a bump or a pothole, that was it. Game over. "Three."

Keith grabbed for the steering wheel, but she was prepared and elbowed him away. And then stepped even harder on the gas.

"If we go off the road, we die. You better pray I don't lose control. Four."

"I don't need a gun to beat you to death. I can choke the life out of you with my bare hands."

She said, "Five."

He rolled the window down and tossed the gun. "Slow down, you stupid bitch! You can barely drive."

"Turns out, I can drive just fine. I can do a lot of things."

"Slow the hell down!"

She wanted to. But if she did, he'd take control of the steering wheel. "Grab some duct tape from the back and tape your hands together."

"I can't tape my own hands together. I need my hands for that!" he shouted.

"Use your mouth, use your knees, do whatever it takes. Can't you do anything?" She repeated the words she'd heard a million times when they'd been together. "I'll slow down when your hands are tied."

He swore again but reached for the duct tape. He used his right hand to wrap the tape around his left wrist, then his mouth to roll the tape around the right. He had nothing to cut with, so the roll hung next to his hands as he dropped them onto his lap. "Happy?"

"Stay in your seat." She eased the speed back to ninety. "The baby I lost is the last thing that you will ever, ever take from me." She dropped the speed to eighty, but didn't slow further until she reached the Oxford exit. She took the exit then pulled into the old, abandoned gas station.

Keith grabbed for her throat before she could come to a full stop next to a Salvation Army drop-off container.

She'd always held back before, because Justin had always been there, and she'd always worried that if things escalated, her son would get hurt. This time, Justin was at home, safe. Wendy jabbed her elbow into Keith's face with all her strength.

He screamed in pain.

She screamed right back. "Don't you ever touch me again!"

Then she cut the engine, took out the keys with her right hand as she rolled her window down with the left. "I got him! I'm coming out. He's unarmed."

She bolted from the van, leaving the door open.

Two dark shapes popped up from the bushes up ahead. Bing aimed his gun at the van as he rushed forward in a crouch. Joe ran for her and dragged her behind the Salvation Army container. Then he just held her, so tight that she could barely breathe. "What happened?"

"Go! Help the captain."

"Chase and Harper are here. That's plenty for one man. Mike would be here too, but he'd gone off to see why you stopped at the other exit. What happened?"

She told him in a rush, her heart banging, adrenalin making her shaky.

The cold fury in Joe's eyes betrayed just how much he wanted to be out there with the others, taking care of Keith. But all he said was, "I'll let the captain know that somebody has to go and find Keith's gun. We can't leave a loaded weapon on the side of the road."

That *I want to kill someone* tone was there in his voice, but he stayed calm, he stayed to protect her. He was nothing like Keith. They were different on a basic level.

Joe was a man Wendy could trust.

A man she would never have to fear.

Joe Kessler was the man she loved.

If her heart had raced before, now it came to a sudden stop, as if it had run into a brick wall. She stared at him. *I love you.*

The thought had the power of a flash-bang grenade going off next to her.

She barely heard when the captain shouted, "We got him!"

Joe kissed her, then let her go at last and stepped forward, calling back two words to her, in the firmest tone possible, "Stay here."

She followed him. And she was glad, because she got to see his expression when he saw Keith duct taped.

Even Bing shot her an impressed look. "If you were one of my officers, I'd award you a commendation. You single-handedly brought in a killer." He grinned at her. "But if it's all the same to you, let's tell Sophie the police saved the day. She'll murder me if she finds out I let this man within a hundred feet of you."

Wendy could almost smile back at him. Almost.

Still more than a little stunned, she watched as a cruiser pulled into the lot, Mike behind the wheel. The captain put Keith in the back seat then got in next to Mike. And then off they went.

Harper and Chase stayed with the black van.

Joe took Wendy's hand and drew her around the building. His car was waiting there in the back. "I'm taking you home."

Home sounded good. Home was where she was with Justin. And Joe. "How long do you think they'll put Keith away for?"

"If Broslin PD has anything to do with it, forever."

"It's over?" The sense of freedom and relief was staggering.

"It is."

The words brought a wave of bliss. Then a small but rapidly growing worry popped up its ugly head.

What would happen now that they didn't need Joe's protection?

What if she'd been just another conquest? She was *in love* with Joe Kessler. But was he really in love with her? Had she been impossibly stupid for falling in love with the hot jock, playboy son of Broslin?

CHAPTER THIRTY-FOUR

THE BROSLIN POLICE STATION FILLED UP BY FIVE P.M. ON JACK Sullivan's last day at work. Everyone was there, whether they were on shift or not. Ashley came with her daughter, Wendy with her son, and Sophie with a tray of cookies. Dozens of outsiders showed up too, people Jack had saved one way or another during his time with the PD.

The captain gave an impromptu speech, finishing with "You can come back anytime you want. These doors will always be open." Then Leila brought out a cake, but before she could cut into it, the captain held up a hand. "I have a few more announcements to make."

Everyone quieted.

"I would like to take this time to announce the promotion of Officer Joe Kessler to detective." He grinned at Joe. "Congratulations."

Joe stood there, stunned. He had *not* expected that. Not yet. "Thank you, Captain."

Then Wendy was giving him a hug, and everyone came over to shake his hand, the captain in the lead.

When that commotion settled down, the captain raised a hand to regain the attention of the room. "Another piece of good news." A smile split his face nearly in two. "My little brother, Hunter, is coming home from Afghanistan. His third tour of duty is finished."

The cheer that rose filled the station. Hunter was a great guy. There wasn't anybody present who hadn't prayed for his safe return.

When that excitement abated at last, and Leila picked up the knife again to cut the cake, the captain said, "Not yet."

Bing took Sophie's hand and tugged her into the middle of the station. And then, as Sophie watched with a puzzled expression, the captain lowered himself to one knee and pulled a red velvet box from his pocket.

The silence was absolute. Even the phones didn't dare ring.

"Sophie Curtis. I don't know why God brought you into my life. Lord knows, I don't deserve you. This place is my second home. These people are my family. The station is a big part of my life. If you take me on, this is what you'll be taking on." He gave a quick, crooked smile. "Fair warning. I mean, take a good look at these goofballs."

Sophie smiled, but her lips were trembling.

"I'm asking you right here," the captain told her. "Do you think you could put up with the middle-of-the-night phone calls and with all my bad habits, and marry me?"

Sophie threw herself into the captain's arms. He caught her and held her. Wild clapping broke out around them. Everybody cheered.

Ah hell. How on earth was a man supposed to top that? Joe looked at Wendy. He wanted her, forever and ever.

The look on her face as she watched the happy couple gave him hope. Her eyes softened. Longing stole into her gaze.

Could she be convinced?

As Leila finally cut the cake, Joe tuned out everything else and began planning his own grand proposal.

"I'll take Justin to the bathroom to change him," Wendy said and walked off with the kid.

An entire minute passed before Joe figured out that this might be his best chance, while Wendy was all softened up, having just witnessed Sophie's unconditional jump into marriage.

So he did what he thought was best and strode off to the bathroom after her.

The ladies' room was empty save for the handicapped stall that also had the diaper-changing station inside.

He stopped outside the stall door. "Wendy?"

"What are you doing in here?"

"Will you marry me?"

The long silence that followed made him sweat.

"Seriously?"

"Yes." He racked his brains for something smart to say, but he was so messed up, he couldn't think of anything.

The stall door opened. Wendy had Justin on her hip. "You are proposing to me in a police station bathroom? Where criminals go to pee?"

"Uh…" He hadn't thought of it like that. He scrambled for a comeback.

She didn't wait for him. "What happened to the suave ladies' man who knows exactly what women want?"

"I don't care what women want. I only care what you want," he said miserably. "Love throws me off my game." At least, he remembered one more thing he meant to tell her. "I want to be a father to Justin. I'm not just saying that in case it helps. You know I love him."

"I do." She leaned forward to press her lips against his.

"Is that a yes?"

"It's a maybe. Yes to living together." She walked by him as Justin blew raspberries behind her back.

Joe wiggled his eyebrows at the kid. "Seriously, partner? That's all the help I get?" Then he asked Wendy, "Living together at my place? It'd be better for me to be in Broslin. For the job. But I can go to Wilmington if you want. I don't mind the commute."

"It'd be nice for Justin to have a yard, and a swing set. And I don't think he'd ever forgive me if I made him leave Pirate Prince behind."

Joe made a mental note to get the cat a gift basket of mice. "I won't take control of your life. I swear. We can put your name on every room."

"You can have the kitchen and the laundry room," she offered magnanimously.

"What, not the bedroom?" He couldn't stop smiling. All his blood was rushing to his groin. "We don't have to stay here long. Nobody would notice if we slipped away. It's almost Justin's bedtime anyway. I'm thinking we should probably leave."

"You don't want Leila's cake?"

He shot her a look he hoped told her exactly what he wanted.

———

The look Joe had shot her at the police station told Wendy exactly what he wanted. But he didn't get it until much later. First, they had to feed Justin his dinner, then play with him, then his bath, then the bedtime story. Then Justin "read" the book back to them. Then they all had to sing and bleat like sheep.

The second Wendy stepped out of the guest bedroom, Joe pulled her into his own room down the hall. "I love you."

There were no guarantees in life, but she knew what she wanted: Detective Joe Kessler.

"I love you too," she told him, and the smoldering look in his eyes made her wonder why she'd waited so long. "I love that you could just look at Justin and love him. No hesitation. That you insisted on being there for me even when you thought the baby wasn't yours. I love that you make me laugh. I love that you never try to make me into something I'm not. I love it that you're Broslin's favorite son. Even if I sometimes think it's gone to your head."

"I don't know what you're talking about. Please continue with your list."

She bit back a laugh. "I love it that you can make my knees go weak with a touch."

He brushed his lips over hers. "Like that?"

Oh no, she wasn't going to let him take control so easily. "I distinctly remember someone saying that I'm the boss of the bedroom. Take off your clothes."

"All right." He grinned that sexy grin of his that made him a town legend. He peeled off his clothes, slowly, holding her gaze the whole time, making a good show of it.

He was secure enough not to have to be in charge all the time. She added that to the long list of things that she loved about him.

He stopped when he was down to his black boxer shorts, hooked his thumb into the waistband, and shot her a questioning look.

"All of it."

He obliged, his enormous erection springing free. Heat flared in his gaze. "Will there be leather involved in this at some point, Madam Dominatrix?"

She choked on laughter.

"Maybe." She was in control, and she liked it.

She stepped closer, walked around him, caressing his shoulders, his back, her hands slipping down to his firm butt, his muscles tightening under her fingers.

Then she moved to face him and brushed his nipples deliberately. His erection grew even bigger, although she wouldn't have thought that was possible.

"Will you be taking your clothes off?" Tension tightened his voice as her fingers danced down his abdomen.

"When I'm ready." She touched her index finger to his tip where a clear drop of liquid beaded.

He jerked against her hand.

She ran her fingers up and down his length. "You'll do anything I say?"

"Anything," he promised in a husky voice, heat pouring off him.

The feel of his silky skin made her nipples tighten. Moisture gathered between her legs.

His tender lovemaking the other night had been perfect, but now she wanted more—the kind of reckless passion women who'd never been hurt by their men were capable of having.

She closed her fingers around him and looked him in the eye. "I don't want slow and sweet."

"Then tell me what you want."

And she did, brazenly, explicitly, enjoying that his gaze darkened with her every word.

He picked her up, carried her to the bed, and saw to it that her every wish was fulfilled.

When they lay there, slick in each other's arms after a lovemaking that went beyond Wendy's wildest dreams, she told him again that she loved him.

"Then you'll marry me?"

"Why?"

"Being with you feels better than scoring a thousand touchdowns."

"Is that football romance?" He could always make her laugh. That was a gift. And yet... "I think I'm going to need a little more time to get comfortable with the idea of marriage." But she could see life with a man, for the first time, without being afraid of losing herself.

"I won't push," he said, "but please consider this. Marriage is not one person gaining power over the other. It's an equal partnership. It's you propping me up when I fall down, and me propping you up when you need it. It's having someone to share the good times with, along with the bad."

Sharing good times with a man sounded utterly foreign, but Wendy could see how it might be possible with Joe. "I'm going to work on becoming the person who can trust a relationship like that."

"I'm not going anywhere." He kissed her lightly on the lips.

"My own, personal Cop Casanova."

"*Detective* Casanova," he said with a grin, then deepened the kiss.

THE END

But...

The guys at Broslin PD would like to cordially invite you to hang out with them a little longer. Chase is about to meet his match. You don't want to miss that! All I can tell you is, he is about to be tried like he's never been tried before. The girl who spread a rumor in high school that he was bad in bed is now all grown up and murdered her boss. (Or did she?) Chase better find out and soon, since he's falling for her again, and he's the investigating officer!

Excerpt:

. . .

Luanne Mayfair might have killed her boss a little. Fine, a lot. Pretty much all the way. God, that sounded bad. But he *was* a sleazebag. Honest. The maids at the Mushroom Mile Motel that Earl Cosgrove managed often prayed for lightning to strike the lecherous bastard. Alas, God had seen fit to send Luanne instead.

Now you've gone and done it, she thought the morning after as she stood on the sidewalk in front of the fifties ranch home she rented in her hometown of Broslin, PA. She squinted against the early summer sun. Her red 1989 Mustang sitting by the curb had come from the used-car lot with its share of nicks and dents. But the damage to the front was new.

Gone and done it.

She'd done a horrible, terrible, despicable thing. Guilt and regret made her knees wobble. Whatever the punishment was, she deserved it.

Except, she couldn't go to prison. She had her four-year-old twin sisters to take care of. She was Mia and Daisy's sole guardian.

Luanne drew air in big, gulping breaths to wrestle down the shock and nausea. *Get moving. One foot in front of the other.* She couldn't stand there and stare all morning. She had to find a way to get away with murder.

...

Keep reading BROSLIN BRIDE here!

And, pretty please, would you sign up for my author newsletter? If you don't, I'll have no way to reach you to let you know when I'm putting on a big sale, or giving away FREE books, or have a new book out. I'd love to keep in touch with you. THANK YOU!!!!!!!!!!!

Dana

Made in the USA
Columbia, SC
12 December 2023

28137692R00153